S0-CFQ-582

The Sandalwood Fan

Books by Katherine Wigmore Eyre

Amy

The Lute and the Glove

Monks' Court

The Sandalwood Fan

THE

Sandalwood Fan

A NOVEL OF SUSPENSE

by KATHERINE WIGMORE EYRE

MEREDITH PRESS ❧ NEW YORK

Copyright © 1968 by Katherine Wigmore Eyre

All rights reserved. No part of this book in excess of five hundred words may be reproduced in any form without permission in writing from the publisher.

No character or place in this story is intended to represent any actual person or place; all the incidents of the story are entirely fictional in nature.

First edition

Library of Congress Catalog Card Number: 68–28723

Manufactured in the United States of America for Meredith Press

The Sandalwood Fan

Chapter one

THE sky was sullen, the choppy, strong-running water of the bay like molten pewter, the wind off the open sea a cold sting of salt on the never-to-be-forgotten day in San Francisco when, for the first time, mystery and terror, grief and love began to be more than words to me as they gathered their forces for an assault on my life.

The February rains, a downpour since dawn, had stopped momentarily, but the gutters of San Francisco's Chinatown were still overflowing at five o'clock on that Saturday afternoon. The tenement room at the top of the rickety stairs I had rushed up so concernedly smelled of damp plaster and rotting wood. There was a smell, too, of red incense candles lighted on my old amah's washstand and of the heavily scented yellow-and-white New Year lilies she had sprouted in a pottery bowl of pebbles and water. But strongest of all was the smell of the burned, crimson paper and gunpowder of celebration firecrackers exploding damply in the alley below.

As I knelt beside an iron cot spread with a thin, worn quilt, I put my arms around a pitifully shrunken body, and tried to make my presence known. "It's Nan," I repeated again and again. "It's Nan. Your Nan, darling Ah Sam."

I thought I was too late, but after a moment or two a skeletal hand reached out for mine and pressed it feebly. For a brief instant vaguely staring, sick black eyes met mine and were cognizant.

"*Gung Hay Fat Choy,* Little Missee . . ."

"Happy New Year to you, too, darling." My voice was unsteady.

After that she lay quietly in my arms for a few moments, her difficult breath a rasp, and then she started up abruptly against her pillow. Wildly, desperately, she tried to tell me something, but this time she was speaking Chinese and her words were meaningless to me. With an indescribable anguish I had to watch her eyes pleading with me to understand as they filled with a terrible longing to communicate, a terrible frustration.

"Dearest Ah Sam, it doesn't matter. Nothing matters. I'm here, I'm right here. . . ."

I turned to the brisk young Chinese doctor who stood at the foot of the bed replacing a thermometer and a stethoscope in his case, and of whom I had hardly been aware before. "What is she trying to tell me? Can you understand?"

The doctor snapped his case shut. "It is a garble of Hunan dialect, and I'm Cantonese—sorry. But it's too late for her to make much sense now, anyway. She is going fast." He glanced at the candles on the washstand and at a little teak table that was set out with a New Year's feast to propitiate the household gods, rice cakes and melon seeds and wine. "She hadn't expected the end so soon, I take it?"

"She wouldn't give in. She wouldn't admit it was anything serious, though she has been terribly ill all week." My arms tightened around Ah Sam. "You see . . . you see, she didn't want to face up to leaving me. She's been with me ever since I was born. She's never been able to realize I'm not a child anymore, or that I could manage without her."

My eyes suddenly brimmed. "It won't be easy. . . ." I held Ah Sam closer. "It's Nan, dear," I began repeating again while I tried to calm her. "Nan. Your Nan. Don't try to talk. Please . . . please. You can tell me some other time. Just know it is Nan . . . with you . . ."

Even as I begged it she was all too still, too suddenly rigid in my arms. The rasp of heavy breathing stopped. The black, anxious eyes filmed over.

I kissed her goodbye, and after a moment I stood up. "Thank you for telephoning me, Doctor Yee. I am glad I was with her. And I'm more than grateful to her neighbors for calling you in."

"They found her collapsed on the stairs with her market basket. One last errand, and one last climb, was too much for her. And as your name was in her purse . . ."

I buttoned my tweed coat, retied a scarf over my windblown hair, and pulled on my gloves, though my eyes were full of tears. "I've come to see her every day, after my job, and I was coming this evening. I've tried to make her stay in bed. I did my best to have her let me put her in a hospital." My voice was unsteady again. "I've realized for a long time how old she was getting, and I knew the slightest illness could be dangerous. But she wouldn't listen to me." I looked around me at the poor, bare room.

"This is where she wanted to be. She insisted, and I had to give in to her. It's a room she rented years ago, to come to on her days off."

"All the old people of my race want to die down here, in their own part of town, Miss Allen. To them, it is the next best thing to dying in China, and being buried with their ancestors."

"I know. But I was so afraid of just this very thing happening."

The doctor took a memorandum pad and pencil from a pocket. "I'll make the necessary reports, but about the funeral arrangements . . . Can I be of any help?"

"Would you be kind enough to call my attorneys? They know Ah Sam. They'll handle it all for me. It's the firm of Marshall, Martin and Hitchcock." I hesitated. "You might ask for Mr. James Bradford in the Trust Department."

I wondered if Dr. Yee had noticed the tiny hesitation, and I turned rather quickly toward the door, and then I stopped to look toward the bed. "If only I knew what she wanted to say then, at the last."

The doctor shrugged as he drew a sheet up over Ah Sam's face.

"I shouldn't let it worry me. The little I could make out was only something about a fan."

"A fan?" I questioned it. "But she looked so troubled. It all seemed so important to her. Surely it was more than just that."

The doctor shrugged again. "As I said, I'm not up on Hunan. And it was all garbled. She was pretty far gone, you know, and after that last hypo——"

I closed the door after me abruptly. I didn't want any clinical details. My eyes filled again as I went down the tenement stairs and out into the alley. Half blinded and fumbling in my bag for a handkerchief, I picked a way past puddles and garbage cans, avoiding the cats, sleek from sorties in rat-infested basements, that wanted to rub against my legs. When I had pushed through a surge of riotous children who were setting off firecrackers and waving punksticks, their pale-saffron moon faces and their hands sticky with blobs of violently pink spun-sugar floss and the dribble of ice-cream cones, I was out on Stockton Street. It was impossible not to stop at a sidewalk flower stall: I bought a miniature tangerine tree bright with orange fruit and wrapped in red-and-gold paper for good luck, and a bunch of the same sweet-smelling lilies that were blooming in the room I had just left. Then, from a shop on the corner, hung with chiming windbells and garish with tinsel festoons and dangling silk tassels, I bought a paper bag of lichee nuts and a little wicker-covered pottery jar of preserved ginger. It all made rather a lot to carry, but I couldn't leave Chinatown empty-handed.

Not today, of all days. For I knew that after this, I would always have to buy these traditional symbols of Chinese New Year for myself. There would be no more Ah Sam to present them, smiling, and bowing ceremoniously, in her best black silk trousers and one of her starched, white cotton, high-necked tunics, her old, old yellow hands so clean, so very clean, and always so eager to reach out and give.

No more Ah Sam who had once said so many Happy New Years to the small child left in her charge to bring up, the child I, Nan Allen, had been.

Never again. I was alone now. Entirely alone. Oh, I had friends, certainly. Good friends. But I had no family, no one in the world to whom I truly belonged, or to whom I mattered, as I had mattered to Ah Sam.

There was Cousin Elizabeth, of course; I wasn't forgetting Cousin Elizabeth. But she wasn't a blood relation—she wasn't an Allen—and she lived an ocean away, sometimes in Honolulu, sometimes in Hong Kong. And anyone as caught up as she in her astonishingly successful business world could hardly be said to count. She simply hadn't the time to give to any sort of companionship. Not just now, at any rate. Though someday, perhaps . . .

As I walked toward the California Street cable car I acknowledged the simple, indisputable fact of my aloneness without self-pity, but with a normal regret and a certain amount of rebelliousness. Everyone was entitled to someone. Surely that was not expecting too much. Just someone to turn to, and even though not family, someone who was a part of you, and of whom you were a part. And surely there was no need to be ashamed of your regret at being alone. There must be thousands of people in this same city with you who felt the same way. Each of them asking for nothing more than just that one close person to be theirs; that one close person to give point and meaning to their existence.

Take these people going home now in the five-o'clock rush, jostling you on the curb, elbowing you, almost crowding the breath out of you on the cable car. Some of them were lucky, undoubtedly; but many, many of them were as lonely as you. Detached. Separate. Living in a vacuum.

The cable car clanked, and balked, and slid backward, as usual to the catcalls of the passengers, and then strained on its way, bells jangling, to the top of Nob Hill and down the slope to Van Ness, where I got off and crossed over to walk to Franklin Street, and down a block or two, and over again toward the bay. Then I shifted my packages and rummaged awkwardly for the door key I kept safety-pinned to the lining of my brown leather bag and let myself into one of the city's few important, late Victorian-Gothic houses that had defied not only the 1906 Fire, but the threat of present-day wrecking crews.

Ugly? Quite hideous, frankly. But a house with personality, all fretsaw gingerbread and turrets and bulging bay windows. It had been newly painted olive green with black shutters, and the black window boxes were stuffed to overflowing with white marguerites.

I was used to the emptiness that had invaded the house this past week—or almost used to it, I realized as I closed the front door behind me and bolted it and put on the night chain. Since Ah Sam's illness and her stay in Chinatown I had even been able to steel myself against the melancholy ticktick of the tall clock in a corner of the hall, and against the shadowiness of the house, with springtime dusk blurring what little light filtered through the purple-and-blue stained-glass window on the stair landing.

Quickly, I switched on lights and walked the length of the hall to the back of the house. It meant going through a mahogany service door and a butler's pantry lined with ceiling-high shelves crowded with gold-rimmed dinner plates and goblets, past a row of long-disused call bells, their clappers rusted. The kitchen, when it was finally reached, was enormous, with scrubbed wooden sink boards and a huge old-fashioned gas range set high on iron legs. As I put down my packages on the table, which was covered with a blue-white oilcloth, I swallowed a lump in my throat.

Ah Sam's pots and pans and pastry board and rolling pin. Ah Sam's rice bowl and chopsticks. One of her aprons dangling from a hook. Neatly aligned jars and bottles on the windowsill, supplied by her favorite herbalist and apothecary, but whose contents had failed to make her well. Powdered sea horse and lizard skins. Nameless liquid mixtures I had never inquired about too deeply. And all the rest.

A cup of tea was what I wanted, I thought. A cup of good strong hot tea to cheer myself. I was wrong. The tin canister of oolong meant Ah Sam again. A glass of sherry seemed a better choice. And later, though I was not in the least hungry, I would look to see what leftover scraps there might be in the refrigerator. It would be the sort of dinner I had satisfied myself with all the past week. Nothing had seemed worth the slightest effort, nor had eating in a restaurant appealed to me. Most of all I had not wanted to bother with friends, and their well-meant kindness.

I was acting foolishly, I knew, but there it was.

With my sherry, I went back through the house to a stiff, fadedly handsome room that could only be called a parlor, with its double sliding doors cutting it in two, its lace curtains at the bay windows, the festooned and fringed gold plush side draperies that matched the upholstery of two rosewood sofas, and six primly arranged, straight-backed rosewood chairs.

There was even a rubber plant, a monstrosity, in a cloisonné jar. I had always disliked it, but taken it for granted; whether it was years and years old, or whether when one plant died, Ah Sam replaced it with another, I never knew. But as long as I could remember she had dusted and polished those gigantic, overpowering, cold-looking leaves.

When I had switched on a center chandelier, where gas jets had once flared in the etched glass globes, I stooped to the marble hearth and lighted a fire in the coal grate.

The parlor, as far as cheer was concerned, was not going to be much of an improvement over the kitchen, I discovered. Too well I remembered that it was Ah Sam who had laid the fire. Against all my remonstrances she had insisted upon lugging up bucket after bucket of coal from the basement. Weekly, she polished the brass fender, the tongs, the poker and shovel.

Always Ah Sam's hands at work for me.

When the paper and kindling had caught and flames were licking up the chimney, I drank my sherry and watched the reflection of firelight in a pair of tall rosewood cabinets crammed with small bibelots of ivory and porcelain and jade and carnelian and cinnabar, and on a Coromandel lacquer screen and a silk wall hanging embroidered with a five-clawed dragon grasping a sun.

The silk was yellow, the Emperor of China's Imperial yellow; always as a romantic child, I had chosen to believe it had once hung in his palace in the Forbidden City.

Ah Sam had reinforced the cracking silk, just as she had darned the lace curtains and washed and ironed them, just as she had waxed the square rosewood piano that had come around the Horn in one of my great-grandfather Allen's sailing ships.

There was still an Allen and Company, Importers and Exporters, in San Francisco, with an office on California Street. But now the main offices were in Hawaii and China, and it was Cousin Elizabeth Beaton who was at the head of the firm, not an Allen anymore.

A fantastic turn of the wheel, when you stopped to think about it.

Cousin Elizabeth had been Southern kin, by marriage, to the Allens, and churchmouse poor. Like me, she had been an orphan. She had lived in this house all her childhood and grown up with the two Allen boys of her generation, John, the elder, and Richard, who, one day, was to be my father. When John went out to China to manage an Allen-owned tea plantation he married a very young English girl, and then sent for Cousin Elizabeth to be a kind of companion-housekeeper for his bride.

Richard, too, had gone out to China, and married an English girl.

Idly, I considered the two brothers, and Cousin Elizabeth, as I often had considered them before. How little I really knew about them. A few bare facts, and nothing more. Both the boys had died in China, killed by guerrilla forces in World War Two. Edith, John's wife, had died of malaria and starvation in a prison camp, and Richard's wife, Anne, my mother, had died in the same camp. She had died giving birth to me. But Cousin Elizabeth had survived the horrors of that camp, and she had seen to it that I survived, too. She couldn't have done it without Ah Sam, the coolie woman who had helped an imprisoned British army doctor, nearly beaten to death by his captors, to deliver me. And from the first moment she held me in her arms, Ah Sam loved me. Widowed and childless and homeless because of the war, she had needed to clutch at something, someone.

There you had it again—loneliness.

From her one blanket she had cut and sewed a sort of sack to keep me warm. Some days, there was a grudgingly allotted ration of canned milk; on the other days, when I wailed with hunger, she used to dip a rag, torn from her clothes, into rice water, and give it to me to suck. When I was old enough to eat solid food, she starved herself to give me the larger share of the rice or noodles in her bowl.

Cousin Elizabeth, too, had gone without that I might live; with the doled-out scraps of fish or meat, and whatever rare, precious bit of vegetable or fat she could bargain for going into broth or spread on a crust of bread.

When the war was over, Cousin Elizabeth brought me and Ah Sam back to San Francisco, and with hope of finding some way to make a living, settled us in the old Allen house that had been unoccupied since Grandfather's death. Not only because it was home to her; it would be a rent-free roof over all our heads.

She thought she was penniless. Letters from Mr. Martin's firm telling her she was Grandfather's heir had never reached her. She couldn't believe it at first, Mr. Martin had told me, but with the realization it was true, and that not only Grandfather's house and money were hers, but Allen and Company as well, an urge for a business career seized her.

The income from the family firm had shrunk to almost nothing in the war years, but Cousin Elizabeth determined to change all that. And she became a kind of splendid Phoenix—that was how I always thought of her as I grew up—rising from the flames and ashes of the war, and winging off, first to Hawaii, and then to China again, to reestablish Allen and Company's Far East contacts. It took the hardest kind of work, and it took time. She was back and forth frequently between San Francisco and Hong Kong for the first few years, but eventually, when she decided to move Allen and Company's headquarters to Hong Kong, her visits home became infrequent, and finally stopped.

Even Cousin Elizabeth found she couldn't, successfully, be in two places at once.

I was seven years old when she left me, here in this house, for the last time, with Ah Sam and a brace of Allen family lawyers to look after me, and sailed away to the Orient. I accepted her departure philosophically, as a child necessarily must accept the actions of adults, and I can just remember waving good-bye to her at the Embarcadero docks. It was my last glimpse of her.

I can remember, too, that Ah Sam had taken my hand when the lines were cast off and the steamer eased into the bay, and we boarded a cable car, and then got off for that treat of treats, a walk through Chinatown.

Ah Sam had bought me a paper bag of candied melon and some wonderful little dried-up nubbins of paper that magically opened into lovely flowers when you floated them in water, and I more or less forgot about Cousin Elizabeth.

It was only sometimes at night, before I fell asleep, when I heard the whistle and toot of a foghorn blowing, that I thought about her, and felt a vague aloneness, a vague bereftness that I was far too young to analyze, and that was too intangible to describe.

I had been duly pleased with Christmas or birthday dolls from her, or skates, or a bicycle, or beautifully bound sets of fairy tales. If, as I began to grow up, I sometimes wished that the accompanying cards were more personal, I was also sensible enough to know that a woman as busy as Cousin Elizabeth couldn't spend much time in toy shops. Her secretaries had to do these things. Still, it would have been nice. And later, when I was even more grown up, I used to think, oh, if just once the checks Cousin Elizabeth sent to the lawyers who looked after my well-being had been accompanied by some little indication of the unswerving interest Cousin Elizabeth took in the young girl she was so conscientiously, so generously supporting.

She paid for the best of schools. I was given dancing and piano lessons. The checks provided for ice-skating lessons when the rink was in vogue. I had horseback-riding instruction. I even had birthday parties; the wife of the senior partner of Marshall, Martin and Hitchcock arranged them. Mrs. Martin saw to it that I had a pretty dress, pretty hairbands, correct patent-leather slippers, a birthday cake with candles, and ice cream. She saw to it that the right children were invited to watch Punch-and-Judy shows and to play Pin the Tail on the Donkey, here in this very same parlor where, tonight, I was staring into the fire.

Later, just before my freshman year at Radcliffe, Cousin Elizabeth paid for my debut. Mrs. Martin presented me at a formal tea that September before I went east. Her big house on Pacific Avenue, as Victorian as the Allen house, was crowded with bronze chrysanthemums stuffed into tall gilt baskets, and with caterers' maids and "the" man from Mr. Martin's club on Nob Hill opened the door. The Old Guard, in white gloves and velvet toques, crowded around a long, lace-covered table with a silver tea set at one end, a coffee urn at the other, and with little silver dishes of salted nuts and chocolate mints and plates of sandwiches and *petits fours.*

Everyone came who was invited, and everyone sent me flowers; I was an Allen, and that still meant something to the older generation of San Franciscans, if not to the new jet setters who were already crowding them out.

In the Christmas vacation I came home to lovely parties. Mrs. Martin arranged a dinner dance for me, just as efficiently and kindly as she had arranged my birthday galas. And she sponsored me for the Cotillion. It meant that in white tulle, I made my official bow in the Garden Court of the Palace Hotel, with Mr. Martin acting as substitute for the father each of the other girls had as partner for the first waltz.

But after my graduation from college, and a summer in Europe, the checks from Cousin Elizabeth became much, much smaller. Mr. Martin called me into his office and explained that Cousin Elizabeth, quite justifiably, and with my best interest at heart, felt she had done enough for me; she would pay for a stenographic course, her house was mine to live in, she would continue to pay the taxes and the upkeep of the house, and Ah Sam's wages, but she had made it quite clear, in a concise letter, that I must stand on my own feet from now on.

This was a difficult and uncertain world; it would be no kindness to encourage a girl without money of her own to live as though she were rich in her own right.

It was a shock, and I felt frightened and terribly unsure of my ability to swim. I was convinced I would sink. Then, luckily, pride came to the rescue, and also a sense of adventure buoyed me. Other girls managed; other girls got a lot of fun out of running their own lives.

Only one thing struck me as impractical on Cousin Elizabeth's part. "I can understand her paying Ah Sam, but why does she want to keep the house going?" I asked Mr. Martin. "Why spend all that money on it, when she never sets foot in it, and when Ah Sam and I could easily find a little inexpensive apartment?"

Mr. Martin had no ready answer. "I can't imagine," he admitted, "unless, as a wild guess, the house has become a sort of, well, a sort of status symbol to her. I have always had an idea that, to her way of looking at it, she was eating bitter bread all those early years as a child, when your grandfather took her in. The 'poor relation' category rubbed her raw when she was a girl—try as she did to hide her feelings; she was as proud as the devil—and I don't imagine she enjoyed playing second fiddle to John's wife, later, in China. Afterward, when her position changed so radically, her inheritance of the Allen house, as well as the Allen money, was an enormous triumph. And now that the house is hers, she isn't going to let go of it. I'm willing to make a large-size bet that she'll come back to it one of these days. It would be the natural reaction of any woman, in similar circumstances, a chance to lord it a little, in the same house where she'd felt herself a nobody for so many years. I can't think of any other reason for her holding on. Business woman that she is, I'd have thought she would long since have torn the house down and built a high rise in its place."

"Did you like her, Mr. Martin?" I put the question curiously. "Did other people like her?"

"She could have had as many friends as she wanted. Her problem was she was too shy and proud, too reserved. It was difficult to reach her. Well, it wasn't much of a bringing up for a child—a houseful of Allen men. Attractive, spoiled, self-assured, every one of them. If your grandmother had been alive . . . But as it was, they rode over her roughshod. No wonder Elizabeth got the idea in her head she was there on charity, for no other reason than that she was a family legacy, who, inconveniently or not, had, in all decency, to be given bed and board."

"Poor Cousin Elizabeth!" I exclaimed it with sincere compassion. For a revealing moment she was someone I actually knew, someone I could understand, as though I were standing in the shoes of the girl she had been.

Inarticulate. Unapproachable. Cold only because she was frozen with pride.

But in a prison camp she had accepted the responsibility of a newborn baby, because of family ties. And even now she was saying, "Don't misjudge me. Don't think me unkind. Know that it is for your own good I am helping you to be independent and to stand on your own feet. One poor relation, one object of charity in the Allen family was enough."

I asked another question. "You told me once that my father and my grandfather quarreled, and that is why all Grandfather's money, and his house, went to Cousin Elizabeth after Uncle John and his wife died childless; but you didn't tell me what the quarrel was about."

"It's no secret; I suppose I simply hadn't realized the subject interested you. It was a lot of to-do about nothing, as a matter of fact. Too bad."

"Whose fault was it?"

"You couldn't pin it on either of them. It was a matter of one generation not seeing eye to eye with the other. Your father was an independent young man, and he didn't take too well to the idea of working in Allen and Company. He wanted to strike out on his own. It was a big disappointment to your grandfather. There were a number of rows, and then a final blowup. Your grandfather lost his temper and said a lot of things I imagine he was sorry for afterwards. But he was too proud to back down. Anyway, your father took off. Well, well, a pity, but it happened a long time ago, and it's past history. And I must say Elizabeth treated you handsomely for a good many years. She needn't have, you know. She's gone out of her way to be generous. And even if she has made you dive into cold water a little suddenly, you'll be all right.

I'll see to it that you are. Just get on with that secretarial course; there are plenty of offices that need a nice, attractive young woman like yourself to meet the customers."

He gave me one of his hearty, warm handshakes, and asked, paternally, how I was doing for beaux, and then I left his office knowing little more about my father than when I came in.

Cousin Elizabeth would be the one to ask. Cousin Elizabeth could tell me about both my parents; she could make them seem real to me, so they'd be people, they'd be "family," to which I could relate myself. It took a woman to come out with all the little bits, the little intimate sidelights I wanted to hear. But Cousin Elizabeth wasn't here—and more than ever, Honolulu and Hong Kong seemed a long way off.

But I had more to think about than Cousin Elizabeth or my parents. I took my business course and worked hard at it.

Mr. Martin helped me to find a receptionist's job. I was at last to be free, at least in part, of my overwhelming dependency on my cousin. The picture Mr. Martin had drawn of Elizabeth's youth made me shudder. And although the water was cold, the plunge breathtakingly sudden, I thanked Cousin Elizabeth over and over for making me take it. I was proud of learning to budget, proud of my tiny but growing savings account, proud of my new self-respect. And if I had not found in my grandfather's house my only sense of identity, my only sense of background and of anchorage, and had not felt a strong pull of family loyalty to it, I would have moved out to a flat, and so ceased, entirely, to be Cousin Elizabeth's dependent. Though I never, of course, could have left Ah Sam.

Now, Ah Sam had left me.

I was Nan Allen, alone. Richard Allen's daughter.

Sitting in front of the fire the night after Ah Sam's death I felt lost as I had never felt lost before. I began to think about my parents again, began to wonder about them as I hadn't wondered since that day in Mr. Martin's office.

What had my father really been like? Would he have loved me had he lived? And what of my mother?

I turned my eyes toward a mirror over the mantel. Mrs. Martin had once commented that my chestnut—no, auburn, dark-auburn hair—must have come from my mother's side of the family. All the Allens were blond. My masses of hair . . . It was bright in sunlight. Men admired it. Girls sometimes asked me what kind of rinse I used.

Were my brown eyes my mother's?

The Martins had never seen her. None of her family had ever come to San Francisco. There were none left to come, after the war.

My brown eyes. *My* red hair. Mine, only. My parents had no reality for me.

I looked away from the mirror. What mattered was the evening ahead. It would be dull, dull. Another glass of sherry. A heated-up can of soup. A dab of leftover tuna on a lettuce leaf, eaten in the kitchen. Bed, and a book.

The dullness was my own fault. I had been foolish to cut myself off from people this past week, foolish to have given way so utterly to my depression, my dread of Ah Sam's approaching death. I had always known she would die sometime, and I should have prepared myself, realistically, sensibly.

One thing was certain; I would not hear from Jim Bradford again in a hurry.

"Mr. James Lowell Bradford of the Trust Department."
He wasn't the sort of man to pursue acquaintanceship
with a girl he had met only once unless the girl showed at
least a modicum of interest in return.

That first meeting had been at a dinner party given by
the Martins, just before Ah Sam's illness. They were
always having new young men from the firm, and always
asking me to sit next to them. Throwing me at them. Mrs.
Martin wouldn't be happy, nor feel her duty done, until
she saw me married.

"You'll wait too long," she used to warn me. "Girls
become entirely too particular and choosy as they get
older. The time comes when no man suits them."

She was a dear, and I didn't really mind her anxious
and obvious attempts to run my life. I just laughed.

The last dinner had been very, very pleasant.

But when, in this past difficult, worrisome week, there
had been two telephone calls from her latest hopefully
introduced prospect, I had been short, almost rude; dis-
interested sounding, certainly. And all because I hadn't
been able to explain to a complete stranger my preoccupation, my total involvement, with Ah Sam. ". . . No, I'm
sorry, I'm busy." That had been all I could manage,
instead of "Please, won't you call me again? The Martins
will explain."

Stupid. Like inarticulate Cousin Elizabeth, pushing
people away because of her foolish pride and unable to
communicate or come close to people, I too, had pushed
someone aside because of an inability to put in words the
concern I was feeling.

When I eventually left the parlor to investigate the
refrigerator, the uninspired bits of food I picked at did
nothing to improve my frame of mind. After I washed the

few dishes I turned off the lights downstairs and went up to my big back bedroom on the second floor, which still had a view of the bay in spite of the tall apartment buildings springing up on every hill.

When I got into the wide, ugly old walnut bed with the carved, towering headboard, which had always made me feel so small, so lost in its vastness, I remembered Ah Sam tucking me in, all the years of my childhood.

Ah Sam, dead . . .

I got up and hunted in a bookcase for a little thin volume of Chinese poetry. When I had found it I got back into bed again and turned on my reading lamp and hunted for a remembered poem. It was a love poem, written more than a thousand years ago, but the first lines made me think of the tenement room I had been in that afternoon.

> Jade incense-burner's fragrance,
> Red candles' tears,
> Unevenly light the decorated chamber's sadness.*

Each line hurt. I put the little book down and turned off the light to lie in darkness and listen to the rain that had again started to fall and was loud against the window-panes.

In Chinatown the crowds under the umbrellas would be lining the curbs waiting for the Dragon Parade to start. I knew exactly what the evening would be like. I had watched the parade year after year as a child, clutching Ah Sam's hand, and taking it all in with big eyes. Sometimes we had stood on a curb waiting, until my pipestem

* From *The Penguin Book of Chinese Verse,* translated by Robert Kotewell and Norman L. Smith. Introduced and edited by A. R. Davis. Baltimore, Maryland, Penguin Books, Inc., 1962.

legs, in white socks, wobbled under me, and then when the singsong whine and clash and thump of flute and cymbal and drum could be heard coming down the street Ah Sam would pick me up and hold me high so I could see over the heads of the crowd. And sometimes we had the choicest of views from the upstairs balcony of a Grant Avenue café, thanks to the proprietor, who was an old friend of Ah Sam's from the Hong Kong days.

It always rained on the Night of the Dragon, the big night of the Chinese New Year celebration. But no one minded. After the block-long crimson-and-gold dragon, spouting fire and smoke, had wound through the streets on centipede legs that were mens' legs under a framework of papier-mâché, the crowds would hurry out of the wet to restaurants and teahouses and homes. They would warm themselves with hot wine, in the traditional manner, or—if they preferred the new way—with gin or vodka or bourbon or scotch. They would gorge, and loosen their belts, or the wrappings of their old-style garments, over duck and chicken and fish and meat-filled doughy buns, over rice and noodles and peapods, and shrimp in batter, and sweet cakes, and ginger and winter melon and custards. There would be plenty of hot dogs and chili beans and French fries eaten, too, by the younger generation.

This year would be little different from any other. Perhaps more sailors from the cruisers and carriers ready to weigh anchor in the bay. More Marines, waiting to be flown out to Vietnam. And the hippies . . .

Everything else would be the same. The firecrackers would only sputter in the dampness, but the drums and cymbals and gongs and flutes would make their usual satisfactory dissonance to drive away evil spirits. Radios and record players and jukeboxes would blare. Tinny-sounding calliopes would grind away. The hot trumpets and saxophones of nightclub bands would wail. In the background would be the click of Mah-Jongg tiles, the click of ivory or bone abacus balls, the money counters that Chinatown's old-timers still used.

Everyone, of all ages, celebrating. Venerable grandparents who had just come from paying for incense to burn before a gilded Buddha. Children bundled in padded, embroidered silk jackets, slung on their mother's backs, or in imitation leather cowboy costumes, brandishing frontier-model guns. Bankers' wives in mink. Dancing girls in see-through plastic raincoats over sequined bikinis.

The rich political big wheels of Chinatown. The sober-minded, quietly prosperous merchants. The wretchedly poor citizens. The influx—by the thousands—of refugees from Red China that Hong Kong didn't want. The gamblers. The heroin and opium addicts. The prostitutes, the holy men. Tourists from the Middle West. Coughing old women who spent their days bent over beadwork in back-alley sweatshops, but who liked it that way, and didn't want the do-gooders—or the unions—to interfere in their lives. The teachers from the Chinatown public schools who turned out slum pupils with the best scholastic records in the city. The little stenographers in their mini skirts and windowpane stockings, arm and arm with their boyfriends. A group of priests from old St. Mary's, where the inscription on the tower clock reads: "Son, observe the time, and flee from evil."

A cross section . . .

Gung Hay Fat Choy!

Happy New Year. Happy New Year!

How valiantly, how lovingly Ah Sam had struggled to

say it for a last time. But how pitifully she had failed to say anything else coherently.

Inconsequential babbling about a fan . . .

I fell asleep with the sound of the rain, like the faint beat of a painted New Year drum in my ears.

Gung Hay Fat Choy!

With my last waking thought I was still remembering that Ah Sam had wanted to say so much more. Had it been so inconsequential, after all, that something about a fan?

What fan . . . ? Whose fan . . . ?

Odd, how desperately Ah Sam had tried. . . . And not only odd. Disturbing, in a curious, nagging way.

Chapter two

THE telephone rang early on Monday morning while I was in the kitchen making a breakfast of sorts. Cold packaged cereal. A glass of milk. Chilly, and horrid, and leaving me empty, and headachy. When Ah Sam had padded around the kitchen in her blue cotton trousers and white tunic and felt slippers, breakfast had been grapefruit, carefully sectioned, with a scalloped rind, and bacon and a boiled egg, and lovely hot toast with guava jelly, and my tea in the prettiest flowery cup the pantry could provide.

This wretched inertia, this stupid "It's too much bother" attitude; I wondered if I'd ever again feel that anything was worthwhile.

It was Mrs. Martin on the telephone. ". . . but my dear child. You simply can't stay on in that huge old house by yourself. We shan't allow it. Oh, now, Nan dear, be reasonable. Well, if you insist . . . for the next few days, perhaps, until we can help you make plans, but not a minute longer."

There was no use arguing with her. I reminded her, as pointedly as possible, that I was a working girl now, who had to get off to an office, and so I got rid of her. Not that I didn't adore Mrs. Martin, not that I wasn't grateful for her concern; but I had no intention of letting her dictate to me. And little as I myself liked the idea of living alone in Cousin Elizabeth's big, empty, echoing house, any decision to leave it must be mine, and mine solely to make.

It was more than time that I learned to take the initiative, and to plan my own life. How completely Ah Sam had spoiled me. I had become an anachronism—a girl utterly out of step with the times. A girl so overprotected that now I was entirely at a loss.

The telephone rang again as I was taking my raincoat from a hook in the hall closet. This time it was Mr. Martin. Ah Sam's funeral would be tomorrow, he told me. And on the following day I could go to her room and dispose as I saw fit of her possessions. She had left a will with him. Everything she owned was to go to me. The money she had saved from twenty-five years of service with Cousin Elizabeth was all mine.

"It's not a great deal. But it's a nice nest egg."

When Mr. Martin rang off, I hung up the telephone receiver and cried. Dear, good, loving Ah Sam.

Month after month of saving, of scrimping. Year after year of doing without. Nothing spent on herself, ever, except the rent of that tiny, miserable room in Chinatown. I could see the sagging mattress on the iron cot, the thin blankets, the coarse sheets that she had laundered herself. Her old black coat, the only coat I could remember ever seeing her wear. The patched cotton tunics so stiff with starch the frayed edges didn't show too badly. The one pair of silk ceremonial trousers that only came out of her bureau drawer at New Year's. She hadn't bought them, herself, I was certain; Cousin Elizabeth had provided them, without any doubt, long ago when Cousin Elizabeth had lived with us.

The hall clock struck and warned me I wasn't free to cry any longer. I daubed at my eyes with cold water and then locked the front door after me and hurried to the office. At my desk, I made a difficult effort to be the smiling, courteous receptionist with just the right answer for whoever stopped at my desk, and I got through the morning well enough, and through a long, gray afternoon, with rain splattering the glass front of the tall building where I worked, and with sea gulls circling in from the sea, a sure sign that more wet weather and wind would be blowing from the west by evening.

Dreary. Dreary. Dreary.

Before I took the cable car back to Cousin Elizabeth's house that afternoon, I stopped at a flower stand and bought branches of flowering quince and almond and took them to Ah Sam in a Chinatown mortuary. She looked very tiny and old in her coffin and very lonely. Poor Ah Sam, so far from the fields of Hunan, the province she used to tell me about, so far from her little wisteria-hung village with its stone paving worn by the feet of pilgrims making their way to the mountain shrine of Nangyu. I knew Nangyu as though I had been there. Poor Ah Sam, so far from the clamor of bronze temple bells, the soughing of wind in dark pines and cypress, the leap of waterfalls, the rush of stream water. So far from the graves of her ancestors. That, more than anything else, would be troubling her now.

She was the first dead person I had ever seen, and I had difficulty in believing in an afterlife for anyone who was lying so still, so unwakable, but when I left the mortuary I stopped at the Buddhist temple. There, I lighted pink and yellow incense sticks for her, and red candles, and I bought from a shop nearby the little cakes and melon seeds and the silver paper coins that, if left at her grave in the morning, would provide for her in the spirit world of her next existence. Always, she had been confident of inhabiting it.

Then it struck me that perhaps a brief stop at Grace Cathedral would not be amiss, either, as long as I'd be passing its bronze doors on my way back to Cousin Elizabeth's house.

I prayed for Ah Sam with all my heart, hoping that Heaven, for her, would be a return to that far away little village in Hunan.

It had begun to rain when I came out of the cathedral, and there was a slanting rain, and a chilly wind off the bay. I crowded onto a cable car again, and then walked the rest of the way to Cousin Elizabeth's with my head scarf and raincoat soaked, my nylons plastered to my legs. There were, of course, no lights on in the house to give me any sort of a cheering welcome when I opened the front door, and I stepped into the shadowy emptiness of the hall with the ticktock, ticktock of the clock much too loud.

Was Mrs. Martin right? Was I going to be able to stay on here alone, after all, in this depressing house?

It struck me, suddenly, that "depressing" described it exactly, and that it always had been just that, as long as I could remember. Even Ah Sam had not been able to lighten the somber, heavy atmosphere I had sensed, as a child, although I could not have put my impression of it into words. It had simply been one more thing to accept.

But now, without Ah Sam, the sense of depression was all at once a weight too heavy for me to carry alone.

For the first time, ever, I began to wonder if the house had been a happy place for the other Allens, the earlier Allens. Yes, as far as I knew, except for Grandfather's quarrels with his son Richard, my father. But what about Cousin Elizabeth's childhood, and her growing-up days, and her young womanhood?

I glanced up the stairs, involuntarily, half expecting to see her, a hand on the banister; half expecting to hear a soft tread on the thick old-fashioned Brussels carpet, and a little chill made me shiver. Then I was thoroughly disgusted with myself. Seeing and hearing things; now, really! And my own unhappiness was sufficient without dredging up the past and long over with problems of Cousin Elizabeth.

As on all the other nights since Ah Sam's illness, I went into the yellow parlor, and trying hard to dispel the chill and the gloom of the house, I lighted the fire. It was a fire I had laid with almost the last of the kindling and coal from the big brass bucket on the hearth. When the bucket was empty, then what? I knew that nothing on earth could induce me to go down into the huge black cave of cellar whose stairs led down from the kitchen. In the old days, the Allen family's Chinese cooks and houseboys had lived in the cellar. The queer, sweetish smell of the opium pipes they smoked there surreptitiously still lingered, at least in my imagination, as did tales of San Francisco's tongs and hatchet men and slave girls, along with the legends of tigers and wolves that Ah Sam used to tell me, and of warlords, swooping down on the villages to eat little children alive.

I used to beg her for more and more stories, and listen

with my heart thumping, and that terrifying exciting cellar, the background of many a childhood nightmare, was still, ridiculously or not, a region I wouldn't dare set foot in.

I tried to laugh at myself. A man around the house was what I needed! One man in particular would be rather a nice adjunct. . . .

When I had eaten another of my make-do dinners off the kitchen table, I went upstairs to bed, once more to stay awake in the darkness, listening, listening, to all the night sounds of an old wooden house.

How completely I now agreed with Mrs. Martin. To stay alone was impossible. I might as well give in gracefully and let her have the fun of running my life. I was only cutting off my nose to spite my face by resisting her kind, well-meant interference. Pack up and move in with the Martins until you find an apartment. Be sensible.

All that creaking and soughing. Only old floorboards, only the wind, but. . . . and the foghorns—those mournful foghorns, and tolling buoys . . .

I was more or less of a wreck the next morning after my sleepless night, by the time Mr. Martin and his driver came for me and we followed Ah Sam's hearse out of town to the Chinese cemetery at Colma. There were no other mourners. The grave diggers shoveled cold, wet earth over a hole in the ground, and I put down the silver paper coins and sweetmeats for which Ah Sam would be so grateful on her long journey to join her ancestors, and turned away.

That was that.

Mr. Martin and I were silent on the drive back to town. Once or twice he cleared his throat and glanced at me tentatively, but he didn't make any attempt at small talk, thank heaven, and I have never liked him more. He left me off at my office building, and for the rest of the morning I smiled, and pressed buttons, and answered the telephone.

The twelve-o'clock ferry building whistle had just gone off and the noon church bells were ringing all over town when Jim Bradford walked up to my desk.

"You've had a rough time, I hear from Mr. Martin," he said without preface. "I'm sorry. And I've come around to see if you'll have dinner with me this evening. It might do you good."

He had nice gray eyes that I had liked the first time I met him, and they were looking at me directly, with something in their expression that told me he was really sorry. I liked his hands, too, just as I had liked them that evening at the Martins'. They were big hands, big-knuckled and hard looking and tanned, and I remembered he had told me he sailed a lot, and kept a small boat across the bay in the Sausalito Yacht Harbor.

He is taller than I, I thought, irrelevantly, when we are standing next to each other. And I was pleased. I am tall myself, and I hate to feel like a beanstalk, as I do with some men.

"May I come for you at seven?" He was not giving me a chance to say No to his invitation. "Have you a favorite restaurant? Would you like to go to Jack's?"

"I'd love to—if it were any other evening, but——"

"But you'd rather go somewhere else tonight?"

"I don't feel like going out anywhere." I was honest with him. The nice gray eyes made it easy. "You're very kind, but——"

"You have to eat dinner somewhere. Why eat in—in that hermitage of yours, alone?"

The "hermitage" didn't sound rude. It was merely his frank opinion of a house that the Martins had undoubtedly described to him. I could hear Mrs. Martin on the subject.

"Seven o'clock?" he persisted. "And we'll make it anyplace you say."

"Do you know Chinatown? Have you been to the Moon Gate?" I asked it on impulse.

"No, but there always has to be a first time. The Moon Gate it is." The nice smile was quick and decisive. With a nod that settled it all, he was on his way to the elevators, and I had lost my chance to change my mind. For which I was glad.

I thought about him all during my noon break. Lunch, more often than not, was an apple and a sandwich put in a paper bag by Ah Sam for me to eat on a bench in Union Square. I had learned, quickly, the very first month of my job, how expensive restaurants or salad bars could be, and I was going to need every penny I could save for shopping, as the clothes Cousin Elizabeth had paid for gradually wore out. Even the best didn't last forever.

Tonight, I'd wear my faithful old black sleeveless wool with the jacket that would make it covered up enough for dining at the Moon Gate. But what did clothes mean to me—or a man taking me to dinner—when Ah Sam had been buried this morning? And why had I suggested the Moon Gate to Jim Bradford?

I knew the answer to the last question. In Chinatown, Ah Sam would seem close, and alive. Briefly, at the Moon Gate, I could forget graveyard earth, shoveled back into a hole.

Ah Sam had first taken me to the Moon Gate when I was a child for *deem sum*, the midmorning tea and buns and assorted sweet and salty tidbits Chinatown loved, on Saturdays after our marketing tours along lower Grant Avenue for the chicken or fish or meat, the fruit and vegetables she crammed into her string bag.

She had always cooked the best of meals for me, but Cousin Elizabeth's household expense money had been spent with the greatest care. She had squeezed every cent—and squeezed every piece of fruit, too. And she had kept her black, peering, sharp old eyes on the scales when anything was weighed out.

That bulging heavy bag—the lolling chicken heads. The wet, slippery, finny mackerel, wrapped in newspaper. The onions, the kale, the sugar peas. The way she shuffled along, little and skinny and withered, staggering under her load, but never allowing me to carry a single bundle, because I was her Little Missee, and bundles were not for a Little Missee, properly brought up, China Old Style.

She had taught me to use chopsticks almost as soon as I had learned to hold a spoon, by slapping my hands until I could manage without spilling so much as a grain of rice, and when we went to the Moon Gate I used them as readily as any of the Chinese around me. We had been there often to dinner, as I grew older and could stay up later, and the glazed duckling, the sweet and sour condiments that accompanied roast pork, the dumplings, the fish with ginger, the custards and almond cakes were the greatest of treats.

Mrs. Martin would have had a fit.

The Moon Gate was no tourist trap, nor a deluxe restaurant catering to well-to-do Chinese. It was the simplest of cafés, but it served wonderful food and was a very real part of Chinatown. There, at a little table spread with a coarse, clean white cloth, and with a soy-sauce bottle in the middle of it, and two big teapots, two deep handleless cups from Canton, Ah Sam and I would sit, smiling and nodding in return of the nods and smiles of the other guests. The merchant down the street who sold silk and kites and goldfish and firecrackers and wicker baskets and Canton plates. A teller from the big bank down the street. A silk-trousered Venerable Grandmother with her grandchildren. And then there was the very rich Chinese gentleman with a wen and a great fat stomach, like a Buddha, who owned apartment houses all over the city, and who hobbled in every evening with his chauffeur, and had to have a gouty foot propped up on a teakwood stool.

The mounds of rice he got away with. His enjoyment of chicken and noodles. The bottles of hot Chinese wine he washed it all down with. The pots of hot tea that made his face glisten as though he were in a steam bath.

We gradually stopped going to the Moon Gate as I outgrew childhood. Mrs. Martin had me firmly in hand by then and didn't leave me time for Saturday-night treats with Ah Sam. But the restaurant was still flourishing, and I had been nostalgic for the old days more than once when I happened to pass it walking through Chinatown.

Tonight, I'd sit at one of those little tables again. Tonight, of all nights, was the time to go back.

Jim called for me, and we had cocktails, first, at the University Club, where he was living until he found an apartment to his liking, and then because it was so short a distance down the hill to Grant Avenue, and not worth the bother of reparking his car or calling a cab, we walked to the Moon Gate.

The hill below the club is steep; at one point I caught my heel in a paving crack, and would have fallen if Jim had not grabbed my arm. He held onto it, firmly, the rest of the way down, and for no reason at all I felt suddenly happy. Absurdly happy.

The waiter at the Moon Gate was new to me, and the proprietor didn't recognize me, nor did we sit at the table in the far corner, against the wall, where Ah Sam and I had always sat, but nevertheless it was the same familiar restaurant.

Ah Sam was almost too close. My brief happiness evaporated. It had been foolish to seek out the Moon Gate again, and self-inflicted pain to attempt to bring Ah Sam back.

Jim sensed my mood. He asked me to do the ordering, saying that a menu of Chinese food was entirely a mystery to him, but he asked for a pleasant Napa Valley white wine, and when it had been poured he raised his glass, his gray eyes quietly understanding. "A little reunion with your Ah Sam, was that what you had in mind when you chose the Moon Gate?"

I nodded. I couldn't speak. His perception, the sympathy I was afraid he might offer, were going to be too much for me. I would disgrace myself in another moment.

He saw me bite my lips, hard, saw the quick, bright start of tears in my eyes.

"Have a drink to her. Wine is a great cheerer-upper. And may I join you? I would have liked her. From what the Martins tell me, she was quite a person."

We drank, and I managed an uncertain smile.

"That's it. Now, shall we talk about you and me? We've a lot to catch up on." He stated it matter-of-factly. "And by the way, may I call you Nan? As I'm the Martin's nephew, and they are your aunt and uncle by proxy, more or less, 'Miss Allen' is ridiculously formal. Nan . . . ." He repeated it consideringly. "You are the first Nan I've ever known. I like the name. There's an old-fashioned sound to it."

"If it is to be Nan for me, than I expect it ought to be Jim for you."

"Right."

We were off then to a running start. It was heaven to put aside for a little while the happenings of the last few weeks, and over our duckling and sugar peas we got on beautifully together. I found we could discuss a hundred subjects, and agree on most of them, but what was better, over the others our differences of opinion or dissimilarity of viewpoint could be argued amiably, comfortably, and with an exchange of laughs.

"You are not only the first Nan I've ever known, you are the first red-haired girl I've ever taken to dinner," he told me, smiling. "I was always afraid of sparks flying, but you seem reasonably good-tempered, in spite of the color of your hair."

"Wait till I'm crossed."

"Thanks for the tip-off. I'll watch my step. But tell me something. I thought red-haired girls always wore green, and had green eyes . . ."

"That's mostly in novels. Black is much more practical for a hard-up working girl to wear, and as I'm not a heroine, I'm stuck with plain everyday brown eyes."

"Brown? You're wrong there. A sort of ambery color is more like it."

The waiter put dumplings in front of us, and he dropped the subject of my eyes. "You are not only the first red-haired girl I ever dined with, you're the first I ever knew who ate with chopsticks. Good Lord, what talent."

"I'm showing off . . ."

I hadn't been really. The chopsticks were there, at my

place, next to the knife and fork, as they were at everyone's place in the Moon Gate, and I had simply picked them up and used them, without thinking, as naturally as I had used them with Ah Sam.

"If you are as much at home in Chinatown as you seem, perhaps you can help me with a shopping problem. I don't know the first thing about rigging out an apartment, and when I find one I'll be wanting the cheapest sort of furniture. How about bamboo or rattan, and a couple of grass mats for rugs? I've got to do it on a shoestring. All my spare cash goes into my boat. She's damnably expensive to keep up."

"What is she, a sail or motorboat?"

"Sail. A ketch. And a beauty."

"What's her name?"

"The *Seabird II*, after a boat I had on the East Coat when I was a kid, and sold when I went into the Navy."

He told me a little then about his service years doing carrier duty, and about Harvard Law School, and his first job in Boston, and then his decision to come west and accept an offer with his uncle. He told me about his parents, too, and his married sisters and brothers and their children.

I envied him all that family life. He'd had a lot of fun growing up, and he hadn't any idea of what loneliness could be. He was one of the lucky people in life.

Our dinner ended with almond-flavored custard and lichee nuts. Jim had seemed to enjoy the Chinese food, but when more of the strong, steeped tea that had been served with every course was offered us, he said enough was enough, and suggested we go up to one of the hotels on Nob Hill for coffee and a brandy.

"I'll make coffee and give you a drink, if you'd like to

see my cousin's house," I offered. "The hermitage might entertain you."

"I've heard it's terrific."

A surge of gratitude welled in me when he enthusiastically accepted my invitation. For a little while, at least, some of the loneliness would be banished from Cousin Elizabeth's house. There would be laughter, louder than the ticktick of the hall clock, and emptiness filled.

We walked back up the hill, and when Jim took my arm a warm lovely happiness again possessed me. The walk was too short. I was sorry to get into the car for the drive to Cousin Elizabeth's house.

"If you'll make a fire, I'll make the coffee," I told Jim as I took him into the parlor. "It won't take a minute. Across the hall, in the dining room, on the sideboard, you'll find some bottles. I'll bring glasses and ice and soda. Take what you like. I'll have a crème de menthe."

When I came back from the kitchen he took my loaded tray and set it down. The last of the coal and kindling from the brass bucket was burning cheerfully. The yellow brocade curtains turned to warm gold. The room was alive as it hadn't been all the past weeks, and enfolding, I thought. Enfolding me—and my love.

He was that to me. My love. Found at last, and instantly recognizable.

He looked very large, and not at all comfortable on one of the rosewood chairs, but he didn't seem to mind its stiffness, and he eyed the lacquer cabinet appreciatively, and the silk dragon hanging and the Coromandel screen, as he drank his Scotch and soda.

We sat a little while, companionably, without much in the way of conversation until he asked unexpectedly, "Do you feel like talking about Ah Sam? Would it help?"

"It might."

"Give it a try."

"I don't know where to start."

"She brought you up?"

"Yes." I turned the stemmed glass I was holding, and firelight on it made the liquor the same green as the jade bibelots in the parlor cabinet. "Every morning of my childhood, and every night as long as I can remember, she was the first person I saw, and the last," I began slowly. "She wakened me when it was time to get up, and she sat in the doorway of my bedroom until I fell asleep. There was always a little night light burning so I could see her. She bathed and dressed me and brushed my hair. She cooked for me and washed my clothes. She played games with me. She told me stories."

"Did she teach you to speak Chinese?"

"No. Oh, I picked up a few phrases. But she couldn't read or write herself. She could draw, though, and she bought me ink and brushes, and showed me how a few strokes could be a bird, or a tree, or a hare, or a temple roof."

I was not minding, now, that my eyes were wet and stinging. "Whenever I tried to thank her for anything, she wouldn't listen. 'Small thing,' she'd say, 'Small thing for Missee.' She lived for me. She hadn't anyone else. Neither did I."

"Your cousin?"

"She had to leave me with Ah Sam. She was starting up the family business again in Hong Kong and Honolulu."

"And the Martins took over?"

"Yes."

"They were never as close, though, as your Ah Sam?"

"Not half."

His sympathetic, quiet questions drew me out until after midnight. The fire burned low; there were only ashes in the grate when Jim stood up. "Tomorrow is another day. I'm due in court with a client the first thing in the morning, and I've got to get back to the club and bone up on some notes. But when are we going to see each other again? Will you come sailing Sunday, if the weather is decent?"

We settled plans; I said I'd bring a picnic lunch, and Jim said we would dine out after our sail.

"More duck and dumplings in Chinatown, if you like—I'm game—or a steak at Jack's or their *sole meunière*. You name it."

We left it undecided, and said good-night at the door. My hand felt very small in his.

I watched him swing down the stairs, and listened to the sound of his footsteps on the sidewalk fade, and then I turned out the parlor and hall lights and went up to bed thinking: This is it; this is it, at last.

In my bedroom, I looked searchingly at myself in the heavily framed old-fashioned mirror that hung over the dressing table.

Probably he thought me too tall and too thin, with eyes too big, in a face that never had much color.

Amber eyes, he had called them. And he needn't have arranged for Sunday—had I begun to mean something to him?

But I was being a fool. I'd been around enough—and long enough—to know better than to clutch at straws.

Chapter three

It was several days later that Mr. Martin sent over the key to Ah Sam's room, and a written legal permission for me to go through her possessions. I climbed the tenement stairs after office hours, and the bareness of that poor, bare room—the bareness for my sake—and the meagerness of her life, touched and humbled me beyond words.

There was so little to do, so little to dispose of. I stripped the bed of its blankets and sheets and made them into a bundle for the Goodwill; but I folded, to keep for myself, the quilt she had made. There were shabby black felt slippers and a Mother Hubbard sort of flannel nightgown that went into the Goodwill bundle, and from the washstand-bureau drawers a jar of the oil of quince pomade she had used to sleek her hair, a comb, and her shabby black plastic purse with my name in it, on a card, and some small change.

Nothing else, at all. Or so I thought, until, reaching far back into each drawer to be sure I had missed nothing, I came on a small bundle in gold tea-paper wrapping, with a scarlet silk cord tied around it.

I opened it, and saw a five-sticked fan made of intricately carved and pierced sandalwood. The sandalwood scent still clung, unmistakably, as I unfurled the fan, and the little room was suddenly filled with a waft of it. A waft of the Orient. A waft of the Old China Ah Sam had known, and that had come to an end for her, just as it had for the Allen family, when Hong Kong fell to the Japanese twenty-five years or more ago.

A fan . . . something about a fan. I stared at it, and did my best to guess why on earth a fan had been of such importance to Ah Sam on her deathbed. Was this the fan she had tried to tell me about? It was old, and most delicately carved, and certainly not a fan that would be easily come by today, in this age of machine-made imported goods. But what other value it might have, or what meaning to Ah Sam, I couldn't imagine.

A thing of sentiment? A relic of the old days in China? Had it belonged to her as a girl? I doubted that; the daughter of a Human coolie, a girl who had hoed in the grain fields and gathered fagots in the forests, was not likely to have owned so exquisitely fashioned and so obviously expensive a fan.

And even if she had, why would Ah Sam, as an old woman, a miserable refugee from her village, stumbling along the road, fleeing from the Japanese as they swarmed down from the north, have held on to such a fan? Ah Sam had existed on tree bark and drunk snow water on that flight; would she have held fast to a fan that might have been traded for a bowl of rice or sacking to wrap around her bleeding feet when her straw sandals wore out to nothing?

It didn't make sense to think so. Ah Sam was the most practical of the practical. A fan such as this in my hand would have been traded off the first thing.

I gave up trying to guess where the fan had come from, but the scent of sandalwood so faintly but so exotically filling Ah Sam's poor little room gave me an understanding of why she had treasured it. Only to flutter it, lightly, was to evocatively fill the small room with the atmosphere of an oriental bazaar.

Jostling crowds. The smell of incense. Lanterns on poles. Cinnabar and silk and ivory. A blue harbor whose hills climbed to the sky. Junks with scarlet sails. Rickshas and sedan chairs.

A world of wonderment and dazzle to Ah Sam's old peasant eyes when she first reached Hong Kong after her flight, and before Hong Kong's prison camp swallowed her up.

I still could not imagine how such an expensive fan could have come into her possession, but I could understand now a possible reason for her last pitiful crying out; with the fan in her hand she would have had a reunion, of sorts, with Old China. Not just with Hong Kong, but with all of China. Even the Province of Hunan would not have seemed so far away, nor Nangyu, her tiny village that was home, and the burial place of her parents and of her revered ancestors.

A farfetched supposition, perhaps, but as good an answer as any.

I put the fan in my purse, left the Goodwill bundle in the hall, found the landlord of the tenement, paid him what was due for the remainder of the month's rent, turned over to him the key to Ah Sam's room, and said an inner good-bye to Chinatown. I wouldn't want to come back ever, I told myself.

I walked over to Columbus Avenue, and with my thoughts deliberately fixed on my meeting with Jim on Sunday, I went all out for an Italian picnic lunch. In one of the cluttered, garlicky-smelling little groceries that catered to after-work shoppers, I bought ravioli that could be heated up in the *Seabird*'s galley, sliced ham, and cheese, long bread sticks, tomatoes, and an avocado.

It was long after dark when I got back to Cousin Elizabeth's house; a bus was irritatingly slow in coming, and then I had a walk of several blocks. I ate an indifferent dinner, and then I forced myself to sit down and write to Cousin Elizabeth about Ah Sam. Mr. Martin would notify her officially, of course, but Cousin Elizabeth would certainly expect to hear from me personally. It would not be an easy letter to write.

How much would Ah Sam's death matter to her? Would she be sorry? I very much doubted it. She had spent years in the Orient, and Ah Sam had always been only a servant in her eyes. A good, honest, entirely dependable servant, the amah whose loyalty and devotion were proverbial. China had always produced thousands of just such amahs.

It was even more difficult than I had anticipated to write my letter. Every word was labored, the result stiff and reserved. My Ah Sam wasn't Cousin Elizabeth's Ah Sam.

If only I could have opened my heart freely as, in a measure, I had opened it to Jim Bradford. If only I could have let myself go . . .

As I sealed the letter and stamped it, I was wondering what Cousin Elizabeth was really like. Something more

43

than a career woman? Something more than a woman who put business and high finance first? I could only hope so.

Should I allow myself to feel resentment against her? Should I feel she had abandoned me, selfishly and inexcusably? Appearances warranted such a viewpoint, but I wanted to believe differently.

Once more I put myself in her place as a girl. There had been humiliations . . . the Allen's charity to thank for the roof over her head and the food she ate: the roof and the food of her San Francisco days and the roof and the food of her life in China . . . living in my uncle's and aunt's house with a younger woman as its mistress and she herself little more than a servant, with pocket money instead of wages.

After that, the prison camp. Wouldn't a prison camp harden any woman? Wouldn't you have to grow the thickest kind of protective shell to survive?

Later, she had worked herself nearly to death, spurred by her ambition, her relentless drive to make Allen and Company again a name that meant something.

I tried hard to muster my memories of her. The quiet eyes—blue? A quiet sweet voice as she said good-night to me each evening in the parlor when Ah Sam sent me down in the silk Chinese pajamas she used to make for me.

"Pleasant dreams, Nan."

I didn't remember her kissing me, ever, but I could still feel her soft hand lightly patting my cheek. "Run along, now. The Sandman is waiting."

It suddenly was easy to forgive her for any seeming abandonment. And, as suddenly, I longed to see her. A psychologist would, I suppose, say that to recompense myself for a long-felt, if subconscious, yearning for the parents I had lost, and for the loss of Ah Sam, I was trying to create a mother-image to take their place.

Perhaps so. In any case my longing to see her was intense. Together, and grown close, after all these years, she and I could both warm ourselves, both be rid of loneliness.

Before I could change my mind, I tore open the envelope I had just sealed and added a postscript to my letter.

I am of course wondering about the house, and your plans for it, now that Ah Sam is dead. I find it very big for one person. I wish so much you could come back to San Francisco if only for a short visit so that I could consult you about my own plans for the future. They are very indefinite. Or, if you can't come, perhaps I could go out to Honolulu on my next two weeks' vacation. It seems the greatest pity that we are such strangers to each other. And I would so much like to thank you, in person, for all you have done for me, for so many years.

I hesitated a moment at that point, and then added,

Please don't feel I am in need of any more financial help. I can manage an apartment easily, if your house continues to seem too big for just me, or if you decide to close it.

I hesitated again. Should I finish my postscript, "With love"? No. "Love" was too much. I was letting myself be carried away on that wave of sudden compassion, sudden longing. "Your grateful and appreciative niece, Nan" would do.

Late as it was, I tossed a coat over my shoulders and ran out of the house to the corner mailbox.

Airmail to Honolulu, airmail back—I'd have an answer in no time.

The house seemed emptier than ever when I came back to it. I wished I had accepted an invitation to dine with the kind, insistent Martins. I wished I had gone to a new Swedish film with the young married couple who often telephoned me when they had an unexpected, out-of-town man on their hands for the evening. I wished I weren't so choosy about the nice-enough but uninteresting men who asked me now and again to go out to dinner, or to a gallery opening, or a charity ball.

Being lonely was my own fault.

When I was in bed listening, as I listened every night now, for the creaking of the house, I determinedly con-centrated on thoughts of Cousin Elizabeth.

When she came back, the sterility of our relationship would end. The remembered quiet blue eyes would smile. The gentle voice would again call me "Nan, dear." Cousin Elizabeth would become my friend.

It became more than wishful thinking; it became a certainty, in my half-awake, half-asleep dream picture.

So much to talk about, so much for us to catch up on. We needn't ever discuss the bad, cruel prison days. I wouldn't ask about my parents. We'd begin with the day Ah Sam had carried me aboard the ship that was sailing for San Francisco with a passengerload of freed Ameri-cans. I knew it was Ah Sam who had held me, following Cousin Elizabeth up the gangplank. Ah Sam had told me so.

Ah Sam the amah, the servant.

I forgot the Cousin Elizabeth of my new imaginings in

a fresh and bitter welling up of grief for what I had lost in Ah Sam.

I got out of bed and opened my dressing-table drawer, and in darkness fumbled for the fan I had brought from Chinatown.

The faint but pervasive scent of sandalwood was all about me when I had unwrapped the gold paper. Old China . . .

Clearly, I could see Ah Sam raising herself on her pillow, could hear her crying out her last, unintelligible, meaningless words. Something about a fan? Cousin Elizabeth who knew China so well, who knew the sound and sight and smell of Old China, would agree with my theory as to why a sandalwood fan had been so important to Ah Sam. She herself was under the spell of the Orient, if her going back time after time to Hong Kong was any proof.

But I wouldn't show her the fan, nor talk about it. It wouldn't interest her. A fan belonging to a mere servant wouldn't mean a thing to her. I rewrapped the fan in its gold paper and retied the scarlet cord and put it back in my dressing-table drawer.

More and more it puzzled me to think how much it had meant to Ah Sam, and puzzling also to find it was beginning to mean something to me. And how strange the lingering of its exotic fragrance in my bedroom. A fragrance that was a kind of speaking out, a trying to speak out.

Ah Sam had tried so hard—but why?

Sandalwood and Ah Sam. Ah Sam and Cousin Elizabeth. Ah Sam and Cousin Elizabeth and the scent of sandalwood. As I lay half asleep, half awake, all three seemed to become, inexplicably, the separate parts of a whole. And I made a fourth part—with the scarlet cord of a gold-paper-wrapped bundle somehow knotting us close.

Drowsily, I considered and reconsidered the fan. It began to take on a dreamlike, out-of-proportion importance. Could it once have belonged to my mother? The remote and fanciful possibility pleased me. I seized upon it gratefully as a defense against the blackness and the emptiness of Cousin Elizabeth's house.

Something of my mother's, something that she had touched . . . Something to make her real to me. In the morning I would laugh at myself, as one so often laughed at night fancies, but for now, just for now . . .

Chapter four

STORM warnings for small craft were being posted from Point Reyes south to Monterey early Sunday morning when I tuned in my kitchen radio as I made toast and tea for breakfast. Momentarily, I expected a telephone call from Jim saying our sail was off, and I was braced for the disappointment, but when he did call it was a quick and surprisingly keen relief to hear him say we would have our day together in spite of the bad weather.

"I'll put you to work. If it doesn't rain you can help me varnish decks. Take it as a compliment. I don't allow just any landlubber to mess around the *Seabird*. Wear your oldest duds, but bring along a change for dinner."

The whole day with him, and an evening ahead, too.

I never sing when I am happy; I whistle. Not always on key, but enthusiastically, with trills coming out as spontaneously as trills from a bird's throat. And I was whistling while I put on the faded yellow slacks, the heavy Irish fisherman's cardigan I garden in when San Francisco's chilly summertime fogs dampen the fuchsia and hydrangeas and pelargonium and ferns, the mildewed roses of Cousin Elizabeth's back yard. I had rubber-soled espadrilles, too, and I tied up my hair in a yellow scarf.

It would have to do; I didn't belong to the Yacht Club crowd, and hadn't any chic nautical getup on hand.

Jim came for me at eight o'clock, and I was ready and waiting with a small suitcase and our picnic lunch in one of Ah Sam's string bags.

"Good girl," he approved. "I like prompt women. But you aren't going to be warm enough. Here. Put on this old pea jacket I brought along."

I knew I was going to be glad of it as we drove across the Golden Gate Bridge and could feel the car sway in a strong westerly wind, and saw the bleak gray sky.

Jim parked the car on a hilltop when we got to Sausalito and we walked down a narrow winding road to the waterfront, and past antique shops and art galleries and restaurants and espresso bars to a small dock.

I was enchanted with the *Seabird* at first sight.

Her hull was white with a gray trim, and her name was scrolled in black on the bow.

"Gorgeous!"

Jim looked pleased as I examined it.

I drew a deep breath of the gusty clean air that smelled of salt and of the tide-washed, barnacled dock pilings and tarred mooring lines. "I should think you'd want to sail away on her and never come back. An office, every day, when you have this?"

"You advise a cruise of the seven seas instead? A search for coral and pearls and spices and all that?"

I drew another long, deep breath. "Sandalwood, too . . ."

"Why sandalwood?"

"I don't know, really. Except that it sounds romantic, and far away. And . . . and mysterious."

"There's tortoise shell to go after, and ambergris, too, as long as you are making a list."

We both laughed, and he helped me aboard *Seabird*.

"I'll show you around and then we'll get to work."

There was a tiny cabin with two bunks, a minute washroom, a tiny galley with a midget stove and icebox.

"Make yourself at home, and I'll stow away the food."

I powdered my nose and redid my lipstick and went on deck. Jim, in his white, paint-smeared ducks, a navy-blue pullover, and sneakers, was prying open a can of varnish.

"I'm not really a slave driver," he grinned. "Sit and watch, if you'd rather. I'd offer you a beer, or a gin and tonic, but it's a little early, don't you think?"

"Much too early."

"Does coffee appeal? You'll freeze, unless you keep moving."

"Give me a brush and tell me where to start."

I won another approving "good girl," from him, and he opened a second can of varnish and gave me a big brush and a pile of cotton waste.

"We'll start aft. You take the lee side. And wipe up in a hurry if you spatter any brasswork."

We both got down on our knees. There was the slap, slap of water against the side of the boat, the creak of her mooring lines, the cry of a gull, perched on the *Seabird's* tall mast, and my involuntary, tuneless whistling.

Once I shifted position and straightened my back.

"Had enough? Holler when you want to call quits."

"I'm fine. I'm having fun." I sat back on my heels and brushed a strand of hair out of my eyes. "I still think you're crazy, not sailing away somewhere. If this were my boat, I'd never put ashore until the galley needed restocking and the drinking water ran dry."

"Where would you head for, the South Seas? The Bahamas? Baja California?"

"Those places could wait. For my first voyage, I'd set the compass for the Sandwich Isles."

Jim laughed. "Or less romantically, Hawaii? Why there, especially?"

I was dabbling my brush in the varnish can aimlessly as I answered, "I don't know why, exactly, but . . ."

Jim glanced at me. "Give me the lowdown." There was curiosity in his voice. "Ever been to the Islands? You want to go back, do you, because you left something—or some-one—behind?"

"I've never seen the islands. I've got friends who go back and forth, but no one there who—well, who counts, except a cousin."

"Male or female? Let's get the suspense over."

"Female."

"That's a big relief! And do you mean the Miss Beaton I've heard about from the Martins?"

"Yes. She brought me up. Or rather, she gave me to Ah Sam to bring up."

It sounded a little bitter, and Jim looked surprised. "She's quite a person, I'd have thought, from what the Martins said. They told me about the prison camp, and what a tiger she was, sticking it out, and seeing you safely back to San Francisco."

"Don't think me ungrateful." I spoke up quickly. "Cousin Elizabeth was wonderful. I owe her more than I can ever say. But——"

"But you could have done with a little more of her company all these years you've been living alone in that big old house—or practically alone? I don't blame you. A raw deal, for a kid. But I can't see why you want to go chasing out to the Islands after someone who's more or less a complete stranger to you."

"I can't explain it—it's just that——"

"What about her side of it?" Jim put the question bluntly. "She'd have come back to San Francisco, wouldn't she, or she'd have sent for you, if she'd wanted to see you?"

"That's just it." I began varnishing the deck assiduously to keep him from seeing a blur of quick, ridiculous tears. Once before, at the Moon Gate, he had sensed tears ready to brim. He'd think me a silly, sentimental crybaby. He'd be disgusted with me. "I'd give anything if she cared even the least bit about me. She's all I've got now. And I loathe being so . . . so detached. It's a beastly feeling."

I shrugged. "But you couldn't possibly understand. You've got a family to tie to. Tons of family. Not just the Martins. You can go back to New England and settle down in a huge nest of parents and brothers and sisters and cousins, from what I've heard."

"And of nieces and nephews," he supplied. "There's a whole clutch of them: my brother's kids, plus my two sisters' contributions to the population explosion. They've overdone it, I feel strongly, around birthday and Christmas shopping time. But what's a bachelor uncle for, after all?"

"You sound a frightfully baked-bean and cod sort of family. Impressive. Back Bay personified."

"And stuffy-sounding as well?"

"A little, maybe."

"We aren't too impossible. You might even learn to like us, given time."

He had been laughing, but now he looked at me

thoughtfully. "You *are* more or less alone. . . . I've never stopped to think before what that would be like. I can see where you might be missing a lot. And you think your cousin—Miss Beaton—would relieve the situation? Is that what you had in mind when you dreamed up this Hawaiian reunion deal?"

"Yes. I . . . well, I suppose you could say I'm homesick for her."

"And she will be glad to see you?"

"It's natural to think so, isn't it? She's as alone in the world as I."

"Alone. But lonely? Those are two different things. If she had wanted you in her life, wouldn't she have shown some sign of it by now?"

"You've been listening to the Martins. They don't seem to see that a business woman hasn't time to bother with a child."

"All right. I see your point. But you aren't a child now."

"I wish the Martins had kept their opinion to themselves."

"Frankly, I agree with them. Your Cousin Elizabeth sounds a damn cold fish to me. I'd forget about her if I were you. I'd skip Hawaii. Not that it's any of my business."

"You're so right. It's nobody's business but my own. And if I choose to go out to Honolulu and look her up, I'll go to Honolulu."

"My, my. A typical redhead, after all. But I don't mind a dash of paprika. It adds that little something, just so long as we're not starting an honest-to-God scrap."

He looked a little anxious.

"Don't worry," I reassured him, my flash of temper cooling quickly. "You'll know if I ever get really mad." I laughed, and Jim flashed a swift relieved grin, and as I dipped my brush in the varnish and resumed working alongside of him, I was whistling again.

After a while Jim glanced at the watch on his sun-browned wrist. "Lunchtime. Let's go. I could eat a horse."

I heated the ravioli, and while I set out the rest of the food, Jim opened a bottle of *vin rosé*. We ate and drank, and talked and laughed. I was happy, happy. And I dared to think Jim was happy too.

After lunch he went ahead with the varnishing, but he wouldn't let me help anymore. "You've done your stint for the day," he declared.

"Didn't you hear me say I was having fun?"

"Don't argue, woman."

I enjoyed being bossed around in that joking sort of way and obeyed orders, contenting myself with cleaning my brush in a turpentine bath, and with cleaning myself; there were splatters of varnish here and there, including a speck on the bridge of my nose that I could only see cross-eyedly, and which Jim obligingly wiped off for me.

The wind blew harder as the afternoon passed, with a sharpness to it, and Jim saw me shiver. "Go below and change. I'll wash my brush, and then I'll take my turn in the cabin, and we'll batten down the hatches and make for Jack's and an early dinner before the usual Sunday night crowd gets there."

I took a brown wool restaurant suit out of my dressing case, and did my hair, and pinned on a flat brown velvet bow, and went on deck. Jim changed quickly and we went ashore.

The sunset was spectacular as we drove back to town, with cars already bumper to bumper on the bridge with weekend traffic. Jim was giving all his attention to his driving, but I looked out to sea, where the darkening green water of the Gate was almost black under its wind-whipped white riffles, and I thought again of those Sandwich Islands, lying westward, where the sky was like fire and smoke, with vermilion holding its own against a bank of gray fog.

One of those islands out there was Oahu: Honolulu was on Oahu. Plane flights from the mainland put down there practically every hour. No longer was it far away—in time. And no longer was a flight too expensive to be out of reach. I could afford an Economy Class ticket, and I wouldn't need new clothes. I already had the cottons and linens I wore down the Peninsula in summer when I was invited to buffet Sunday lunches, a yellow chiffon for supper dances at the club, and I had a bathing suit.

I had a lot to think about and did no more talking than Jim until we reached the parking lot next to Jack's restaurant and went inside.

The headwaiter knew Jim and gave us a good table. Jim did the ordering, and instead of duck and sugar peas and soy sauce and dumplings, we dined this time on crab cocktails and the *sole meunière* that was his favorite dish, and artichokes with Hollandaise, and drank a Riesling. For dessert, Jim took crackers and cheese and I had zabaglione.

It was over coffee that he brought up the subject of the islands again.

"I'm butting in for the second time around, and you won't like it, but you meant it, did you, really meant it about Honolulu? You're seriously thinking of taking off?"

"Yes."

"When?"

"It all depends. I don't know, yet. I'm waiting. I expect a letter. I won't decide anything until it comes."

"If you go, how long will you stay?"

"I've only got two weeks' vacation coming."

"Would you stay longer if you could? Would you want to stay?"

His eyes were on me steadily. I couldn't meet them.

"No—no, I wouldn't want to stay longer." I looked away and stirred my coffee.

"Good!" He called the waiter abruptly and paid the bill, and we left.

He drove out Sacramento Street and turned onto Grant Avenue. Chinatown was as crowded and noisy as always on Sunday evenings. We crept along in the one-way traffic, and I was liking him more than ever for his quiet perception in putting just the finishing touch on a perfect day.

Ah Sam's Chinatown, but mine, too.

We heard the singsong of voices and the harsh clash and whine of Chinese music as a theater door opened. There was the familiar smell of incense, of the musty straw of packing barrels just in off the wharves that permeates everything, the smell of fish and frying noodles. It smelled of damp basements and alley tenements, with wretched rooms like Ah Sam's. But it excited me. Stirred me. Lured me.

When we reached Cousin Elizabeth's house, I asked Jim if he would like to come in for more coffee and perhaps a whisky and soda. He said No, tomorrow was another day. Monday, at that. With a glance into the dark hall, he frowned. "You oughtn't to live here, alone in this big empty house. I don't like your coming back to it at night, this way."

"You sound like the Martins."

I said it lightly, scoffingly, but nevertheless I was doing the usual, putting on the light, hurriedly.

He stepped inside. "You don't like it yourself. And it's not right. Not necessary." He put a hand on my sleeve. "You know it's not necessary, don't you, Nan? You know there are other places you could live? You know you needn't be alone anymore? I think you do . . ."

He suddenly leaned down and kissed my mouth, hard. "I'm not proposing. It's too soon. You'd think we hadn't known each other nearly long enough. And we haven't, if we want to be sensible. But one of these days . . ."

His mouth was on mine again and then he ran down the steps to his car.

I went up to bed in a daze. He was in love with me. Jim Bradford, that attractive, wonderful man was in love with me. With me, of all people, when he had the whole world of girls to choose from. I couldn't make myself believe it was true. When I had undressed and was in my night-gown, I sat in front of my mirror and brushed my hair, still disbelieving, and still marveling.

It would mean Jim and me in that apartment he was looking for. I met the eyes of the girl whose glowing face looked back at me from the dressing-table mirror, thinking: She won't be Nan Allen anymore. She will belong to the Bradford family.

A lovely word, "family." I smiled at my reflection, and was glad, remembering something. "The begetting Bradfords." If I was lucky, I'd have children.

But the "begetting Bradfords" were, as well, the Back Bay, Beacon Hill Bradfords, the Groton and Harvard and North Shore Bradfords. Would that spoil things? A small cloud of apprehension dimmed my happiness for an instant. What would those Bradfords think of Jim's marriage to a girl from way out in San Francisco who had no family of her own for background? The name Allen wouldn't mean a thing to them. Even here it carried no importance to the influx of new people who had changed the city so much in the last few years. Only in the close but thinning ranks of the old-timers did it carry weight.

Oh, yes, the Martins would speak up for me, but to those Bostonians I would still seem no one in particular. They might not be intentional snobs, but I'd be merely one more of those detached girls that could be found by the thousands in any big city.

That hurt. Not my pride, exactly; it was just that I had a sense of regret for my parents' sake, more than my own. They would be sorry not to be here, and so provide a conventional, satisfactory background for their daughter.

Well, they weren't here.

But what about Cousin Elizabeth acting in their place? She would be far better than no family at all. She must come back. She must.

I was able to convince myself she would see it that way herself. And with that reassuringly settled, my happiness rushed over me again in full tide. I began to brush my hair again, and as the thick, bright abundance of it fell around my shoulders (it was my one vanity), I thought: I hope Jim will like seeing it hang loose. I thought, too: I must buy some very special nightgowns, white and sheer, cut Empire, with pale-blue satin ribbons tying under my breasts.

Jim, dear Jim who loved me, and whom I loved. I was going to marry him. I would never again be lonely or depressed. And Cousin Elizabeth's old, empty house could creak all it chose to creak; the clock in the hall could tick as loudly as it liked. The stairs could wind up, and up, into eerie, scary shadows. No longer would any of that matter. Because I wouldn't be here. I would be with Jim.

"You need never be afraid again," I told the happy-eyed girl in the mirror. "Not of anything, or anyone, in the world."

Never again afraid.

No assumption could have been more mistaken. But how could I have known better? I had as yet no inkling of the emissary Cousin Elizabeth was sending out from Hong Kong instead of a letter. I had as yet no warning that under his chilling, inscrutable gaze I would come to feel like a hapless, impaled butterfly, who for all its frantic fluttering could not loose itself from the pin that held it fast.

Chapter five

WORD from Cousin Elizabeth—a cable, I hoped for, optimistically, or certainly an immediate letter in answer to mine—became an obsession with me. Every day I hurried home from the office to snatch up the mail the postman had dropped through the slot in the front door. Standing in the hall, still in my raincoat and soaked head-scarf, and dripping on the rug, because rain had drenched the city all week, I scrabbled through a handful of envelopes, and only then took off my wet things. Gas and electricity and water bills, advertisements, charity pleas, cocktail invitations. Never mind, I told myself with confidence, tomorrow. There will be word from Cousin Elizabeth tomorrow.

With each disappointing day an almost unbearable desire mounted in me to hear from her, and so to have even the slightest beginning of a rapport established between us. My detachment from normal family ties would come to an end. I would have my cousin, Miss Elizabeth Beaton.

I allowed myself the ultimate in wistful thinking. Immediately on receipt of my letter she would come rushing back to San Francisco, as eager for a reunion as I. She had only needed to be reminded of me, she had only needed a hint of my loneliness.

Miss Elizabeth Beaton
announces the marriage of her niece
Miss Anne Rathbun Allen
to
Mr. James Lowell Bradford III

As though those announcements were on my desk, stamped, ready to send out, I could see them. I could see the cards, engraved on Shreve's most correct ivory vellum. I could see the fluttering tissue paper of the inner envelopes when people opened them.

No longer would I be merely "the girl who lives by herself in that old Victorian monstrosity," or "that girl the Martins always have in tow." Not after Cousin Elizabeth's arrival, dynamic Cousin Elizabeth's impact on the San Francisco she used to call home. And the announcements, going back east to Jim's family and friends, would establish me as a girl with family ties and roots of her own.

But still no letter came. And beside my inordinate longing to hear, a longing grew daily to know more about my parents, to have their barely-sketched-in figures outlined for me with stronger pencil strokes and be given perspective against the canvas on which Mr. Martin and Ah Sam had delineated them so lightly. I remembered I had once asked Ah Sam what my mother had looked like. She had pretended not to hear. I had persisted, but she still was deaf, and I realized, quickly, that she didn't want to talk about my mother. To keep at it would only hurt her.

Over and over, all those long ten days of waiting, I caught myself glancing into every mirror I passed, whether in my bedroom or bathroom or in the parlor, or in the glass of a shop window. Was my red hair my mother's red hair? My eyes, hazel or amber, call them what one chose, her eyes? And the words "my mother" took on an importance they had never before held for me. Now Anne Allen had become the woman whose fan was in my dressing-table drawer and so was real to me for the first time in my life.

There were a good many times, of course, when neither Anne Allen or Cousin Elizabeth engrossed my thoughts. To be with Jim meant to think of no one else. We saw each other every evening. We went to restaurants and to foreign films and to a symphony concert, to galleries, and to the Chinese Theater on the last night of its New Year's celebration run. We avoided the Martins as much as we could, politely, and cocktail parties. We only wanted to be alone together.

It was saying good-night to him that became increasingly hard. Not only because I was so much in love, but because when he left me, Cousin Elizabeth's house began more and more to depress me. And frighten me, though Mrs. Martin, with all her fussing over the way I lived couldn't have wrung the confession from me.

There was one evening in particular. Jim left, and after I bolted the front door and was walking through to the kitchen to make sure the back door was securely fastened, I stopped, and stood very still, with my heart thumping, and a feeling that someone beside Jim and me had been in the house, or was still in the house. Someone who had come in while we were out.

Jim smoked a pipe, and I wasn't smelling a pipe tobacco that I recognized. This whiff, this almost nonexistent whiff, was different. A cigarette . . .?

I stood motionless a long time, listening, waiting, expecting anything. Finally I convinced myself I had got jumpy over nothing, and had turned into the world's worst coward. But I left all the lights flaring on the first floor, and almost ran up to my bedroom.

The hall had never seemed so long, the stairs so winding and shadowy and unending. When I bolted myself in, I was shaking. Someone beside myself and Jim . . .

It was sheer nerves, I knew, a bad case of silly jitters. And I didn't tell Jim when I saw him next. I was too ashamed. Ashamed, but not entirely self-convinced.

Someone. You can sense when there has been a stealthy intruder in a house that has been familiar to you all your life. An intruder leaves part of himself behind, something alien.

All of which, of course, was just too, too . . . Forget it, I told myself. Be your age, Nan Allen. You will be counting the Allen's silver forks and spoons, the next thing you know, and looking for burglars under your bed.

We spent a very special, very momentous evening together, finally. I had invited Jim for dinner at Cousin Elizabeth's, and I was going to do the cooking. Not really the cooking, the serving would be more accurate. I gave him a choice ahead of time of steak or of Chinese food and was relieved when he chose the latter. It meant I wouldn't have to struggle ineptly over the monstrous kitchen stove with thoroughly unattractive results. Instead, I could order and bring back a delicious entrée and perfectly cooked vegetables from the Moon Gate that needed only to be heated, and I knew I could manage rice. I had seen Ah Sam do it a thousand times; the rice went into a heavy iron pot and was just barely covered with water. Then the lid was pressed down tight with an old flatiron. When you could hear the water boiling—talking, as Ah Sam said, the rice was done, and each grain of it plump and dry and separate.

I set the table, with a pot of red New Year azaleas for a centerpiece, banked with good-luck pomelos from a Chinatown fruit stand, and then I ran upstairs and changed into a yellow silk *cheong-sam*, one of the Chinese dresses, slit up the sides and fastened high at the neck with braid frogs, which I often wore at home in the evenings, and put on black velvet, beaded Chinatown slippers.

At seven o'clock Jim arrived with a bottle of white wine, smoked salmon on brown bread from his club for an hors d'oeuvre, and, of all things, a bakery-shop apple pie and large wedges of yellow mousetrap cheese.

"I thought we'd go all out American for at least one course," he explained with a twinkle. "And since I'm hungry——"

"And not too sure whether or not you'd have to sit down to bird's-nest soup, or chicken feet with ginger, or turnip cakes, you thought you'd play safe for at least one course?"

"I haven't been hungry only for food all day." He was suddenly holding me close, and kissing me, and I was returning his kisses, and then we were becoming engaged, precipitously, rashly, delightfully, and inevitably.

Afterward, a long while afterward, Jim opened the wine and I put the rice and chicken almond and bean sprouts on an old round, flowery-patterned Canton platter from a top shelf in the pantry. We used the Allen family's best dinner plates, too, of celadon-green Export Ware, all raised-enamel butterflies and peonies. This was a feast. A celestial feast. Were not Ah Sam's gods and goddesses smiling on me? Was I not experiencing Heavenly Happiness?

To my mind, it was a private New Year's celebration. To me, the dining room seemed strung with lanterns and tassels and windbells. To me, firecrackers were going off, drums were beating, and the dragon was dancing again.

How could anyone be so happy, happy?

After dinner we took our coffee into the parlor, and Jim produced a paper bag of fortune cookies. ". . . just in case the pie might not have struck the right note."

He opened one of the cookies and read aloud its saying. It was short, but very much to the point. "The water is deep and cold, but you can swim." How we laughed. Could anything be more apropos, or offer more comforting reassurance for a man about to give up his bachelor status and plunge into matrimony?

It was my turn to choose a cookie. "To believe all is to be foolish. To doubt is to be wise."

"So, you are a philanderer, are you?" I teased Jim. "And I'm a poor girl who ought to be on guard before she is led astray?"

There was more laughter between us, and a good deal more kissing as we made plans. If Jim could take his vacation now, it would do nicely for a honeymoon, but we'd have to find an apartment as soon as possible.

"If we have children—if they come along, we'll buy a house," Jim said.

"You sound rather rich. Do you know what houses cost nowadays in San Francisco? The earth."

"We'll sell the *Seabird,* and get a rowboat instead, if

necessary. But it's not likely to come to that. I'm not rich, really rich, but praise the Lord I'm well-heeled, thanks to choosing the right grandfather."

"I chose the right one too, but it didn't do me any good, in the end. . . ." I told him about my grandfather's will, and he said, to hell with the Allens; I had the Bradfords now to look after me.

He was kissing me again when the telephone rang. "Let whoever it is call some other time," he suggested, but I have never been able to listen to a persistent ringing, without my curiosity getting the better of me. I tore myself out of his arms and went to the hall cloakroom, where the only telephone in the house has always been since it was first installed in my grandfather's day.

"Hello?"

When I heard who it was, my excitement and delight were overwhelming. Not Cousin Elizabeth, but almost as perfect—a Mr. Yin Wah introduced himself as a close business associate of Cousin Elizabeth's, here from Hong Kong. Cousin Elizabeth, in Hong Kong herself at the moment, had received my letter, forwarded from Honolulu, and had given him a message for me. Might he call on me tomorrow at Cousin Elizabeth's house, after my office hours, or would I prefer to meet him in the lounge of the Fairmont Hotel, where he was staying?

The Fairmont, at the reservation desk, at half past five, was decided on, and I hung up the receiver, thrilled. This was wonderful. A hundred times better than a letter. Cousin Elizabeth's personal messenger. And what other news could he be bringing than that Cousin Elizabeth herself would soon be flying into San Francisco?

I rushed back to the parlor and gave Jim an excited account of the letter I had sent off, and of its result.

"What does the bloke sound like? A nice guy?"

"Nice enough." I hesitated. "Not exactly, well, polished. A bit on the abrupt side. But that doesn't matter. Just think, Cousin Elizabeth caring enough to send him all that way."

Jim was sweet about my excitement, but I could not help feeling he was just a little bit jealous.

"Your cousin means all that to you, does she?"

"She is all I have of family, remember."

"A fiancé doesn't rate? A husband-to-be doesn't fill the void?"

"Oh, darling. Don't be silly. This is different. I wish I could make you understand."

"Aren't you counting your chickens before they're hatched, being so certain she'll turn up? Why a go-between, if she's on her way? Why not a cable? Or speaking of being rich, why didn't she pick up a telephone in Hong Kong and give you the word direct?"

I refused to let him take the edge off my anticipation. "She may have called and called when I was out, for all you know."

"All right. All right. You win. But let's talk about us now. Let's talk about the future Mr. and Mrs. Bradford. Know something? I'm going to like being married. What about you?"

I gave him a satisfactory answer, and there was no further discussion about Cousin Elizabeth, and no further argument. Not that evening.

Chapter six

I got up earlier than usual the next morning and did the night-before dinner dishes in my dressing gown. Then I put on my best brown suit, new brown calf Italian pumps with brass buckles, and a brown velvet pillbox, and as I picked up an alligator bag left from the extravagant days of Cousin Elizabeth's clothes allowance, and a pair of *café-au-lait*, luxuriously wrinkling gloves that I kept for special occasions, I took a last glance in my bedroom mirror. Would Mr. Yin Wah, with a male Oriental's traditional prejudice against red hair, consider me a too frightfully ugly and repulsive girl? I very much hoped not. His approval of me was vital. I wanted the most complimentary of reports to go back to Cousin Elizabeth.

When five o'clock came that afternoon, I washed my hands and inspected my manicure, and put on fresh lipstick, and then took a cable car to the top of Nob Hill. At the Fairmont I pushed through the revolving door and crossed the deliberately Edwardian and flamboyantly rococo lobby. At sight of a Chinese man standing at the reception desk, obviously waiting for someone, I slipped behind one of the marbled pillars that rose up from a welter of scrolled, thick-piled crimson carpeting for a quiet, unobserved appraisal.

Cousin Elizabeth's messenger.

He was a coarse-featured, heavy-jowled man, perhaps fifty years old, wearing horn-rimmed, thick-lensed glasses. A Cantonese, I judged from his short stature and stockiness—the northern Chinese are taller—but there was also a look of mixed blood about him. What might be termed a Latin swarthiness; his pockmarked complexion was several shades darker than the ivory-to-saffron skin I was used to seeing in Chinatown. As I went up to him, I wondered if perhaps he were part Portuguese. From Macao, possibly; that was only a ferry ride's distance from Hong Kong . . .

"Mr. Yin Wah?" I ventured it tentatively, and put out my hand. "I am Anne Allen."

His acknowledgment was a kind of grunt. Ignoring my hand, and without any waste of time on civilities, he nodded to a window alcove, where two chairs behind potted Edwardian palms allowed for private conversations. "Over there . . ."

I did not like him. And nothing could make me like him. My mind was made up to it as I sat down next to him. I had not liked him on the telephone the night before, either—not his voice, not his approach—although I wouldn't have admitted it to Jim, and had not even admitted it to myself, until now. What could Cousin Elizabeth see in him? Even though he might be the cleverest of businessmen, he had no manners, and looked thoroughly unattractive.

The glasses magnified his eyes so enormously that they made me think of dark fish, swimming sluggishly behind those thick lenses. But in spite of my instant distaste for his appearance I leaned forward in my chair. My own eyes, my whole face, must be alive with anticipation, I thought, and my inner excitement must surely shine outwardly.

"Will my cousin be coming to San Francisco soon?" I plunged ahead with the question, hurrying to get to the whole point of our meeting. "I am longing to see her. She is the only family I have, and——" It sounded incredibly childish and sentimental, and I dropped it to ask, "Has she set a definite date for coming? Oh, I hope so."

Mr. Yin Wah took his time about answering. He was rolling a yellow-papered cigarette, and before he put it between thick lips to light it, he spat, disgustingly, into a brass jardiniere that held one of the palms, and as casually as he might have spat into a Chinatown—or Hong Kong —gutter.

"Miss Beaton will not be coming to San Francisco in the near future." His voice was curiously high-pitched and thin, and a faintly British accent suggested years of a Crown Colony background. "Miss Beaton has requested me to tell you she is much involved in business affairs, and has no time at present for a journey to San Francisco." The statement came flatly, and with finality. It was like a slap in the face.

"No time . . . ?" I echoed it weakly as I sank back in my chair. I could feel myself shrivel inwardly. All my foolishly optimistic, soaring hopes of a reunion with Cousin Elizabeth crashed like those fragile paper kites sold in Chinatown shops that become just so much torn bright paper and shattered sticks when they plummet.

"But I'd counted on her coming. . . ." It sounded like the protest of a bewildered child, punished unfairly. What must this man think of me? My pride came to the rescue, and I leaned forward on the edge of the chair again. "It doesn't matter. I understand—I know how busy she is. But please tell her that as she can't come here to see me, I can perfectly well fly out to see her. Honolulu, Hong Kong—either place."

Mr. Yin Wah flicked a grain of tobacco from a pendulous underlip. "Miss Beaton has no time for you. To attempt seeing her would be useless. And a great mistake."

"But that's ridiculous! I know she'd see me if I came." I flung it at him, angry and humiliated. "Of course she'd see me."

With deliberation he ground out his cigarette in the moist earth around the palm—ground it out with unnecessary emphasis, it seemed to me. A frightening emphasis. If the cigarette, instead of being a cigarette, were a person he wanted to be rid of—someone who for any reason didn't suit his plans . . .

I sat there, dismissed. Dismissed by an uncouth boor whose dark eyes behind those thick glasses chilled me and, strangely enough and for no real reason, made me feel all at once very much alone in the world. More than that, perilously adrift in strange waters . . .

His good-bye to me was another grunt. Then he walked away. I watched him go to the desk. He beckoned a bellboy to pick up a suitcase and went out the lobby door, his arms, which were too long for his body, swinging like an ape's, and his fat, soft-looking, huge hands an unpleasant dangle.

Ugh. Those hands. How could Cousin Elizabeth stand having him around?

Wondering it, I left the hotel and started back to the house. Cousin Elizabeth's house. Just a house. That was the way I thought of it. Never as "home" now. A dreary, empty house, and nothing more, without Ah Sam.

In all the Nob Hill apartments the lights were on, yellow and warm, through the first drifting in of thick fog that was banked heavily beyond the Gate. And there were lights in the big brownstone Pacific Union Club that had survived the earthquake and fire, opposite the hotel, and where, doubtless, Mr. Martin and his cronies were playing dominoes and having a drink or two before they went in to dinner. Down the hill, at the University Club, the lights would be on, too, and Chinatown would be neon bright against the early evening darkness. Ah Sam's Chinatown. My Chinatown.

In contrast, when I reached Cousin Elizabeth's, the hall seemed all the gloomier in its unlighted darkness, all the more depressing. A veritable forcing-house for curious apprehensions, already sprouted and growing.

Jim was to take me out to dinner—but dinnertime was an hour ahead. With the ticktick of the hall clock emphasizing the emptiness, the loneliness of the house, I wanted Jim. I ached for him. I had to be with someone. I had to talk to someone.

I couldn't get to the telephone quickly enough, dial quickly enough, but in my rush I fumbled, and had to dial twice. It seemed to take ages to have Jim paged at his club.

"Hello?"

At the sound of his voice I tried to make a little joke. "It's me—just yours truly—ungrammatically speaking . . ."

My voice shook in spite of my attempt to be facetious.

"Nan! What's wrong?"

"Nothing—nothing much. Just this empty house. If you could come a little earlier . . ."

"Hold everything. I was in the shower. Give me ten minutes."

I heard the receiver slam down, and I blessed him.

When he ran up the front steps and I opened the door, he looked grim. Inside the hall he was laying down the law to me even before he kissed me. "You're moving out of here, Nan. And you are marrying me the minute we can get a license."

He pulled me to him. "Three days for a license and a physical. But you are to pack up now—right now—and we'll ask the Martins to take you in. You're not staying another night in this mausoleum."

"I can't marry you, not in three days." I broke away from his arms. To my utter astonishment I heard myself say, "I'm going out to see Cousin Elizabeth first. But I'll be gone only two weeks, and I'll marry you the day I get back."

"Two weeks!" It sounded more like two years as he exclaimed it. "You mean, instead of our being married the minute we can, you'd take off for Honolulu and that cousin of yours?" Then he laughed, and pulled me to him. "I almost believed you. I don't like that kind of joke."

"It wasn't a joke. . . ."

"It must have been; just think, darling, in three days from now . . ."

"No, Jim. In two weeks. Please! Please! You've got to listen. You've got to try and see it my way."

He let me go, and it was awful to have his arms drop away, and to stand, alone, and know an unbridgeable gap had begun to widen between us.

"You had better have some foolproof arguments lined up, that's all I can say."

The case I tried to make out for myself could not have been weaker, but my whole heart was in it, and I hoped that would count with him. I did my best to explain my longing for someone to call family, my longing to know Cousin Elizabeth.

I told him, then, in detail, about my meeting with Mr. Yin Wah, my disappointment, and sense of letdown, and about the dislike I had taken to Cousin Elizabeth's puzzling ambassador. "He puts me off; if you saw him, you'd feel the same. And there is something wrong, somewhere, something untrue, about what he says. It doesn't ring right. I don't believe for a minute that Cousin Elizabeth sent that sort of message. It's just not true." I was vehemently confident. "It couldn't be true."

"Why should he lie to you?"

"I don't know. But there was just something. . . ." I was honest with Jim, but the honesty bogged me down; all of it sounded silly in the telling, and made me feel an idiot.

"So, just because you didn't like the poor fellow's face or manner, you are down on him, and have made a bogeyman out of him? Personally, I hand it to him for telling a straight story, and giving you the word, out and out, that your cousin isn't interested in you any longer. It couldn't have been an easy or pleasant job. And now that you know the truth, why still insist on chasing after her? That's what I don't get."

"The man was crude and ugly. Disgusting . . . But that wasn't what upset me. He—he frightened me." I confessed it with a small shiver, and was glad of Jim's arms around me. "I couldn't say why, but . . . And I keep wondering if he frightens Cousin Elizabeth, too. Somebody ought to find out. She's so far away—and there's only me to go."

"Two frightened ladies?" Jim smiled and kissed me. "And one of them in need of immediate succor? Isn't that being rather superimaginative, my darling, precious girl? And, in any case, your cousin wasn't born yesterday. She can take care of herself. So be sensible, sweetheart. Forget this Yin Wah character. If he is anyone's problem—which I doubt—he is your cousin's. And someday we shall go out to Hawaii together: Mr. and Mrs. Bradford on a trip; I like the sound of that a thousand times better than your idea."

He tried to bring me around with kisses, but when he realized he couldn't shake my determination, or laugh away my distrust of Mr. Yin Wah, he tried reasoning with me again. The reasoning turned to argument. It only made me more stubborn.

"All right. If that's the way it is, and you won't listen, let's drop it. Come on—I've a table at Jack's."

It was an armistice over dinner, but the divine food was wasted. We hardly ate a thing. Jim had a third martini and I drank more than enough wine, because sipping was easier than trying to choke down all the lovely stuff Jim had ordered ahead. A wretched evening. Even our waiter, who was an old friend now, sensed the strain between us. One glance at each of us, and he was a clam, instead of his usual voluble French self, with reports of his falling arches, or his latest grandchild, or the place he was buying in the Sonoma Valley for his old age, with grandchildren and grapevines and a fig tree and a tomato patch.

Eventually Jim saw me back to Cousin Elizabeth's, but at first he wouldn't come in with me. "I'll call you tomorrow," he said stiffly, and started to leave barely before I had the light on, but then snatched at me and began kissing me, and I was kissing him.

It was late when he left.

"Make up your mind, Nan," he said to me the last thing. "It's that ridiculous goose chase to Honolulu, or it's me and our wedding Friday. I mean it." His voice was firm, his eyes serious. "Because you are not thinking straight. You are mixed up. You've lost your sense of values."

When I went upstairs and turned on the dressing-table light, I saw myself in the mirror. I was flushed. My eyes were enormous. My throat showed the hard pressure of Jim's kisses. And yet I was not thinking of him when I opened a bureau drawer and took out Ah Sam's fan.

The scarlet cord of the gold-paper wrapping was not only knotting the fan and Ah Sam and Cousin Elizabeth and me together; in some curious, puzzling way, it was knotting us to Mr. Yin Wah. I could feel the knot tightening as the faint breath of sandalwood made itself known.

All of us tied together, inseparably. But why, why? And where were the scissors that would cut the knot?

Things unseen, things to come—premonition of them weighted me when I put the fan away again and drew back my curtains and opened my windows. I shivered involuntarily, but the shiver had nothing to do with the cold night air, the fog, laid like a clammy hand on the city.

I tried to laugh at my foolishness, but I was cold in bed for a long time.

And all for no reason, I told myself. Three days from now I could be married, and then no more loneliness or fear ever. I would belong to Jim. And he was right to have issued an ultimatum. Cousin Elizabeth was looming much too large in my life. I was allowing myself to wallow in stupid sentimentality. What was Cousin Elizabeth to me, when I came right down to it? A figure out of my childhood, nothing more. And almost as unreal as my mother. Even gratitude could be overdone. Cousin Elizabeth had been generous because she chose to be generous; I owed her dutiful thanks and a large, unpayable debt of gratitude. But this . . . this yearning—and you could only call it that—this dominating, persistent longing to see her, to bridge the past and the present, to make her part of my life now, as an adult, was going too far.

Thousands and thousands of girls were alone in the world and got on well enough. And anyway, if I married Jim, I wouldn't be alone. Perhaps, though, by flying out to Cousin Elizabeth I'd get her out of my system. Perhaps the flight wouldn't be a silly, childish gesture, after all. It might be a kind of intelligent therapy. A true growing up. A true maturity, with me finding out, beyond a question, that I needed Cousin Elizabeth as little as she needed me.

Cousin Elizabeth needing anyone at all? Not she. Not strong, self-sufficient Cousin Elizabeth, who had gone her own way so long.

I would put a few questions to her about my parents, just to bring them into focus. I would express the simple, natural wish that she might be in the Cathedral's Chapel of Grace when I married Jim, and I would express no more than a normal regret if she chose not to come for my wedding. And then I would fly home—with home meaning wherever Jim was.

Jim, all the family I wanted. And beginning now, from this very moment, I would stop imagining things.

It sounded easy—until I began thinking again, against my will, about Mr. Yin Wah.

Who was he but a hawking, spitting coolie? That was the troubling part; he was only a coolie in manner, but he had got to the top of the ladder somehow, and somehow he had made himself important to Cousin Elizabeth. Close enough to her to become a business associate. A coolie from Macao—if my guess was right. I had read about Macao, sinister, shady Macao, a tiny world of its own, a world of intrigue and undercurrent.

Might he have some sort of vicious hold on Cousin Elizabeth? She was even more alone in the world than I now. I had Jim to look after me, but she . . .

Mr. Yin Wah's heavy, coarse face seemed to fill my bedroom as though it were a face I was seeing on a huge film screen from a seat too far forward.

Lying in bed, sleepless, I was convinced that Cousin Elizabeth needed family standing by much, much more than I had ever needed family. And it stood to reason she would clutch at me gratefully if I went out to her as an ally. And she had saved me once, in that prison camp, so now it was my turn to save her.

Save? A ridiculously melodramatic word. But the pock-marked face on the screen loomed larger, those dark eyes, like fish, swimming sluggishly.

The fish I thought of were sharks. Sharks, swimming lazily in deep, oriental waters.

I was certain I heard Cousin Elizabeth call out to me, imploringly.

Deep, deep water—and sharks.

I had, of course, fallen asleep. And when I started up in bed, my nightgown was soaked with the sweat of my nightmare. Had I still been a child, still Ah Sam's Little Missee, I could have cried out, and Ah Sam would have come running to quiet my terror. She would even have succeeded in making me laugh at my foolish nightmare, and knowing she was there, knowing she'd let no harm befall me, my eyes would close again, this time in quiet sleep.

But there was no Ah Sam in Cousin Elizabeth's house any longer. There was nothing of her left, just a few pots and pans and rice bowls, and an apron dangling from a kitchen hook. Nothing else, except her sandalwood fan, over there in the dressing-table drawer.

I turned on my bedside lamp, and to forget Mr. Yin Wah, I made a penciled list, on paper torn from an engagement pad, of all the details a flight to Hong Kong or Honolulu would entail. I even made a list for my packing, and with my clothes, I included the sandalwood fan.

To have the fan with me would be a little like having Ah Sam close. At this very moment Ah Sam was probably beseeching any number of benevolent spirits to look after both me and Cousin Elizabeth.

It was a pleasant if childish thought to go back to sleep on. Unfortunately I couldn't help wondering if Mr. Yin Wah would be in Honolulu or Hong Kong when I arrived.

I began to think about sharks again. And I couldn't get warm even after I pulled up my silk puff.

Chapter seven

A week later I was on my way. In minutes, the plane would be in the air, with Honolulu only four hours distant. I couldn't believe it, couldn't take it in, when my flight number was finally called, and I walked along the concourse to the departure gate. The fastening of my seat belt was unreal, and the revving up of motors, and the taxiing down the runway for a takeoff.

On my way. I had stood firm in the face of Jim's arguments—and logic—and of the Martins' candid disapproval. "Quixotic and sentimental" had expressed their viewpoint.

But I was paying for my stubborn stand with a heartache; the night before, after Jim and I had dined, and come back to Cousin Elizabeth's house, we had quarreled miserably and unhappily, and stupidly.

So silly! So . . . so wasteful, two people in love, wrangling, and parting.

"You won't change your mind?" he had asked.

"No. It's settled. Don't keep at me, Jim. Please don't."

"I won't. Never fear." He got up from his chair in Cousin Elizabeth's parlor. "And this had better be good-bye. I doubt if I'll be down to see you off on your Voyage of Discovery. I wouldn't feel like waving. . . ."

"Oh, Jim, don't be so . . . so stuffy. Don't make such a *thing* about my going. What are two weeks? I'll be back before you know I've gone."

"It's not the two weeks—or not only the two weeks. It's your childishness that gets me. No one could be more grateful than I for the strong ties I have with my family, even though I do more or less take them for granted; it's terrific luck to feel you can reach out, and latch on, whenever you feel like it, to people who are your own. But this Cousin Elizabeth business is something else again. It has gotten out of hand. You are being downright neurotic."

"I'm not . . . I'm not!"

"But you are, darling, with this choice you have made between a husband and a cousin."

"I haven't made a choice! It's not a question of choosing. You are one person, and Cousin Elizabeth is another, and why can't there be room for you both in my life?"

At this point, in the frustrated knowledge that Jim's viewpoint and mine were impossibly far apart, I lost my temper.

"Just like a man—always right! If only you'd try, just try, to be reasonable. And I'm going out to Cousin Elizabeth, no matter what you think. Even if . . . even if it means a breakup. . . ."

"Is that the way you want it?" He waited. "You are sure, Nan?"

I was fool enough not to answer. I turned away from him and poked the fire.

"So that's settled. And I don't suppose you'll be sending me any of those 'wish-you-were-here' postcards; anyway, I wouldn't want you to bother. Because, frankly, I shan't be giving the smallest Goddamn how you are making out in Honolulu. Which is a lie, but . . ."

He closed the front door after him with an exaggeratedly quiet politeness, but I heard him slam his car door, hard.

There was a hard lump in my throat as I went back over it all. Up until the very last moment, while I had coffee and a sandwich at one of the airport counters, I had hoped—and believed—I would be paged for a telephone call. Jim would forgive my burst of temper. He would get over his hurt, and be reasonable. He would meet me more than halfway, and admit I had no alternative than to do what I felt was right.

And I, in turn, would apologize. The making up would be sweet. . . .

I had regrets, too, about the Martins' attitude. They had overwhelmed me by announcing they intended to give me the trip as a present, and I realized they were competing, pathetically, even if unconsciously, against Cousin Elizabeth's hold on my loyalty and affection. But they hadn't come to see me off, although they had sent me to the airport in their car. From both of them there had been vague excuses, something about a conference, and a bridge party. They had made it very plain that they were not in the least pleased at my running away from their nephew. They adored Jim, who, in their eyes, couldn't be more eligible as a husband. And why, of all things, should I go chasing off after an almost mythical cousin—not even a real cousin—who had shown no wish whatever, for such ages, to keep in any sort of personal contact with me?

The plane rocketed and zoomed west, and we were over the Pacific, high above the clouds.

Before I finished looking through a magazine I had bought at the airport, the pilot was announcing our position: The halfway mile had been reached, that point of no return, when there is no going back.

For me, the no-going-back meant no Jim, ever again. I didn't dare ask myself if seeing Cousin Elizabeth was worth that; I knew the answer. It did not bear dwelling on, and anyhow, it was too late to change my mind, even though I had come to my senses. So much for that. There was nothing now but to make the best of what my stubbornness had got me into.

The stewardesses changed from their blue gabardine mainland uniforms to bright-flowered muumuus. They offered cocktails or pineapple or guava or papaya juice, and passed baskets of tropical fruit. The radio played Hawaiian music.

The plane's cabins were sprayed with an insecticide, the passengers were reminded of the strict Agriculture Department rulings regarding imported plant material, and then we were circling the island of Oahu. There it was, its mountains grooved with dark, deeply cleft canyons, green with forests, its lowlands lush with sugarcane and pineapple fields, and the tall white buildings of downtown Honolulu reaching to the bluest and cleanest of skies, while the loveliest water I had ever imagined lapped at their feet.

Turquoise water, lapis and amethyst and jade water, streaked with white where spumy foam broke over jagged coral reefs, and when gigantic waves curled, and broke, and rushed high on a scallop of palm-fringed beaches.

The plane put down and taxied to a stop. When I had

unfastened my seat belt and walked down the landing steps, the heat and glare of the asphalt airstrip struck like a blow after San Francisco's chilliness and made me a little giddy, but once I was in the shade of the terminal I forgot the heat, and the sight of women and children in muumuus or kimonos, with flower leis around their necks, and of men in bright shirts and flower-wreathed straw hats, smiling and calling greetings, and playing ukeleles and steel guitars as they strolled, delighted me.

Hawaiians, Chinese, Portuguese, Filipinos, Japanese.

Big-boned, tall people. Small people. Enormous dark eyes. Slant eyes. Fat, waddling people, men and women with beautiful bodies.

Those Alohas! Those bare feet! The general gaudiness!

It was touristy, terribly touristy—some of the leis were only made of paper, some of the alohas were meaningless, but in that first glimpse of Hawaii I found far more than merely the cheap or the tacky; how agreeable everyone was, how courteous, how seemingly content and relaxed, and on what a smiling, live-and-let-live basis. And even the assault of the sun was something I suddenly welcomed, something I discovered I had unknowingly craved.

Honolulu was for me! Already, I adored it.

The soft wind that blew my hair and skirts, and rustled the fronds of tall coconut palms, planted everywhere, smelled of all the flowers—gardenias and carnations and tuberoses were a few I knew by name—that everyone was wearing or buying, giving or receiving.

The wind smelled of the sea, too, of salt and seaweed and fish, and all of it was a scent equally compounded of languor and briskness.

A small shower of rain suddenly wet me, and as suddenly stopped. Miraculously, I was dry in seconds, and so was the airport asphalt. Through big rents in the heavy clouds, I could see the sky, bluer than ever—so blue it made me want to write a poem about it, and toward the mountains an unbelievable rainbow curved. I had never before seen a double arc, and never seen a prism of colors so vivid.

A very large, very brown, fat-stomached Hawaiian taxi driver with bare feet, the tail of his flower-print shirt hanging out over old khaki army trousers, saw me wondering what to do about my bags, and took me in charge. The dearest man; as soon as he realized I was alone, with no one to meet me, no one to present me with a lei, he bought one for me, a garland of tiny mauve orchids.

For all I know, the smiling old woman who sold it to him was his grandmother, and the transaction a cut-rate family affair, or perhaps he added the price of the lei onto my fare; never mind. The gesture was heart-warming, and that was what counted.

I got into his car, an outsize, shiny black limousine, of which he was the owner, he told me with pride, and being a conversationalist, he pointed out all the sights along the way as we drove to the hotel. A new shopping center, new office buildings, condominiums going up everywhere, a pineapple factory, the Yacht Harbor . . . And then, when we turned off Kalakaua Avenue, crowded with the tourists from Waikiki Beach, and turned into an acre or more of tropical gardens, we were at the Royal, the huge, luxurious, traditional hotel—the Martins' idea of a nice hotel, and where they had insisted upon making reservations for me, as their guest.

At first sight I knew the hotel would be more than merely to my liking. It charmed me. Of pink stucco, all fretwork and balconies and elaborate grilling, with a tower on top, it was set in lawns where flocks of doves cooed, and dark-plumaged birds with yellow beaks were making the most fearful racket. They were myna birds, my taxi driver informed me.

Everywhere, there were tall palms, and tree ferns, and the pink- and white- and red-flowering trees I was later to know as plumeria, just as I was to recognize all the other plants and vines that crammed the hotel garden with color and fragrance: croton, and spider lily, and ginger, and bird-of-paradise, anthurium, and ti, and cup of gold.

The lobby, too, was filled with flowers; all sorts of orchids made a gorgeous mass, growing in fern and bark, reflected over and over in handsome gold-framed mirrors. The place was crammed with people, all prosperous-looking tourists, I suspected, the women in linen or silk or cotton sleeveless, backless dresses, or obviously new muumuus, the men a little self-conscious looking, but comfortable, in expensive duplicates of the flowered shirts at the airport. Most of them were carrying cameras or attractively wrapped packages. I was quite sure there was not a true Island resident among them.

A bellboy took me past jewelry shops, curio shops, dress shops, antique shops. There were superb old porcelains, and lacquer boxes to look at, sari cloth and brocade, carved wooden salad bowls and trays, woven straw place mats, sequined evening dresses, cotton shifts, strings of shells, ropes of real pearls, lime-green semiprecious stones, with cards saying they were aventurines, found in the Islands. There were bathing suits and feather-banded men's hats.

I would have enjoyed my progress through the lobby a great deal more had I not almost immediately caught sight of Mr. Yin Wah sitting in a big chair, ostensibly reading a newspaper. It was an unpleasant shock. I stopped, with a hastily checked startled gasp, and went on, shaken. His chair was too well placed to suit me; he could see whoever entered an elevator, or came out of one. Mr. Yin Wah, back from Hong Kong?

Had he been watching for me? Deliberately keeping track of me, for some reason or other? Or was it coincidence, his happening to sit there just in time for my arrival? I wanted to think so. But was that busy lobby the sort of place a man would choose for the quiet perusal of a paper, the quiet enjoyment of the drink in his hand?

I couldn't believe so, with the sea to look at if he turned his chair to face the other way, and with any number of umbrella-sheltered tables invitingly arranged on a wide terrace just behind him.

He didn't look up when I passed his chair.

One could only hope there was a spittoon handy, if not a jardiniere, I thought, and tried to tell myself I disliked him merely for his boorishness, and that my fear of him, unreasoning, inexplicable fear, had nothing to do with my hurrying a little toward the elevator.

After all, he was probably waiting in a convenient spot for a business acquaintance, perhaps the arrival of an out-of-towner, coming in on any one of a dozen hourly Mainland or international flights.

I almost forgot Mr. Yin Wah in quick delight when the bellboy showed me my room and pulled up the venetian blinds. I was facing the sea, and the iron-railed balcony outside the wide windows, festooned with vines, overlooked a magnificent sweep of beach.

Swimmers were drying off with huge striped towels under yellow and blue and pink and orange umbrellas. Children, in next to nothing, dug at the water's edge with bright buckets and shovels, or tossed balls, some of them with the telltale pallidness of brand-new arrivals, some the lobster red of a first whole day in the sun, some a lovely tan.

A lot of native beach boys, as brown as the carved wood in the lobby shops, were rubbing sun oil on the legs and arms and shoulders of bosomy girls in bikinis, who lolled on the sand with quantities of bleached blond hair loose around their faces.

Beyond the beach, where huge waves, breaking farther out, rushed shoreward in white foam, surfers were balancing on their boards, and the bows of outrigger canoes and blue-sailed catamarans were thrusting into water so beautiful I had no words to describe it to myself.

I longed to plunge into that jewel-colored water. The temptation was almost irresistible, but I wanted, even more, to get in touch with Cousin Elizabeth or find out how to reach her.

Her telephone number was listed in the directory on the bedside table, but before I dialed it, I changed my mind. Thanks to Mr. Yin Wah, and the seeds of distrust he had planted, a shrinking from rebuff held me back in spite of all of my much-vaunted faith in a welcome from Cousin Elizabeth.

A servant, in all likelihood, would answer the telephone and inquire my name. And when Cousin Elizabeth heard it . . . ? Would the servant come back on the line with a polite "Miss Beaton is not at home," or "Miss Beaton is out of town"?

Instead of telephoning I would go to her house. Somehow, I would get past any servant who might open the door, and once I was inside, surely she wouldn't refuse to see me. This was a good time of day for a try, too; there was a chance that by this late in the afternoon she would be home, no matter what business affairs might have filled her day earlier.

Just keep my fingers crossed, and hope she was still in Honolulu, as Mr. Martin had found out for me, and hadn't taken off again for another of her Hong Kong trips.

I didn't waste time unpacking except to take a white linen dress and white sandals out of my suitcase, and a pair of huge, white-framed, expensive sunglasses from Saks that I had not been able to resist.

When I had changed, I went down to the lobby to arrange for the rental of a small car, and to inquire at the desk if anyone could tell me the way to Miss Elizabeth Beaton's house.

"You want her Nuuanu Pali house, or her beach house?" a clerk asked.

"I don't know, Where would I be most apt to find her?"

"You ought to telephone for an appointment, she's hard to see."

"I'll take a chance."

"Then the Nuuanu Pali house is your best bet."

The clerk gave me directions, and explained that her beach house was seldom used by Miss Beaton. "She's too busy to enjoy it, I guess. Not that she couldn't get there in half an hour or so. It's just beyond the Pali."

"What is the Pali?"

"Our big tourist attraction, a scenic highway you don't want to miss."

"Do you know Miss Beaton?"

"Everyone in Honolulu knows her by name. She's one of the Islands' biggest money-makers, and just about top of the list when it comes to forking out for a good cause."

"You mean for charities?"

"Yes, and for the museums and the Art Academy, and the Aquarium, and the Zoo—you name it."

I, too, had been a good cause, once upon a time, I reflected wryly. An outlet for Cousin Elizabeth's very evident generosity. Had I ever been anything more to her? I wondered, as I got into my little car.

There was a nice little guidebook full of maps and general information in the glove compartment, and when I had studied it for a moment I drove out of the hotel grounds and turned left, along Kalakaua Avenue. Then I was in an older part of the city, I could tell by the buildings, and the big trees, and finally, blocks and blocks from Waikiki, I was driving northwest, toward the mountains on a gradually climbing highway with pleasant-looking houses and apartments on either side of it and small gardens bright with yellow and pink and red hibiscus, and clambering flowering vines. It started to shower again, and another double rainbow put on a show for me, but in a moment there was sunshine once more and a steamy fragrance of growing things, and of wet earth, as though I were in a conservatory with a temperamental overhead sprinkling system, now on, now off.

Toward the crest of the grade there was a change in the landscape. I had turned right at a signpost, following the desk clerk's directions and one of the guidebook maps, and instead of driving along a busy highway I was on a narrow, two-lane, solitary road with the sea behind me and out of sight, as were the houses and apartments.

On both sides of me coarse, dark ferns and shrubs thrust up at the base of even darker forest trees that met overhead and were impenetrably laced with long, twining, sinuous strands of leather-leafed vines, thick as rope. Everywhere, little streams and waterfalls gushed, but the water had no sparkle, because there was no sunlight. Not a ray. Just a heavy gloom, and the dankness of a recent rain.

I found myself continually glancing in my rear-view mirror. Had I been walking, I would have taken nervous glances over my shoulder, and hurried a little.

But I couldn't hurry, in the car. I had to drive slowly to watch for a mailbox with "Beaton" on it.

Such a lonely road, and how easily the gloom and the solitude could swallow me. When I came to the mailbox, I was unashamedly thankful. I stopped and got out of the car to open a wood-and-iron gate—a Chinese compound gate. Then I drove on through more of the gloom until, surprisingly, the trees gave way to a clearing of lush garden and green lawns noisy with more of those chattering myna birds like the ones at the hotel.

And there was a house. A fantastic house. Built of some kind of dark, heavy wood, with a blue tiled roof and gilded, red-lacquer, sharply up-curved eaves, it was a replica of the handsomest of classic Chinese dwellings.

I parked my car in the driveway and crossed a tile-floored terrace that stretched the width of the house to a teakwood door guarded by two enormous, writhing, green-glazed ceramic dragons. The door hung on brass hinges and was embossed with the nailheads and scrolling of antique Chinese hardware, and I could imagine the size of the key on the inside, and the thickness of the bolts and bars to keep people out.

Or to keep them in—which was an odd thought to go through my head.

There was a temple gong beside the door, a thin bronze disk, suspended with its leather-padded striker from a carved teakwood frame that served, apparently, instead of a conventional doorbell. I took a chance on it, and struck the disk lightly.

Bong! While the reverberation died away and I waited, I was acutely conscious that no human sound was to be heard. The harsh chatter of the birds on the lawn didn't count, nor the much softer chirp and trill of a dozen or more brightly feathered little birds in a pair of large gilt, pagoda-shaped cages that hung where the two opposite open ends of the terrace made a breezeway.

Voices were what I wanted to hear. The silence put my nerves even more on edge after the solitary gloom of the road. And what was worse: Was the utter silence a portent? Was I going to fail in my mission to see Cousin Elizabeth?

I suddenly felt a very long way away from San Francisco. Or, rather, from Jim. What was I doing here? Who was Cousin Elizabeth compared to all that I had left behind?

Had I been completely out of my mind to come?

I refused to answer the question by telling myself I had never smelled anything so delicious as the fragrance of the wet garden, lying in a thin, watery shaft of sunlight. Masses of white flowers bloomed everywhere; hedges of gardenias; stephanotis that, in San Francisco, you saw only in florist shops, were hanging from the eaves of Cousin Elizabeth's house and rampantly draping the verdigris bronze rain gutters. And that tall-stalked plant, growing in great clumps—was it ginger?

While I drew in long breaths of the exciting, seductive sweetness, I took appreciative notice of the terrace tiles. Cousin Elizabeth must have had them shipped in from China; they looked old, old, and were the blue of Peking glass beads, with inlays of pale, faded coral, in a design of flying cranes.

Cranes are a Chinese symbol of long life and happiness, I had been taught by Ah Sam, long ago; she had embroidered cranes on the silk sleep coats she used to make for me when I was a little girl. To see them here pleased and reassured me. It seemed a favorable omen that Cousin Elizabeth should have chosen a crane motif for the tiles of her entrance terrace as a happy salutation to whoever approached her door. Or even if she had not chosen the cranes deliberately for their symbolism, she must at least have liked the design; which meant our mutual appreciation of things Chinese gave us an interest in common. We would have that to start with, if nothing else.

Now if only the first difficult moments of my self-introduction were over . . .

When a white-jacketed, black-silk-trousered, elderly Chinese opened the door, I put on a brave front. "Is Miss Beaton in?" I asked, but before he could answer, and perhaps say No, I walked boldly past him. Pushed past him, would be more correct. "Please tell her Miss Allen, from San Francisco wishes to see her." I hoped it sounded impressively confident, but he shook his head.

"You wait, please. I go find out. Missee Beaton, she maybe not home."

"Not home to you," was what he meant, and he had given away the all-important fact that she was in the house. And nothing could stop me now.

"I'll go with you." I wasn't caring about manners—or my lack of them.

"No, please; you wait, lady."

"I am going with you."

I was being firm. The situation was seemingly beyond him, and when he padded off in his black felt slippers, undoubtedly to report an interloper, I brashly hurried after him across a wide hall with a bare polished floor, and I know enough about Chinese furnishings to have recognized panels of old, ice-blue Nanking silk that belonged in a museum. A tall cabinet of the rarest, dark, cinnabar-red lacquer stood against one wall. Opposite were two matching lacquer chairs that flanked a painting on silk of deer, their delicate little hooves imprinting a fall of snow, the clouds and mists of the traditional fairy mountains swirling around their antlers.

We passed several large rooms, from which I gathered a quick impression of superb Chinese furnishings, and then the servant was opening a screen door onto another terrace—"terrace" as I then called it, but what I now know Islanders term a lanai.

A quiet-faced woman wearing a plum-colored silk *cheong sam,* her dark hair drawn back from her forehead and thrust through with long jade pins, was sitting in a wickerwork chair, its high back flaring extravagantly, like a peacock's spread tail.

A small black lacquer and mother-of-pearl box on a rosewood table beside her spilled skeins of embroidery silks; with slender fingers tipped with long, almond-shaped nails, she was darning the frayed gold brocade of what might have been an old altar cloth.

She was a woman in her late fifties, I thought, or she may have been older. It was difficult to tell. The calm, serene face and brow were unlined. Which isn't to say there was anything insipid or characterless about her. Far from it. She had strength and self-discipline and enormous dignity and assurance written all over her. You saw, at once, that she had always known where she was going, and that she got there. But she wasn't in any way formidable or unapproachable looking. I dared hope, with my first sight of her, that she would be understanding, and sympathetic, and even if she didn't need me, as I felt I needed her, she wouldn't turn away from me, she wouldn't shut me out.

As the screen door opened, she glanced toward it, and took off a pair of tortoise-shell-rimmed glasses to look at me surprisedly, and to raise a questioning, rebuking eyebrow at her servant.

Blue eyes—my memory had been correct. Dark-blue eyes, very large and clear.

Before the Chinese could explain, her name burst from my lips. "Cousin Elizabeth!" I was certain it was she. It had to be. "I'm Nan. Nan Allen."

"My dear child." She stood up, letting the strip of brocade fall to the floor, and there was not a second of hesitation before she put out both hands and seized mine. "So you have come. I have been more than half expecting you. Mr. Yin Wah reported that you are an extremely determined young woman when it comes to getting your own way." She smiled, and with the softening of her face, the curve of her mouth was a curve I remembered, with a rush of gladness, from my childhood.

"You don't mind my having come?" I blurted it, half afraid of what an honest answer might be, and yet longing to know where I stood.

"Why should I mind, my dear?"

"Mr. Yin Wah told me you——"

"He told you I was a busy person, with no time for anything but commuting between here and Hong Kong? It is true, I am busy, but Mr. Yin Wah must be taken with a grain of salt. He looks after my interests so devotedly that I can never be quite certain whom he keeps away from my door. And I am glad you didn't listen to him. Very glad."

Glad! Cousin Elizabeth was glad. Oh, I had known it would turn out this way.

She spoke to her houseboy. "Move a chair over for Miss Allen, please, Fong."

I sat down next to her in another peacock chair, and without effort or shyness on my part, without any awkwardness between us, we were talking, talking, to make up for all our years apart. Years? It became difficult to remember how long it had been. She was Cousin Elizabeth, and I was Nan, an adult Nan; able now to meet on the same level, we took it from there.

"Your job is going well?" she asked at one point. "Have you learned, by now, how satisfying it is to be independent? And you don't resent my insistence that you make your own way?"

"It was a jolt," I answered honestly. "It wasn't easy to accept."

"Try not to think me harsh. For a woman to be independent is a fetish of mine."

"I'll always be only a secretary; I haven't the brains to be anywhere near as successful as you, Cousin Elizabeth."

"Any woman can be successful—if she makes intelligent use of her opportunities. She can get anywhere, if she wants to enough."

The long, hot, humid afternoon, scented so heavily with steaming forest growth and garden flowers, was drawing to an end, but still we talked. We were on the way to a friendship, Cousin Elizabeth and I; I could dare to think of us in the future as not just cousins, but new-found friends. It was too good to be true, but it was true.

All this way to find her, all this way to let her know she didn't stand alone, that I was close, if she needed me.

In front of the lanai where we sat, talking so directly, clearing up so much, there was a lily pond where red and gold carp swam, and mauve lotus flowers floated, and beyond the pond a thicket of tall dark trees encircled the garden.

I was again conscious of the aloofness of the house, its set-apart-ness, and I began to dislike the dark, encircling trees. Fancifully, I began to imagine them as trees taken from the illustrations of a book of Chinese fairy tales. The painted pagoda eaves of the house, the dragons at the door, the temple gong, the cranes, the lotus pond, and Cousin Elizabeth in her *cheong sam* had stepped from the illustrations, too. And if Cousin Elizabeth was easily recognized as a Lady of the Imperial Court, Mr. Yin Wah, had he been there, would have been equally identifiable. Put him in oriental dress, and who else would he be but the traditional Wicked One?

I had read a great many Chinese fairy tales; often they were cruel, often they had frightened me.

An infantile train of thought. It was a relief all the same when Fong appeared and gave me something else to think about as he padded softly about the garden lighting a flare of tall, oil-burning torches everywhere, to keep away the mosquitoes, Cousin Elizabeth explained.

He disappeared, and came back with a tray of icy drinks and hot hors d'oeuvres. There were shrimps in batter, to dip in soy sauce, and rum and pineapple juice to drink from widemouthed frosted goblets, each topped with a gardenia.

With the arrival of the tray I realized, belatedly, what time it had gotten to be, and how long I had stayed. I jumped up with a flurry of apologies, but Cousin Elizabeth refused to let me leave. With her gentle, remembered smile, she insisted I stay for dinner. "In fact, my dear, you shall stay the night. I don't want you driving back to town alone, after dark. But better yet, you must be my house guest while you are in Honolulu. I'll send for your bags in the morning."

"I couldn't. Not possibly. I mustn't——"

"You would deprive me of so much pleasure?"

"But Mr. Yin Wah said——"

"Remember my telling you he is oversolicitous? It's true I am busy. I have an office in town to which I go every day, and soon I shall have to fly off to Hong Kong again. But meanwhile we could have the evenings together. Say you will stay." She reached out and gave my hand a little pat. "Do!"

"If you are certain I shan't be in the way."

"You will never be that, I promise you." Her gentle smile was a little sad, I thought. "A long time ago I planned my life; now it's the old story of everything having a price. In my case, the price—or part of it—is never having enough time. But a little is far better than none."

"You enjoy your life, though, don't you, in spite of the rush and hard work? And aren't you terribly proud of all you've done?"

"Proud?" She echoed the question without answering it as she stood up. "Come along. I shall show you your room. And we'll see what my maid can find for you in the way of night things."

A small, old, cheerful Chinese woman, Lui Lung,

bustled about, chattering in pidgin English, and making me comfortable in a guest room with robin's-egg-blue silk curtains, thin as gauze, and a wide, low bedspread with a blue-satin gold-thread-embroidered cover that looked as though it might once have been a Chinese wall hanging.

The polished wooden floor was bare. There was little other furniture besides the bed. A tall teakwood wardrobe with drawers and shelves. A blue, painted pigskin chest with black iron handles that served as a nightstand, and held a number of books. A long, carved teakwood table strewn with the ivory comb and brush and powder box and hand glass of an old-fashioned toilet set, and over it an eighteenth-century Chinese Chippendale mirror, framed in gilded black lacquer, and hanging from a thick, heavily tasseled blue rope.

The whole effect was one of coolness and tranquillity, and a revelation of Cousin Elizabeth's liking for things Oriental—and of her wealth.

I washed, and put on fresh lipstick, and combed my hair in the most modern and luxurious of American bathrooms, and then Cousin Elizabeth knocked at the door and we went down to dinner.

She had changed into a long jade brocade housecoat. It was lovely with her dark hair that she wore coiled high and had thrust through with Chinese pins of gold filigree and pearl and carnelian. Her matching earrings and wide, high choker necklace and wide bracelets would have cost a fortune in any San Francisco shop. How Gump's would have coveted them! Romantically I enjoyed imagining they had come from behind the Bamboo Curtain, and once had belonged to some beautiful Peking Number-One wife.

It was also a romantic fancy to visualize Cousin Elizabeth not as a Court Lady this time, but as a female War Lord or brigand riding down from some mountain fastness to seize whatever caught her eye. I could see the steed she rode; one of those chunky T'ang Dynasty horses you see in museums, prancing and tossing their manes.

A brigand; wryly, I told myself that was exactly what Mr. Martin and Jim thought her. Aggressive, selfish, ruthless, even though they conceded her courage. They had no liking for women of that sort.

Not that she would care what they thought. She had got what she wanted out of life. Those divine pearls and carnelians. This divine house. To many women they would seem well worth a little drive and push and singlemindedness.

Without actual envy, I thought of my salary as a novice receptionist, my tiny backlog of savings, my frugal lunches, my careful shopping. Even without a rent burden that most girls had to pay, I barely came out even at the end of every month.

Quite a contrast. I was a little envious, after all.

Fong and another houseboy circled the table passing food and filling our wine glasses. The menu was strictly continental. I had expected something more exotic, but the only concession either to an oriental or Hawaiian touch was little hot biscuits made, Cousin Elizabeth told me, from Island taro root, pounded into a paste. I liked them very much. I enjoyed the French wine, too.

I began to think I should have said No, thank you, to the wine, after the rum drinks on the lanai, when the dining room became a blur of painted scrolls and Coromandel screens, and of candles in brass sticks, with moths fluttering in their yellow flame.

But this was such a very special occasion. The most special of my life, next to the first time Jim told me he loved me. But it wouldn't do to think of Jim, and I let my glass be filled again.

When dinner was over, we had coffee on the lanai. The evening was still warm, and drenched with the smell of flowers. We had a moon and the Southern Cross above us. I thought I heard the sound of the sea, but Cousin Elizabeth said the sea was too distant, and I was only hearing a wind in the trees. She named the trees for me. *Kukui. Hau*. Ironwood. *Koa*. Mango. They were some of the trees of the forest I had driven through, the arching, vine-hung, jungly trees.

I told her how beautiful I had found the Island when my plane flew in, and how entranced I had been by the reefs and the waves and the curving shoreline.

"It seems too bad you can't be at your beach house more often, Cousin Elizabeth."

"Where did you hear I had a beach house?"

"A clerk at the hotel mentioned it. An Island beach house sounds terrific. Perfect." I was getting carried away. "That clean white sand. The palm trees. The shells. I always wanted to start a shell collection. And such gorgeous water to swim in. I'd give anything if——" I checked myself abruptly. My enthusiasm was innocently spontaneous. I hadn't been hinting for an invitation to Cousin Elizabeth's beach house, but I suddenly felt pushy.

There was the tiniest pause, I remember now as I look back, while Cousin Elizabeth put her coffee cup on a small table, with a regret that my preconceived idea of her beach property was much in need of correcting. "You would find it all terribly disappointing. I wouldn't dream of letting you see it. It's not at all a choice spot, compared to other sites on the Island. I bought it solely because of a little house that is on it, a relic of the old days—the missionary days. I did not want a subdivider to get hold of it. And it will go to the city when I die. In the meanwhile I have a thoroughly unsatisfactory caretaker. He has let the garden go disgracefully. Not that he is permanent; I shall be getting rid of him one of these days, when I get around to it."

"But the beach itself?" I asked with persistent interest. "Nothing could spoil white sand and blue water, I should think."

"There is almost no beach at all. No sandy beach, that is. The water comes up to a seawall in front of the house, and there is too much coral for good swimming. Infection from a coral cut can be extremely serious, you know. Stingrays are a menace, too. And recently the local fishermen reported seeing sharks inside the reef, close to shore. And there are dangerous currents. But if you especially enjoy swimming, you must use the pool here at the end of the garden, as much as you like. Or, if you prefer sea bathing, and surf, you can always use the beach in front of the Royal, and also I shall be delighted to give you a card to an excellent beach club."

I thanked her, but I had shuddered at the mention of sharks, remembering my nightmare, and it was pleasant to let the conversation drift to other subjects as we went on with our catching up, our discovery of each other, until Cousin Elizabeth declared it to be bedtime. "We Islanders make an early start every morning to get ahead of the heat. I shall have breakfast in my room at six tomorrow morning as usual, but you may ring for yours anytime you choose."

I yawned, and apologized. "It's been a long day."

"And a most eventful one, as far as I am concerned. I doubt if I sleep a wink, thinking about your arrival, my dear."

Cousin Elizabeth saw me to the guest room which was at one end of the house, with the length of the lanai between it and her own suite at the other end.

"Good night, child. I hope you will be comfortable." Cousin Elizabeth kissed my cheek lightly. "Though 'child' is hardly the word. I can't take it in! To think I have Nan Allen, a grown-up young woman on my hands after all these years. I do hope I can cope. I shall have to put my mind on it."

She smiled, and I smiled, too, and promised not to be more of a bother than I could possibly help.

Just before she left me, I saw, from the bedroom doorway, our reflection in the lacquer mirror. There we were, together, at last. She with her air of dignity, and strength, and poise, her unlined face so calm it could almost be described as impassive, and that coupled with her clothes and the pins in her hair gave her so strong a look of the East. I, so eager-faced, so thrilled, so unreservedly delighted with our reunion.

On impulse I asked a question. "Do I look like my mother, Cousin Elizabeth?"

For a moment she didn't answer while she studied my reflection in the mirror and then searched the face I lifted to her with a wistfulness I made no attempt to disguise.

"You are very like her," she stated quietly. "Anyone who ever knew your mother would recognize you as her daughter. I am quite sure of it. It struck me immediately, the first moment I saw you."

I was inexpressibly moved, and I thought Cousin Elizabeth was much moved too. She turned away with nothing more said, and I wondered if my mother had been especially close to her, especially dear. Her favorite, perhaps, of the two English girls who had married the Allen brothers?

It was immortality, of a sort, to pass on your features, your expression, to a child; if ever I had a daughter, would my mother's face, and mine, be again repeated? But I wouldn't have a daughter; Jim didn't love me anymore, and if I could not have Jim, I wouldn't marry any other man.

I went into the bedroom and began undressing. The borrowed nightgown and peignoir folded on the bed were of sheer white batiste—not nylon—and were exquisitely hand-embroidered, hand-tucked. Washed and ironed by hand, too, with the same patient, painstaking care Ah Sam used to give my things.

Obviously Cousin Elizabeth enjoyed luxury of every sort, I reflected as I took my bath in a deep, long, blue-tiled tub, and dried myself with enormous monogrammed towels, as voluminous as those great wrap-around things you find in the best Paris hotels.

But who wouldn't crave the luxury that would help obliterate memories of a wartime prison camp? That awful camp. It was because I was more tired than I realized, and because of the rum and the wine, I suppose, but I wanted to cry a little for my mother who had died with a filthy, thin blanket under her for a mattress when she gave birth to her baby.

That starving, whimpering baby in Hong Kong so long ago made me think of Ah Sam, and as I put on Cousin Elizabeth's deliciously smooth, cool nightgown, I was far happier going back to our Little Missee, amah days, than

I was to reflect on Mr. Yin Wah, who had come to mind with the thought of Hong Kong.

Mr. Yin Wah, possibly of Macao, but currently of Honolulu. Mr. Yin Wah managing to watch people's coming and going, in spite of a spread newspaper.

One of these days a true knowledge of what he was would have to be faced. I knew it, deep inside me, deep in my bones.

The wind was warning me, too, the soft, warm, showery wind that just now was gently blowing the blue gauzy curtains of the guest room, gently murmuring like the sea in those dark trees that enclosed Cousin Elizabeth's garden.

I drew together the windows' bamboo blinds before I got into bed. I did not want to lie and look out toward the garden's boundaries. Again, for me, the trees and Mr. Yin Wah had become illustrations from a frightening Chinese fairy tale.

Chapter eight

THE next morning Cousin Elizabeth's chauffeur drove her into town and came back with my bags. While Lui Lung unpacked and arranged my things in the wardrobe, I watched her, exulting. Here I was, thanks to my own stubborn determination, my sensible, action-taking decisions. If Jim and the Martins could see me, being settled in. If they knew how much at home I was already beginning to feel.

It wasn't really much fun to gloat. I missed Jim too much. But there was so much to see, and such charm and novelty in Cousin Elizabeth's house and garden that the day passed both pleasantly and swiftly. And there was the evening to look forward to, and tomorrow and tomorrow to help make up for all those years when Cousin Elizabeth had been lost to me.

So after the third day's stay with Cousin Elizabeth I established a little routine for myself. Each morning I went out to what I thought of as the "cranes for happiness" terrace and said good-morning and good-bye to Cousin Elizabeth as she came out of the house and got in her car. She was always in a fresh, immaculate linen or shantung suit and cotton gloves. Her handsome straw bag had a tortoise-shell clasp, her straw slippers tortoise-shell buckles. She always wore a hat, a Panama, rolled on one side and draped with a chiffon scarf to match the color of whatever suit she had chosen. She had an elegance and a terrific lot of individual style, and I hoped I would look half as distinguished when I was her age.

When I heard the car turn into the drive in the late afternoons, I always ran to meet her with a sense of relief that she had actually come back and had not chosen again to vanish from my sight, my life.

Between her departure and arrival I tried to content myself with exploring the house and the garden and swimming in the pool, but I could not forget Jim.

Lunch would be brought out to me by Fong or Wing if there were none of the heavy, drenching showers—they were downpours, now and again—that seemed to be part of the normal weather pattern in the Nuuanu-Pali part of the Island. There would be papaya with quartered lime to squeeze over it, both picked from the garden, and cold chicken, and salad and iced tea. I always saved a lettuce leaf for the birds in the pagoda cages on the terrace. They were finches of various rare varieties, Cousin Elizabeth had told me, and I enjoyed their engaging tameness and cheerful song. There were moments when their cheeriness was more than welcome.

After Cousin Elizabeth got home, she rested in her bedroom, and then we would meet on the lanai just in time to watch the lotus blossoms in the pond close their stiff, waxy petals, and to see white moonflowers open among the tangle of flowering vines that hung from the eaves. Their fragrance was too poignant, too much of a hurt, though. Jim—Jim . . .

Later, we would go in to dinner, and afterward there would be another talk on the lanai until we went to bed. Not once had we been at a loss for conversation. Not once had Cousin Elizabeth seemed anything but quietly pleased about our reunion. And with her light, quick kiss on my cheek when we said good-night, it was always, "Dear Nan."

If only I could have had Jim, too, I would think. If only . . . if only—oh, why, why, couldn't anything ever be entirely perfect?

The fifth day of my stay was oppressively hot and muggy. But the swimming pool did not appeal; I longed for the sea, longed to have the coolness of its jewel-toned water flow over me. But instead of promptly driving down to the hotel, I began to think about Cousin Elizabeth's beach-house property. If I went to Waikiki and swam, I would be just another tourist, and if I stayed here, in the garden, wouldn't I be wasting a chance to see a little something more of the Island? Foolish, when my visit was so short.

Cousin Elizabeth's beach place meant a drive over the Pali, which the hotel clerk had said I shouldn't miss. As for the coral and the current, and the stingrays, even the sharks—well, I needn't go really swimming. I could simply wade at the water's edge. I wouldn't take my suit along, just the rubber-soled sandals I used around the pool.

That heavenly water—and so close. I could drive to the beach house in leisurely fashion, perhaps even drive farther along the coast, and still get back in plenty of time before Cousin Elizabeth returned from town. She needn't even know that my longing for the sea—and my curiosity—had been too much for me. There was no real reason for me even to mention having gone to her beach house.

Naturally, I wouldn't feel entirely comfortable, sneaking off behind her back—because that was what it would amount to. Though what was really wrong about it, actually?

I argued a case for myself so successfully that by the time I had finished breakfast, my mind was made up, and justified by the thought of a long, solitary, and just a little dull day ahead of me if I stayed in the garden, or again wandered through Cousin Elizabeth's house, looking at her treasures. I told Fong and Wing not to expect me for lunch, and got my car out of the garage.

Before I drove off, I studied the map of the little guidebook in the glove compartment, and read a page that described the Pali.

. . . one of the geological wonders of the world. A ridge of the Koolau Mountains, sharp as a knife, that rises to a height of some two thousand feet or more. Today, a modern highway tunnels through the mountains, but by a short detour leading to the Lookout View point of the old road, with its rock parapet, there may be seen a straight drop of five hundred feet to the valley slopes below. Still to be found in the valley are the bones of those Oahuan warriors who, after a desperate struggle, with their backs to the drop, were pushed over the cliff by the forces of the Polynesian king, Kamehameha I, in his conquest of Oahu in 1795, and as part of his bloody and successful campaign to unite the Hawaiian Islands into a single empire.

It was more than enough to interest me in making the detour so that I could look over the parapet to that awesome graveyard below, and get a thrill out of thinking I could hear echoes of old battle cries, and of shell horns, and the shouted commands of ruthlessly advancing chieftains in red-and-yellow feather robes.

It only took five minutes or so to make the detour onto the old road and get to its Lookout, as there was no traffic, and I presumed that sightseers only came later in the morning.

When I opened the car door to get out and look over the parapet, I almost wished I hadn't come, for all the magnificence of the view, and the historical interest of the spot. A wind, funnelling up through a gap in the mountains, and stronger than any wind I have ever felt, all but knocked me off my feet. I took one quick look at the valley below, and fought my way back to the car. The wind tore at the door, and I had to tug with all my strength before I could close it after me.

A terrifying wind, and an altogether terrifying spot; I wouldn't ever want to come back. Think of those five hundred feet below the parapet. Think of skidding, in one of those sudden, unexpected Island downpours.

My little car was swaying crazily, and I was more than glad to be done with the detour and get back on the excellent highway that gradually descended to the sea.

With every passing mile I congratulated myself on having the good sense to explore the Island a bit, instead of just sitting. Everywhere, there was something of interest to see, with the water on my right, blue as blue could be, and on my left, a profusion of trees and plants and vines to exclaim over, growing at the red lava base, and up the sides, of tall, rough mountains whose peaks were lost in steel-gray mists.

With the help of the guidebook, I was beginning to recognize some of the rampant growth. It was a little game to guess *guava,* or *hau,* or *kiawe* or *kukui,* or iron-wood, or *lauhala,* and patches of sugarcane and taro, and then to stop briefly by the side of the road and check with the book.

I had been gone a little over three quarters of an hour, and had passed several small settlements, when I decided to pull up at a combined grocery store and gasoline station and ask, on the off chance, if the young man at the pump could direct me to Cousin Elizabeth's house.

He knew her name immediately, and without hesitation, gave me simple directions. I need only drive five miles farther until I came to a large banana grove, then take the first turn toward the ocean, and watch for her name on the gatepost of a private drive.

I started off again, and soon the road was running along a quiet shore, deserted except for an occasional fisherman casting his line, or wading out with a net to deeper water. And eventually I was calmly ignoring a sign that said, in Hawaiian, *"Kapu,"* and in English, "Keep out. Private property. No trespassing," to push open a rustic bamboo gate and drive down a lane that was only a rut cut through hundreds of banana trees—a jungle of them, it seemed to me, with their enormous, wind-frayed leaves brushing the sides of the car and rustling overhead, to enclose me in a sweltering, breathless green tent.

I had been hot enough, already; now I was dripping, and sticky. At one point the rut divided, with "Caretaker" painted in white on a pointing arrow, and "Owner" on another. I followed the "Owner" arrow, but without much real enthusiasm about going any farther. However, as there was no place to turn around, I had to keep driving.

The highway was beginning to seem much too far behind me. It was idiotic to imagine myself trapped, but I did, all the same, with a sudden panicky impulse to abandon the car, and walk back to the gasoline station where people were, and not just the quietly rustling desolation of this empty, stifling jungle.

It was fortunate that the rear of a small, white-painted wooden house appeared around a turn in the rut just when it did; I was ready to jump out of my skin with silly nerves. But the house was a diversion, especially as there was a turning space alongside of it.

Cousin Elizabeth's rescued relic of missionary days; there it was, a New England saltbox house, with its only concession to Island living a wide screened porch tacked on, I made a guess, to let the trade winds blow through a hot kitchen.

It was an unwelcoming house, with tightly closed wooden shutters at its windows, but with the turning area giving me courage to take a look around, as long as I had come this far, I got out of the car and started on a tour.

The small simple garden was not as neglected-looking as I had expected from Cousin Elizabeth's description, nor as unattractive; its small lawn of a coarse sea grass was bordered with yellow day lilies, and thick plantings of yellow-flowering plumeria trees tried hard to soften the plain severity of the house with masses of sweet-smelling bloom. I was walking on blossoms; the ones that had dropped from the boughs were a thick carpet.

Directly in front of the saltbox I came on the sea, alluringly beautiful, and tempting me to plunge into it despite all the dangers Cousin Elizabeth had enumerated.

Shallow, waveless water, of the palest jade color, and curving so deeply into the shore line as to be almost a lagoon, was quietly *ssh, ssh-ing*, against the wall she had mentioned, and looking down into its glass clearness I could see the darting of tiny quicksilver fish.

These weren't stingrays, these weren't sharks. And there wasn't too much coral down there, either, only a few white, jagged clumps that could easily be avoided. The currents? As to that, I couldn't say, though no water could have looked safer, even far out, a long way out, where small combers were breaking in white foam over a reef.

How perfect a swim would be! But Cousin Elizabeth knew best, of course. Resignedly, I put a swim out of mind, and substituting the rubber pool slippers for my white sandals, I scrambled over the wall, and with my skirts hitched high, and watching for coral, I had a deliciously cool, splashy wade.

The rock seawall extended for perhaps a hundred yards to an overhang of some kind of thick-leafed, densely growing shore shrub, and when I rounded the bushes it was a surprise to come on a little crescent of white, sandy beach, far narrower than the beach at the hotel, but still a beach.

The sand ran up to the door of another house—a hut, rather, smothered in hibiscus bushes and up on stilts, and with a tin roof, and with palm leaves tacked against its board sides.

A little grass shack . . . Was it the caretaker's? I wondered.

An outrigger canoe was pulled high on the sand beyond any rush of tidewater, and not far from it a man and a girl were stretched out on their backs under the shade of three tall cocopalms. The girl wore a sarong of blue-and-white printed cotton, the man wore faded, no-color swimming shorts. Both had hats of woven *lauhala* leaves tilted over their faces. A bandanna, matching her sarong, was around the girl's hat, and a lei of yellow plumeria blossoms was around her neck. They were lying very close. Earlier, they may have been even closer. The lei looked crushed.

Feeling decidedly *de trop*, I turned my back on them, but evidently they had heard my splashing, because before I reached the shrubs that had made the little sandy beach a hideaway the man holloed, and when I glanced over my shoulder I saw he and the girl were sitting up.

He holloed again. "Hold on." He got to his feet and sauntered toward me. "Were you looking for someone?"

"Isn't this Miss Elizabeth Beaton's property?"

"Right. Sorry, though, she's not in residence."

Was there a thinly disguised jeer to that? I was pretty sure of it, and it annoyed me, and so did the glance of his hard blue eyes, looking me up and down. It made me drop my skirt in a hurry.

His voice was British, and educated, but he wasn't a man easy to type. He was tall and well-built, and sunbrowned. There were pouches under the blue eyes, and heavy lines dug deeply on both sides of his nose and the straight-lipped mouth I could see under a small, clipped moustache. The hair on his arms and legs and chest looked as though it had been brass bright, once, but now it was almost as grizzled as the hair of his head. Thicker, though.

He didn't look like a man who had had an easy life. He looked battered. Tough and strong, but battered. There was still a kind of swagger about him, and a good many women would have found him attractive. And though I didn't happen to be one of them, he admittedly had just that something, that indefinable something . . .

"I am Nan Allen, Miss Beaton's cousin," I introduced myself, "and——"

"And you are a tourist, and you have dropped by looking for a bit of local color, is that it? I don't doubt Miss Beaton gave you a fairly accurate idea of what you would find."

"I don't know what you mean. I came to see her house and her beach."

"The local color I refer to is myself: Phillip Fenton, caretaker by necessity, beachcomber by choice, and occupant of the abode you see yonder. And this"—he beckoned to the girl to join him, and put an arm easily around her—"this is Miss Lani Ahkina, flower of all the Islands, toast of Oahu, and sweet sharer of my bed. Do be sure to tell Miss Beaton you have met us both."

He must be drunk. Or was he? No. And there was a deliberateness to the mockery of his smile; he was enjoying trying to shock Miss Elizabeth Beaton's cousin.

The girl? She was crazy about him, I could tell at once. And how could any man be other than wild for her? She was gorgeous. Absolutely gorgeous.

A great mass of thick black hair waved loosely about her brown-skinned face and rippled to her waist. Her dark eyes were soft and liquid, and, at the same time, as bright and lively and happy as those of a merry child.

Her teeth were small and very white, her hands and feet exquisite. The sarong left her smooth brown shoulders bare—the brown was a goldy brown, an ice-tea brown is as near as I can come to it—and outlined the swell of small, lifted breasts. It wrapped tightly her rounded hips and flat stomach, and fell in slit folds to show long, slim, straight legs. She was the Hawaiian girl people hear about and don't believe exists until they see for themselves.

Uncannily, the man seemed to read my thoughts. "Smile

for the lady, sweet Lani, and give her a great big welcoming Aloha! Nice and loud, now—Chamber of Commerce style. And, Miss Allen, I am quite sure you recognize Lani, our Sugarcane and Pineapple Queen, our Hula Maiden of the advertisements and travel-bureau folders?"

The sarcasm was heavy, and the girl laughed. "Da man, he all time make beeg joke," she explained to me, but she looked pleased.

She interested me. I wished I knew more about her. Did she really live with this man? He interested me too. Hardly the usual caretaker. I was surprised at Cousin Elizabeth's choice. But then, hadn't something else surprised me about Cousin Elizabeth's beach place, and puzzled me, just a little?

I couldn't resist the opportunity to put out a feeler. "The water looks lovely," I said, directing myself to the girl. "It's too bad the swimming is so dangerous."

The girl's big, expressive eyes questioned me. She didn't know what I was talking about.

"Because of all the coral, and the currents, and the sharks and stingrays, I mean."

The man spoke up. "Who ever told you that, laid it on a bit thick."

"But . . ." I decided not to argue it with him. Probably Cousin Elizabeth had been overcautious in her warning to me because of my being so completely a stranger to the Island and totally unaware of any swimming risks I might run.

While I explained it to myself, the girl was smiling at me, and she put a question, like a friendly child to a new girl in a schoolyard.

"You like sweem?"

"I'm crazy about it."

"If I go for a sweem, you go, too, maybe?"

"I wish I could, but I haven't a bathing suit with me, and anyway, I wouldn't have time."

"You got lotsa time. You got all day."

"I have to go back to Nuuanu in just a little while."

"O.K. So maybe we sweem *wikiwiki?*"

"*Wikiwiki?*"

"Right now, quick! And why you want suit for this kind beach, where no people come? I don' wear suit—see?"

She began to unwrap her sarong. I was taken aback, to put it mildly, and must have shown it, because the man looked amused.

"Not so fast, Lani. The lady isn't used to Island ways." He turned to me. "If you would like to swim, Lani can find you something to wear, though it may not be entirely orthodox."

"Yes. You come my house, I feex." The girl held out her hand. Again she was like a child. Only a child would have offered, as simply, to lead a friend home. I took her hand, and went with her.

I have wondered at myself ever since. But from its beginning, that entire morning was astonishing. First, I had deliberately chosen to go behind Cousin Elizabeth's back, next I had listened to the persuasiveness of a girl I had never laid eyes on before, and now I was intending to ignore all of Cousin Elizabeth's explicit warnings. Then I was undressing in a beachcomber's shack, with his Hawaiian mistress giggling as she outfitted me for a swim in the very same water Cousin Elizabeth had tried so hard to keep me out of.

As to what I looked like . . . No wonder the girl was giggling. She had tied a big bandanna, like the one around her hat, into a halter bra for me, and handed me a pair of white duck shorts, a man's shorts, miles too big for me, and when I was in them, she bunched up the excess material and knotted it with a piece of string.

If that man dared laugh! Plainly he was entertained by having Miss Elizabeth Beaton's cousin turn up. And he didn't like Cousin Elizabeth. That was plain, too. Wondering what accounted for that faint jeering note, I felt disloyal at having stayed on, and thoroughly ashamed of myself on several accounts. I would have made an about-face, and left at once, if it had not been for the girl. I could not have hurt her, or spoiled her fun, anymore than I could have spoiled things for a child. And she was just that now, with her giggling over a game of "Let's dress up."

"Playing house" was another game she evidently took part in, but its adult implications could not be missed; the shack had only one room, except for a lean-to kitchen and bathroom, and it was dominated by a wide couch—a *hikea*, to Islanders—that was heaped with tumbled pillows laid upon pillows. And one or two of the creamy yellow flowers from around the girl's neck had fallen among those pillows.

I looked away, feeling like a Peeping Tom, and took in the rest of the room. It was clean, but untidy, and the matting-covered floor was gritty with beach sand no one had bothered to sweep up. A big wooden table that looked like an old house door, planed, and put on legs with home carpentry, was littered with squeezed tubes of oil paint, paint-smeared rags, a tomato can crammed with brushes, a pipe, and a tin of tobacco.

A small transistor radio and a ukulele took up more space on the table and crowded a big wooden bowl of nuts and fruits; the macadamias and lichees, the pineapples and papayas and avocados, the bananas, the mangoes, the limes that I could buy at supermarkets in San Francisco, but that could be picked right off the trees here in the Islands.

What apparently was the eating end of the table was spread with broad green leaves for mats, and places were set for two with dime-store knives and forks and spoons.

One corner of the room seemed to be a studio; several canvases were piled on the floor, and another, on an easel, and still wet, drew me to it.

A seabird, its wings spread, was defying the buffet of wind and rain. The wings were gray against a darker-gray sky. The rain was a gray slant. The gunmetal waves the bird was flying over were streaked with the sullen, blackish green of a full-running tide.

A strong picture, moodily effective. And the bird had been painted with the meticulous sharpness and authenticity of an ornithological etching.

A stunning picture. Terrific, hung in the right room.

The almost illegible initials "P.F." in the corner? For Phillip Fenton?

A big kerosene lamp hung over the table on a pull-up-and-down chain, and another hung in the kitchen, where there was an old, black wood-burning stove, an ancient wooden icebox, and a galvanized iron sink.

As I had seen neither any poles for electricity, nor tanks of bottled gas outside the shack, I supposed ice would be brought in from the store on the highway. Ice to chill the man's beer—there was a plastic wastebasket full of cans.

A dented coffeepot stood on the sink and two thick white mugs. Over the sink there was a shelf crowded with shells. A shabby, navy-blue, brass-buttoned blazer with a pocket emblem of crossed cricket bats hung from a wall hook, and there were more clothes behind a skimpy width of cheap cotton material that made a closet.

Something was simmering in a pot on the stove; fish, from the smell, and the shack was suffocatingly hot. I couldn't possibly have resisted a swim, anymore than I could resist the girl's attractiveness, her naturalness, the spontaneity of her acceptance of me on sight. The acceptance was touchingly childlike, but it was flattering also. I suppose everyone likes to be liked.

When the girl had finished outfitting me, she flung off her sarong and ran out of the shack, naked, and laughing, to the water's edge. Wading far out through the shallow clearness until she was over her depth, she dived into deep, translucent water, more emerald-green than jade, and streaked with lapis.

When she came up, she was laughing again, as she tossed back strands of long wet hair. The hibiscus flower had washed away, but the lei was still around her neck. She was like a dolphin, playing in that crystalline water as she dived again and again, but not at all like a mermaid; to me, mermaids have always seemed so sad, so lovelorn, singing on their lonely rocks.

There was nothing sad about this girl, nor lovesick, either. If I wasn't actually envious of her, I was close to it as I ran into the water after her, clutching at my borrowed shorts, and relieved to see that Cousin Elizabeth's caretaker was down the beach, stretched out under the palm trees again.

The water felt divine as I waded in, cautiously, a little deeper, a little deeper. I was still wearing my rubber slippers, but they touched nothing but smooth, firm sand. Coral? I saw only one lump. Currents? When I had waded out over my head, and was floating on my back in deliciously buoyant water, deliciously lulling water, I scarcely drifted. Easily, I would be able to swim back to wading depth again.

Sharks? Had they been a menace, would an Island girl who knew all the risks have dared swim out so far, toward the foam-white water of the reef?

Stingrays? The girl didn't seem to be afraid of them, either, or did Islanders simply ignore the dangers of the sea, and take their chances with it? It wasn't a question worth trying to answer, at the moment. I just wanted to float. I could have stayed in that beautiful water forever.

The girl swam back to me. "You like?"

"It's heaven. But I have to go in, now."

"Quick, quick, go in?"

"Yes. *Wikiwiki*."

She liked that. She laughed and laughed.

"Very smart haole! You learn Island talk fast. Maybe you come again, make other visit? Then I teach you more."

We swam ashore, and back in the shack I dried myself with a ragged but clean towel Lani produced. She herself didn't bother with a towel. When she had rewrapped her sarong over her brown, smooth-skinned body that still glistened with seawater, she ran outside again and picked fresh hibiscus blossoms from a bush at the door of the shack for her own hair, and insisted on thrusting a big, yellow-ruffled flower into mine. I made it stay with a bobby pin.

While I dressed, she stared at my underthings, and seemed to think them pretty but superfluous.

She urged me to stay for lunch—for *kau-kau* as she called it. I explained again that I must leave, and in a hurry.

"You come back soon?" she persisted.

"Would you be here if I came? Do you live here?"

"Sure theeng I live here. Good place!"

"You like the Major?"

"He my numba-one fella. I *too* much like! No can help."

She took my hand again and led me outside, and then let go to swoop down on a shell that a high tide had cast on the beach.

"Not find this kind every day. Here, you take."

She pressed it on me as we walked along the sand toward the car. It meant we had to pass the canoe. The man had just started to push it into the water, but when the girl called out to him, he turned to give me one of those sardonic smiles of his.

"You must come again, Miss Allen." He studied me appraisingly, but with a certain objectivity. "Now if I went in for portraits . . ." His eyes narrowed, his head was a little on one side. I felt like I was under a microscope. "Mahogany hair. Dark eyebrows. Eyes—*hmm,* I don't quite know—sable-brown, and a touch of ocheryellow to lighten them, might do the trick. You don't have usual coloring, you know."

He dropped the subject of my personal appearance to ask, "By any chance could it have been Miss Beaton who mentioned sharks and currents and coral? Not sporting of her to slander our little Island paradise, eh, Lani? If she doesn't want you contaminated by bad company, tell her to come out and say so. And she has my permission to tell you all about me. Though I doubt she will—not everything. In fact, I am jolly well certain she won't."

He gave the canoe a quick shove to free it from the sand, and when it was afloat he swung over the side and began to paddle.

"Where is he going?" I asked the girl.

"Same like every day, he go feesh for *ama-ama*" (which was mullet, Lani explained, when I interrupted her to ask), "and he go paint. Some day he gonna make lotsa poi money with pictures."

I had heard about poi from friends who had visited the Islands. Some said it tasted like the scrapbook paste of their schooldays, others like it, served with plenty of soy sauce and raw fish. It was cheap, and a staple with Islanders, as rice was to the Chinese. If a girl and a man lived on poi, and the fish they caught, and on Island fruits, "lotsa money" would go a long way.

I wondered if the man's pictures would ever sell; I'd like to buy the seabird picture myself. I'd like to take it back to Jim. It could make our whole apartment, when we found one. Only, unfortunately, there wasn't going to be an apartment.

I got in my car. "Good-bye, Lani. Thank you for the shell, and my flowers."

"Good-bye, Mees Allen. You my friend now, huh?"

"Yes. And you are mine."

She waved to me when I drove off and called an aloha. I can see her still as she stood there, smiling. Dear Lani.

When I had gotten through the banana grove and was back on the highway, I stopped at the gasoline station again with the excuse of needing my windshield wiped.

"I found Miss Beaton's house," I told the young man who had directed me to it, and he gave me exactly the information I was angling for.

"Run into the Doc, did you?"

"The Doc?"

"The caretaker guy."

"Is he a doctor?"

"He was, once. Used to be a major in the British Army, and blew in here from Hong Kong a couple months back."

"Who is the girl?"

"Lani? Say, isn't she good-looking? And she's a real good kid, too."

"Is she Hawaiian?"

"Yeah, except for maybe a little *pake*."

"*Pake?*"

"Chinese."

"Hasn't she any family to keep an eye on her?"

"Sure, she's got a family. Her mother and her dad and ten, maybe eleven, brothers and sisters." The young man grinned. "Some tight squeeze when they all pile into their old man's pickup and take off for church on Sundays. Lani and a couple others of 'em sing in the choir."

"Where do they live?"

"Down the beach a ways from Miss Beaton's place."

"Ten or eleven children! How do they manage to eat?"

"They do all right. Lani's old man drives a truck, when he ain't off fishing. You can eat good on mullet and *u'u* and barracuda. Her old lady takes orders for quilted bedspreads. The real thing. You know—the handmade old-fashioned stuff. And all the kids rustle up jobs doing yard work or baby-sitting."

"Don't the girl's parents object to—well, to what is going on?"

"Hell, no. It was them fixed it up. Lani's old man got a fishhook in his hand and the Doc took it out for free, see, so they say 'Thanks, pal,' by sending Lani over to cook his *kau-kau* and wash his shirts." The young man grinned again. "What do you wanna bet the Doc didn't put up much of a fight?"

"But that's dreadful!"

The young man shrugged. "You're new here, aren't you?" he asked as he squirted glass cleaner.

"Yes, but what's that got to do with it?"

"If you stay long enough, you might get to understand people like Lani's folks. Time to get on the beach, time to make music, and plenty of Happy Time—if you know what I mean—is what counts to them. And Lani's folks are real glad they got it fixed up that way for her, with everything what you might call congenial."

"I still say it's dreadful, handing her over like that."

"Like I say, they was just paying back the Doc. That's how they are, always wanting to give you the shirt off their back, and never worrying about nothing."

When the windshield had been polished, I drove off with a good deal to think about, and Lani Ahkina and Phillip Fenton occupied my thoughts for the entire drive over the Pali.

Lani and her Happy Time. What a way to put it! But again I was envious of her. She was getting a lot more out of life than I was, wasn't she?

It was only after I drove through Cousin Elizabeth's moongate that her warnings about the coral and the sharks and the stingrays and the currents puzzled me again. Quite evidently none of them were a really serious drawback to her beach, so why had she stressed them? And if it was because she wanted to make certain I stayed away from the beach, did the intimacy of her caretaker with the enchanting, if amoral, Lani warrant such exaggeration?

She had exaggerated the condition of the garden, too, come to think of it, and was that still another attempt to make the whole place unattractive to me?

I wouldn't have thought it a bit like her. Even knowing

her as slightly as I did, she seemed much too forthright for evasions of any situation, no matter how awkward.

And what would she say if I told her I had gone to the beach and not only defied her warnings, but made a friend of the girl who was sleeping with her caretaker?

I wouldn't dream of telling her. I would keep the details of my highly unconventional day to myself. It would be the safest way to avoid even the smallest con-tretemps. The bond between Cousin Elizabeth and myself, so newly forged, was to me, at least, precious beyond words; I wouldn't risk a break of the smallest link.

Chapter nine

I did not look forward to the cocktail hour. When I had changed into a lime-green, sleeveless linen shift and matching sandals and gone out to the lanai to wait for Cousin Elizabeth to appear from her room, I substituted a spray of jasmine for the hibiscus Lani had thrust in my hair, and I tossed away the hibiscus afraid that Cousin Elizabeth might ask, idly, if I had picked it in the garden.

When we sat down opposite each other in our peacock chairs and were sipping our rum and pineapple juice, I felt as though her large, clear eyes with their direct gaze were looking straight through me as she asked, "You hadn't too long and lonely a day, I hope? The heat wasn't too much for you? We shall be getting our seasonal winds back soon to improve matters. At any rate, you had the pool. You swam, of course?"

"Yes." Answering her with a technical truth, and in a rush to avoid any further discussion of my day, I asked questions of my own. "You had as busy a time as usual,

Cousin Elizabeth? Will your next trip to Hong Kong bore you, as you have been there so often? Or is Hong Kong as exciting as it sounds? What is it like?"

"I wouldn't know where to begin." Cousin Elizabeth lighted a cigarette and inhaled deeply, and then a waft of tobacco was added to the scent of jasmine and plumeria and ginger, heavily sweet on the moist warm air. "The harbor is crowded with ships of all nations, and with native junks and sampans and barges, and the mountain that comes down to it is equally crowded with houses at every level, going up and up, in long rows."

"Cities always seem to have a smell all their own. Has Hong Kong?"

"I'd recognize it blindfolded. The temple incense. Wine fumes. Factory furnaces. The sweet, sickish smell of opium. The reek of fish in hot weather. The crowding masses of people, and their filth. Their pork and their cabbage and garlic and sugary almond cakes and their charcoal stoves. But there is no smell of garbage; too many people are snatching it out of the refuse cans."

Cousin Elizabeth inhaled again. "You can smell money. Oh, yes. It has a distinct smell. It's in the exhausts from the cars that choke the streets—the Mercedes Benzes and the Bentleys and the Rollses. It is given off by the French perfumes, the caviar, the furs, the silks and pearls and woolens in the luxury shops. 'What is Hong Kong like?' I could go on forever: the internal political maneuvers, the international manipulations. The labor situation; the riots and dock fights. And the beauty—camellia bushes rooftop high in gardens with thousand-year-old shrines. The extravagance: the parties in private houses and clubs, given with a glamour and elegance you no longer can find anywhere else in the world."

"Where does all the money come from?"

"It's there, waiting for anyone who wants it, wants it badly enough. Anyone, that is, who is willing to take risks, and who has the right connections."

"When you go back, will Mr. Yin Wah go with you?"

"He wouldn't dream of letting me go by myself." Cousin Elizabeth smiled behind a pale haze of smoke. "I call him my watchdog. My Foo watchdog. He reminds me exactly of one of those goggle-eyed, clumsy, and oh, so fierce pottery lion-dogs I am sure you have seen in Chinatown. And he is forever at my side."

"Have you known him long?"

"Only a year or so. Various business interests brought us together."

"What do you export?"

"Silk. Cotton. Porcelain. Tea. Rattan furniture. Plastic flowers. Sequined dresses, beaded sweaters and bags, and embroideries that I have done in my own workshops."

Cousin Elizabeth picked up her glass. "I could go on with the list. But that does it, in general."

"Doesn't Mr. Yin Wah seem rather—well, rather crude?"

"I ignore the crudities. Ever since he came to me—with a number of ideas, which I had the capital to back—we have had an extremely profitable association, and that is all that concerns me."

"Do you trust him?" I came out with it bluntly.

"Why shouldn't I?" Her gentle, pretty laugh was sincerely amused. "If I didn't, if I thought for one moment I couldn't—well, my dear, it doesn't bear thinking of."

"I know you will think I'm silly, but he frightens me." This I blurted, too, and was glad to have it off my mind.

"Frightens you? Why?"

"I don't know. He just does. There's just something. One reason I wanted to come out to Honolulu was to be sure everything was all right with you."

"You had your doubts?"

"Not until I met him, not until I saw how determined he was to put up a barrier between you and me." I hesitated, with a glance toward the trees at the foot of the garden, so dark, so enclosing, silhouetted against the flaming sunset sky. "A barrier to keep me out, and to keep you in. He made me feel that anything at all could have been happening to you, way off here, or in Hong Kong, without your family knowing. And as family means me—because you and I only have each other—I couldn't do anything else but come and see that everything was all right with you."

"You absurd child. What an imagination! And all because my Foo dog was simply trying to fend off a persistent young woman who might take up too much of my time! Might even take my mind off the business presently at hand—which, as a partner, he has no intention of allowing. But it was sweet of you to be concerned, and I appreciate it."

It all sounded reasonable enough, but it didn't convince me. To me, Mr. Yin Wah remained more than a watchdog, lightly and humorously described and overjealous in guarding his own and Cousin Elizabeth's interests. But she might not like it—or might merely laugh—if I said anything more. Determinedly, I looked away from those shutting, and shutting-out trees, and gave myself up to the pleasantness of the hour.

All of it unreal: the scent of the gardenia floating in my frosty goblet; the wide arc of sky, where stars were pricking through; the languorous warm stillness of the garden, with only the whisper of silk when Cousin Elizabeth stirred in her chair to reach for another cigarette; and the pad of felt slippers as Fong came out on the lanai to refill our glasses.

If only Jim could have been there . . .

I remembered another Chinese poem:

Birds in their nest know the wind's chill;
Beasts in their caves feel the sunless rain,
But if you have never endured separation,
How can you know the yearning for an absent friend?[*]

Only, Jim was more than an absent friend.

The rum, again, I told myself. Jim was nothing to me, anymore. Nothing. That is, from his choice. Not mine. Not mine.

In due course—and high time—we went in to dinner. My day, spent alone, as Cousin Elizabeth thought, was not again referred to, I thanked goodness. And afterward, as we went through the hall to go back to the lanai, and passed the curio cabinet I had noticed on my arrival at Cousin Elizabeth's, I was inspired to think of still another subject that would keep conversation going and ward off the possibility of further questions from Cousin Elizabeth as to how I had occupied myself in her absence.

"I have something to show you, Cousin Elizabeth. One minute . . ." I hurried off to my room and came back with Ah Sam's sandalwood fan. I held it out. "I found it among Ah Sam's things after she died. Where do you suppose she ever got it?"

[*] From *The Penguin Book of Chinese Verse, translated* by Robert Kotewell and Norman L. Smith. Introduced and edited by A. R. Davis. Baltimore, Maryland, Penguin Books, Inc., 1962.

"She couldn't have bought it, certainly." Cousin Elizabeth unfurled the fan. "Carving like that is rare today. The fan would be worth a good deal of money, to a connoisseur."

"She was trying to tell me something about it when she was dying. Something terribly important to her, and troubling. It broke my heart to listen to her try. But she was speaking Hunanese dialect, and the doctor could only understand a few garbled words."

"She was troubled, you say?"

"She desperately wanted to explain about a fan, as far as the doctor could make out. She was frantic. I can't tell you how pitiful she was, how frustrated."

"Why didn't she speak English?"

"She was too ill to make the effort, the doctor said. Words just came the easiest way."

"There was nothing at all in English?"

"Nothing."

The question had something of persistence in it, I remember thinking at the time. Only a hint. Perhaps I was mistaken. Because for what possible reason should she sound overinterested, a shade anxious, waiting for my answer?

She was playing with the fan, absently opening and closing it. A queer little silence fell between us, and then, casually, she commented, "Deathbed scenes are never pleasant." She closed the fan abruptly, and there was a tiny sound of a stick cracking. "My dear. I *am* sorry. You must let me have it mended."

I took it from her, distressed out of all proportion to the damage done, but the cracked stick would have hurt Ah Sam, and Ah Sam seemed very close to me, strangely close, as the scent of sandalwood mingled with all the other evening fragrances that made the air so sweetly disturbing.

Nostalgia for my childhood, when Ah Sam had been everything to me, as well as an adult sense of loss, brought a quick rush of tears to my eyes. I had never looked closely at the fan before, but now I held it under one of the big paper lanterns and examined the broken stick carefully, and a little resentfully. The way Ah Sam had treasured it in its careful wrappings—and now this done to it.

In the yellow glow of the lantern the carving and inlay work were startlingly clear.

"Look!" I exclaimed excitedly. "Look, Cousin Elizabeth. Lettering. A letter on each stick. And down the end stick, numbers. A date: 1937!"

The date, of inlaid ivory, and the five letters, one to each stick, were so elaborately scrolled, so intricately entwined with the delicate carved work of the sandalwood that it was no wonder I had missed them entirely on the other occasions I had unwrapped the fan, and now it was by the merest chance they had caught my eye.

"Look—the letters! They spell out a name. *E-d-i-t-h* Edith. Why, that was the name of Uncle John Allen's wife."

"So it was."

"Nineteen hundred thirty-seven. Was it an anniversary?"

"I've always been stupid about remembering dates, I am afraid."

"If it was an anniversary, I wonder why Aunt Edith gave the fan away to Ah Sam."

"Edith is not an uncommon name. It needn't have been your aunt's fan at all."

"Oh, but I'm sure it was. It makes sense! I'm rather sorry; I have hoped so much, ever since I came across it, that it might have been my mother's."

My disappointment was enormous, and I couldn't keep it out of my voice.

"You do have an imagination! And what a sentimental young thing you are. Don't you realize there is only one chance in a thousand the fan was Edith Allen's? But whoever it belonged to, I insist on having it mended."

Cousin Elizabeth reached to take the fan from me. To this day I don't know why I refused to part with it. "Don't trouble," I told her. Quickly, I wrapped the fan in its gold paper again and tied its red cord. "The break is so small, it really doesn't show."

"But I shan't feel right about it unless I have it repaired. They do magnificent work of that sort in Hong Kong, you know, and for pennies."

I had the oddest feeling we had become adversaries over possession of the fan, and that for some reason Cousin Elizabeth wanted it in her hands now as strongly as I wanted it in mine.

"Just as you say." Cousin Elizabeth's interest in the fan seemed to wane. She yawned, and put a hand over her mouth. "It's late."

I sighed, half to myself. "If only the doctor could have understood what Ah Sam was trying to tell me. I'll never stop wondering. Never."

"I doubt if there is any great mystery to be solved." Cousin Elizabeth yawned again. "Excuse me . . ."

"Did you ever see Aunt Edith Allen and Ah Sam together in camp?"

"See them?" Cousin Elizabeth snubbed out her cigarette. "Not that I remember. But it was all so long ago.

However, I don't doubt for a moment Ah Sam stole the fan from some Edith or other; we were always hungry, and with luck it would have bought a bowl of rice from the guards."

"Ah Sam could never have been a thief," I protested indignantly.

"Life in a prison camp changes many people's morals, my dear girl."

"Someone gave it to her, I'm sure. And before they went to camp. Who would take a fan to prison?"

"We were herded off to camp on a moment's notice. There were women prisoners who snatched up and carried with them the first thing they thought of as precious. Photograph albums. Baby bootees, cast in silverplate. Birds in cages. Dogs. Cats. Fish bowls. One woman brought along a potted plant. Another, too stunned and rattlebrained to bring an extra coat, carried along a golf trophy of her husband's. It sounds incredible. But faced with prison camp, they went blank."

"What did you take, Cousin Elizabeth?"

"Cigarettes. Aspirin. A blanket. My fur coat. And some American gold dollars I had hoarded for months, with just this sort of emergency in mind."

Naturally. She had shown the practicality you would expect of her. But if I was sentimental and romantic, so was Aunt Edith; no matter what else she may have snatched up, she had refused to leave a treasured fan behind. I liked her for it.

Her treasure of treasures. What had the year 1937 meant to her?

"Still worrying your head about the fan?"

"Not worrying. Just trying to puzzle it out. And I still say the fan must have been given to Ah Sam. She'd never, never have stolen it."

Cousin Elizabeth shrugged. "Keep your illusions, my dear. They become the young. And don't think I am being too hard on Ah Sam. As I said, standards change as circumstances change. Hunger can be a terrible spur. Hunger of any sort. And for some people a bowl of rice—or its equivalent—is more irresistible than to others. Temptation, like so many other things, is comparative. And given sufficient motivation, none of us would be as strong as we might wish. But now, then, that's enough of my middle-aged cynicism. Good night, dear Nan. I am going to bed. Pleasant dreams. They are infinitely desirable."

She kissed me lightly.

I stayed on the lanai, alone, an hour or more after Fong had appeared to snuff out the candles in the paper lanterns, and while the garden torches burned low. While I could entirely understand the practicality and the logic of Cousin Elizabeth's thinking, I was wishing she had not so matter-of-factly labeled Ah Sam a thief. Not Ah Sam, no matter what.

I pictured the prison camp; it had always been real to me, a place I almost remembered, so often had Ah Sam told me about it. The barbed wire. The heavily booted guards kicking prisoners, smashing their heads open with rifle butts. Frightened children sobbing. Newborn infants, such as I, had been wailing, wailing. The humiliations. The degradations. The filth. The heat. The cold. The hunger that was a perpetual, terrible gnawing.

Perhaps it was only common sense to admit Ah Sam might have stolen the fan. But honest, or dishonest, would she have recognized the negotiable value of carved sandalwood and inlaid ivory? I strongly doubted it. To Ah Sam, as to any coolie woman, a fan would be just that, a fan; something to stir a breeze, or keep flies away. No. Ah

Sam had not stolen the fan to exchange it for a bowl of rice. If she had taken it at all, it would have been to keep it as a memento of some dead fellow prisoner. Or, again, it might have been left her by the same dead prisoner, in pathetic gratitude for kindness shown her.

Theory. All theory.

Over and over in my thoughts the name Edith re-occured. Was it too much of a coincidence, the fan having belonged to Edith Allen? Ah Sam had never spoken of her to me. I had always supposed she had never seen my uncle's wife; I knew, from her description, that the camp was divided into fenced-off yards, like cattle pens, that separated the prisoners as effectively as though they had been in entirely different camps. Besides, Ah Sam would have had little time to give Aunt Edith Allen, dying of hunger and dysentery. Her entire attention, her full devotion, had been given to me, the starving infant born to that other Allen wife, Anne.

I was making something out of nothing. I was raising questions of no import. Easy to tell myself that. And yet I couldn't dismiss my memory of Ah Sam's deathbed frustration. Nor could I dismiss the curious feeling that if Cousin Elizabeth had got her hands on the fan a second time, not only one fragile stick, but all of them would have crunched with the fierceness of her grip.

Ah Sam was not the only one to whom the fan had its puzzling importance. That was plain. Though why on earth it should mean anything to Cousin Elizabeth, I couldn't begin to guess.

Chapter ten

I went back to the beach the next day and the next and the next. It was easy to slip away. The servants took for granted, naturally, that I was free to come and go whenever and wherever I chose, and Cousin Elizabeth, after a day in town, never put awkward questions. I never had to lie outright to her, for which I was thankful. She would merely ask, "You have been able to amuse yourself, child? The day hasn't been too long and dull for you?" And before she left the house each morning, she would urge, hospitably, "Help yourself to any of the books in the library. See that the yard boys put up the umbrella at the pool, and ask Fong or Wing to bring you what you like for lunch and keep you supplied with cold drinks. Lui Lung will give you towels and hang up your bathing suit, don't forget."

She considered not only my daily comfort, but was concerned with my social life—or lack of it. "You are not seeing the Islands as you should," she told me one evening after dinner. "Each of them is different, and each in its own way delightful. How I wish I might show them to you. And I ought to be entertaining you. Your timing was terribly unfortunate, my dear. You couldn't have arrived when I was busier. But never mind. Perhaps you will come again. I hope so. At any rate, I can introduce you to a few people at the end of the week. Friends of mine who live at Diamond Head are giving a large buffet supper Friday evening, and I have asked them if I might bring you."

I was appreciative, but not too interested. I wasn't in a party mood. Even so, the evening might prove entertaining. I had always heard a great deal about Diamond Head and the people who lived there, the close little circle of long-time residents—*Kamaainas*, as they were called, to differentiate them from the newcomers to the Islands, who loomed large among Honolulu's important citizens. Their hospitality was fabulous—a legend. But a party, no matter how lavish and gay, without Jim? I took a dim view.

The only thing at all that took me out of myself and gave me true pleasure were my daily swims at the beach. Each morning when I wakened I would think, "Another chance to plunge into that delicious cool, cool water." The lure of it was irresistible.

I knew it was silly not to be honest with Cousin Elizabeth. Why shouldn't I swim at a shore Lani had assured me again and again was as safe as any on the Island? I was an adult, wasn't I? And Cousin Elizabeth really had no right to lay down the law to me. Not that she intended to. Her putting it off bounds had been only for my safety. And, of course, I was trespassing, by using her private beach without express permission, and I was breaking all the rules of common courtesy by ignoring my hostess's plainly posted "Keep Off" signs.

But oh, that turquoise water, that indigo, that lapis-lazuli water, on these hot days that to me, after San Francisco, were so enervating in the daytime, no matter how delicious at sunset.

And Lani, that amusing, enchanting Lani, so full of surprises, so changing of mood. "Like seesta, now," she told me after a number of my surreptitious visits to the beach. "Before you come, I have seven brudda but only three seestas. Now, I get four seestas. 'Lucky Lani,' my new name! First, dey bring me my Doc, den dey bring you."

"Dey"? Who was she talking about?

We were in the kitchen eating mangoes, with juice running all over us, and as she wiped her mouth with the back of her hand, she was looking reflective, and humbly grateful.

"You know what? All dem on my side." She made a wide, encompassing gesture. "All dem . . . !"

" 'Dem'? Who are 'dem'?" I was more than just idly curious. The humbleness, the obvious gratitude asked for an answer.

"You no savvy 'dem'? Say, where you been, all time since you born?"

"I'm just a *haole*, don't forget." That, of course, excused my ignorance.

" 'Dem' is Akua. An' evvytheeng good come, if Akua like you. But if dey *huhu* . . ."

"What does '*huhu*' mean?"

"Tha's angry—mad. Dat means you catch it, seesta!"

I was making a wild guess to myself. Were "dem"—the Akua—Lani's gods? Had that wide gesture meant that to her, they were everywhere? In Heaven—in the sea—in all nature? I didn't want to ask her—I didn't want to pry so intimately, but I put another question.

"How do you make 'dem' like you?"

"You all time talk nice. Dey like 'please' and 'thank you.' And presents, sometimes."

She let it go at that, and got up from the table to bring a pitcher of pineapple juice from the icebox, but I noticed an unmistakable little air of private conviction about her.

"Dem, out there." So Lani prayed to them, did she, and offered them grateful—and placating—gifts? I glanced through the doorway to the ocean. I had seen Lani take off a lei, now and again, and toss it back into the water as we waded to shore after a swim. And this was the same Lani who piled into her father's car on Sunday mornings with her mother and brothers and sisters to sing hymns in a Christian church?

Well, she certainly was playing it safe.

It had its humorous side, but I didn't laugh. I found it touching. And when we went outside, after the mango and juice that had been a second breakfast for me, after my early drive from Cousin Elizabeth's house, I gave another glance toward the sea. "Dem"—some of them, at least—were definitely out there. *Haole* or not, I was ready to believe it. In the sound of the waves you could hear their chant. That is, if you really listened. Oh, undoubtedly, Island magic was casting its spell.

We were gathering shells along the water's edge when Major Fenton beached his canoe, and strolled toward us. He had been out painting since sunup, Lani told me.

I hadn't seen him since our first meeting, and I felt foolish under the entertained gaze of his blue eyes, because Lani had draped my bathing suit with seaweed that hung like a hula skirt over my thighs, and hung a lei of fragrant creamy yellow plumeria flowers around my neck. She had picked them from the trees that shaded my car, and from the hibiscus shrubs that grew around the shack she had picked a huge ruffled red blossom for my hair.

"Back again, Miss Allen? Soaking up local color, are you? And not afraid of going native yourself? It's a calculated risk, you know, for anyone who takes to the beach. But I fancy Miss Beaton has warned you."

His glance, then, was all at once impersonal, and he was studying my face, with the seaweed and the flowers of no interest to him. "That coloring of yours . . . I wish I could think—but it will come to me."

He turned his attention to unloading the canoe and tossed a big, slippery fish to Lani. "Supper, my Pearl of Pearls."

With Lani all giggles, the fish clutched in both arms, she and I went back to the shack.

"You come tomorrow?" Lani asked it as she plunked the fish on the kitchen sinkboard and began scaling it before cutting it up. "Next day, too?"

"If you'll let me. But I shall have to leave early tomorrow. I'm going to a party in the evening and I ought to get my hair done. All this swimming! I wish I looked like you when I come out of the water."

I was going on about girls with naturally wavy hair who had all the breaks over girls with permanents when Major Fenton walked in through the open door and took a glass and a bottle from the shelf over the sink.

"A party? I heard you mention a party? The beach one day, High Society another, on the premise that variety is, indeed, the spice of life, Miss Allen?"

Before I could think of any sort of answer scathing enough, Lani broke in. "I go to party tomorrow night too.

My brudda Hanale and his friend Keoki make music, and I make hula at Diamond Head."

"Lani and her brother earn a few dollars entertaining at private houses, now and then," the Major explained.

"Are you going to people named Morrow by any chance, Lani? That's where I'm going, to a Mr. and Mrs. Morrow's house."

"Then you and me go same party. What you know about that!" Lani gave the big silvery fish a hearty thwack. "Hey feesh, you hear what Mees Allen say? The same party! She wait, she see! On Friday I make number-one hula for her, and Hanale and Keoki, they make number-one music—da best. That right, feesh?"

"And here I'll sit, alone in my little grass shack, with only the sad sea waves for company. It seems rather a pity."

The Major took a long drink from his glass, and when the fish was on the stove, Lani and I went out on the beach again. We had another swim—my second. When we came back to the house for lunch, Major Fenton, in gray slacks and the navy-blue blazer from the hook on the kitchen wall, was just leaving. "Anything you want from town, Lani, my love? Coffee, etc., etc.? If you're a good girl and promise to have a couple of big kisses for me when I get back, I'll bring you some of those frozen lick-em things, on sticks."

I might have guessed that Lani would promptly give him the kisses in advance, and I know Major Fenton expected me to look shocked and disgusted, but I didn't give him the satisfaction. As a matter-of-fact, it didn't bother me, except to make me feel terribly sorry for Lani. Such a child—kisses, in return for ice cream on a stick.

It was midafternoon when she walked to my car with

me. I had been in swimming again, and stayed too long in that divine water. If I didn't get going that minute, I would be in danger of meeting Cousin Elizabeth's car turning in at her front gate.

I kept just to the speed limit once I was on the highway and I got back with only minutes to spare; I had garaged my car and was hurrying along the hall to my room when I heard tires on the graveled driveway, and a car stop.

Cousin Elizabeth would be getting out, the door held open for her by her driver, Sing. He was a good-looking young man, hardly more than a boy, with the suavest of correct manners, but with something just a little cocky about him, in my opinion, something that could be impudence if it were a shade more pronounced, and if he hadn't been smart enough not to step over the line. "New China," I told myself, as opposed to Fong and Wing and the others in the house. He was spoiled, I had concluded. His head had been turned. Cousin Elizabeth had brought him from Hong Kong only a few weeks ago. He not only was a splendid driver, she had explained, but the cleverest of mechanics with any of the modern makes of cars, which was more than could be said of some of the older Chinese chauffeurs.

In my rush to get back, I had forgotten to take off my plumeria lei, and though it was very much the worse for all that swimming (the flower in my hair had fallen out at my first dive), I hung it over a chairback. It was still fragrant, and, even yet, much too pretty for a wastebasket.

When I had taken a shower and rinsed the salt out of my hair and let a few pinned-up ends dry, it was time to dress for dinner, and go out to the lanai.

Cousin Elizabeth was there before me. I found her leaning back in her peacock chair, her eyes closed. Her face was white and drawn, but when she heard me, and opened her eyes, she smiled. "I wasn't asleep. Come and sit down."

"You look exhausted!" I blurted it out truthfully, if not tactfully.

"It was just one of those days. A cocktail will put me to rights again."

"Must you work so hard?"

"Don't worry about me. I shall be able to relax shortly. The immediate pressure will be off. And now here is Fong, thank goodness."

The frosty drink, and a second, did her good. I couldn't see, in the gathering dusk, whether the drawn look had gone, and if her color was better, but she was animated and cheerful, and full of questions about San Francisco and the many changes there since she had left so many years ago, and about my job and friends.

She asked if I were interested in men, and any man in particular, and I told her a half-truth. Men were fun, I said, but there was no one who meant anything to me. I don't know that she believed me, but at least she didn't pry.

"I am afraid the evenings here are dreadfully boring for you," she said after a little pause, when Fong had refilled our glasses and padded away and we were congenially alone, with the scent of the garden all around us, and my enjoyment of her company so great that the closing in of the tall trees hardly bothered me at all.

"Even tomorrow night won't be a bit exciting. There will be no one your age, only older people, unfortunately."

"You are quite sure your friends want me? I'm not being a nuisance, or making things awkward for you?"

"Hardly." She laughed, shortly. "I shall not only have

brought a most attractive new girl to the party, I shall have produced that rarity, that prize of prizes, an extra man."

"You went to all the trouble of hunting one up for me?"

"I did nothing. It was an unexpected acquisition, for which I had to make no effort at all." She didn't explain, but her amused laugh grated, and I was vaguely conscious of something under the surface.

"Tell me about the people I shall be meeting tomorrow," I asked to fill a little silence. "Who will be at the party?"

"Any number of important people." Her answer was concise. But she elaborated on it, and I gathered that just about everyone who, in her opinion, was anyone in Honolulu's social and cultural and business and civic world, would be the Morrows' guests on Diamond Head. She enjoyed moving in her world of the Top Brass, I could see.

The party began to sound interesting. It would be a look-in for me at the people who made the life of the Island go round, and I was still thinking about it after dinner when we had finished our usual coffee and liqueurs on the lanai. "What shall I wear tomorrow evening?" I asked Cousin Elizabeth as we were saying good-night. "I didn't bring anything very special. Do you suppose I ought to go shopping in the morning? I want to do you proud, you know. It's going to be a big evening for me." I said it lightly, but in my heart I meant it. I had begun to realize I was thrilled at the thought of going to a party with Cousin Elizabeth. It would be my very first, ever, under the wing of someone who was family.

"Would you like to show me what you brought?"

We walked down the hall to my room and I took the

yellow chiffon from the closet. This was fun, too, the greatest fun, having family to pass on my dress.

But Cousin Elizabeth was not interested in the yellow chiffon; as I held it up, she was looking at the plumeria lei I had left hanging on the chairback.

Oh, Lord! Now I was in for it.

"A lei? Where did that come from, my dear? Did you buy it? I didn't know you had gone into town today."

She waited for an answer, and I simply couldn't lie to her. "I wasn't in town. I took a drive to your beach house, Cousin Elizabeth," I confessed honestly. I felt much better when it was out, but embarrassed, and apologetic. "Your pool is lovely, but I've been thinking about the sea ever since I came here," I tried to explain. "I caught a glimpse of it from the plane, and the hotel, and to be in Hawaii and not get into that gorgeous water—I couldn't resist. Actually, I've been going to your beach every morning." I came out with the whole truth, stumbling over it, and my embarrassment worse every moment as Cousin Elizabeth stood there, looking at me out of those large, quiet eyes.

"I thought I mentioned coral and currents and sharks?"

"You did, but . . ."

"But what?"

"When I got there, I thought I must have misunderstood you—that there was some mistake, because—because . . ."

"Go on. Because?"

"Because your caretaker and—and a friend of his—said it was perfectly safe."

"And you took their word against mine?"

Before I could answer, Cousin Elizabeth smiled faintly. "Never mind. Don't look so upset. You haven't committed a crime, child. The thing is, I felt the beach house wasn't the proper place for you, and I admit I elaborated on the dangers of swimming to keep you away. But I forgot that you were no longer little Nan, the child I remembered from the old days. How silly of me to have thought of you as a child. But you see, my dear, I have heard rumors of what goes on at my beach, and until I find out whether or not they are true, I thought it much the best thing to put it out of bounds."

"I shouldn't have gone there, behind your back."

"What's done is done. And as a matter of fact, you will be meeting my beachcomber caretaker again tomorrow night—unfortunately, I might add, and against my better judgment, but——"

"Tomorrow? You mean at the party?" I couldn't believe I had heard her say it.

"He happens to be the extra man I spoke of. He came into the office this afternoon—something about repairs on the beach-house roof. I caught a glimpse of him waiting to see my secretary when I came in from a lunch conference, and on the spur of the moment I invited him. He is a rather good artist. I've seen his work, and I think he just might have a future. But he needs a boost up. A big boost. And there will be one or two people at the Morrows who can give it to him, it suddenly occurred to me. An Academy of Arts director, for instance, who is a private collector, and another friend who owns an important gallery."

As I stood there, flabbergasted, Cousin Elizabeth went on, "Don't think I admire his type, my dear. He's impossible, but extremely talented." She picked up the lei. "Plumeria from my trees? And 'his friend,' as you put it, that little girl he is supposed to keep, made it? And I suppose you are young enough to find the situation romantic? Personally, I find it sordid. But there. What can you expect of an old fogy of my generation?"

She let the lei drop back on the chair, and then she was saying in her gentle, sweet voice, that was a little amused, "Good night, my dear."

As she closed my door I was staring after her.

Major Fenton a protégé, now, of Cousin Elizabeth's? That dissolute-looking, battered-looking beachcomber with those hard blue eyes a man she would sponsor socially?

Well, you simply never knew about people.

That man, and Mr. Yin Wah. My word, what odd men she collected.

In a way, her association with Mr. Yin Wah was understandable. He was at least clever in a business way, she had said. But Major Fenton? What had he in his favor? In the first place he didn't look the sort of man who put himself under obligation to anyone, and a protégé was always in that position.

And what would Cousin Elizabeth get out of the relationship? Obviously his pictures didn't sell, or he wouldn't be caretaking.

That was what really puzzled me, because I couldn't blind myself to the fact that Cousin Elizabeth was not an altruistic woman. Much as I admired her, and devoted as I was to her, I wasn't that undiscerning.

I hung the chiffon away, frowning thoughtfully. Perhaps she found him a challenge? Perhaps launching him, helping him to sell was exciting to her? It would be, undoubtedly, if you were her type, with all that drive, and energy and ambition. Still . . .

The idea of Major Fenton as an extra man produced by

Miss Elizabeth Beaton at a stylish Diamond Head party was beyond me. I just couldn't see it. And why hadn't she arranged opportunities before this for him to meet people who could give him that boost up, that big boost?

No matter how hard I tried, I couldn't think of an answer, and so I gave up trying and went to bed, and dreamed about Jim.

Jim was calling me darling, and saying we were going to be together always.

So sweet, so wonderfully sweet a dream . . . But it ended, and when I woke I could have wept, had I not been too proud.

Chapter eleven

I didn't go to the beach the next morning. Cousin Elizabeth didn't mention my visits when I came out onto the front terrace to wave her off to the office, but I thought it might be in order for me to stay in the garden this once at least, and confine my swimming to Cousin Elizabeth's pool.

The prospect should have contented me, but as the hours wore on, I became bored, and the hot, languorous morning seemed endless. One moment the sun shone, the next moment there were showers. Then there were showers and sunshine mixed, which brought rainbows, superb rainbows, but I scarcely looked at them. In fact I resented them, childishly, and I resented the scent of wet garden flowers. I resented the beautiful blue-tiled pool into which the water flowed from a series of cascades, shaded with tall tree ferns, like the splashing, mist-veiled pouring down of mountain falls.

A stage-set swimming pool, I told myself. I resented the

perfectly cooked and served lunch Fong brought out on a tray. What good was any of the beauty and the luxury without someone to share it with?

The dream of the night before was still a hurt, and finally I couldn't stand the emptiness of the day a minute longer. In desperation I got into my car and drove to town and had my hair and nails done at the Royal, and when I saw that it was still only early afternoon, I wandered through the Royal gardens to window-shop on Kalakaua Avenue. It was hot, and there was a bright sun, and I stopped and bought a Japanese paper parasol at a big drugstore that sold everything from bathing caps and snorkels and fins to waffles with blueberry syrup, and those awful rubber hula dolls that shake all over in the back windows of cars.

There were dozens of paperbacks, too, and I bought one, making a choice between a crossword puzzle and a murder mystery. I took the crossword puzzle, knowing I didn't really care much for murder stories unless the surroundings were just right—an English butler, a manor house, and all that.

Murder. A chilling word, when you thought about it, even when you knew it would never touch you. I remember a queer little inexplicable shiver I gave, involuntarily, before I sat down at a counter stool and ordered one of the waffles. I was hungry. I hadn't felt like eating more than a bite of the lunch Fong had brought me, and I found it rather a relief to be served something a little more plebeian, a little less rarefied, than Cousin Elizabeth's exquisitely presented meals.

I was in a mood to feel I had almost had a surfeit of elegance and luxury. Just as the swimming pool was a stage set, so were those meals, especially the dinners, with

Cousin Elizabeth and I opposite each other. The silver and porcelain and crystal. The lacy mats. The overabundance of exotic flowers. Cousin Elizabeth in her jade and brocade, always the Court Lady, done in enamel, or fine brushwork. Whichever the medium, still only an outline, even after this long week—more than a week, of our reacquaintance.

I still didn't know her. I still didn't know whether or not she gave a hang for me. It was the stage setting that made me uncertain. There was just too much glamour about it all to let you be certain of the realness behind it. Now if Cousin Elizabeth would walk on the stage only long enough to sit here, on a stool next to me, and order, let's say, a hamburger and a malted milk. . . .

The absurd picture made me laugh to myself and cheered me up for a moment, and then I was down in the depths again, wishing I were at Cousin Elizabeth's beach —that was real enough—wishing I were in my bathing suit and racing toward the sea, with Lani ahead of me, her hair streaming in a breeze that was rustling the fronds of the coco palms.

I would make a shallow dive, only just cleaving the water that was as vari-hued and clear as though every blue and green gem I could name were heaped in a glass bowl, and then I would surface, to turn on my back and float and float, looking up at the cumulous cobalt sky, and thinking about Jim.

Though where that would get me . . . I couldn't finish the waffle. A waffle eaten alone was every bit as tasteless as the chilled consommé, the thin toast rounds spread with *pâté*, the cold chicken and iced papaya Fong had served me.

I was feeling terribly sorry for myself, but as you can't

very well let yourself become teary in a drugstore where at least a hundred people would stare interestedly, I paid my check, and got my car out of the Royal parking lot, and drove back to Cousin Elizabeth's.

Getting dressed for the Diamond Head party gave me a lift in spite of myself—I expect every girl enjoys getting herself done up in pretty clothes, and the yellow chiffon *was* pretty, and I couldn't help knowing it suited me, with all those long floaty panels that are good on a tall, slender girl, and the color was nice with my hair. Cousin Elizabeth needn't be ashamed of me.

When it was time to leave for the party I met her at the front door, and she said that I looked very charming indeed, and that my dress was exactly right.

As to how she looked, well, she was absolutely stunning in one of her long Manchu princess dresses; an aqua satin I hadn't seen on her before, with broad bands of embroidery on the cuffs that almost covered her hands. She certainly knew her own style, I thought admiringly, as I had so often before, and when she smiled at me and said, "I shall be proud to present my cousin," I felt a quick, comforting glow of pleasure that helped erase my despondency of the afternoon.

Of course I meant something to her! And even though I had lost Jim, I had found Cousin Elizabeth, and that was a great deal better than having no one.

Sing was waiting by the car, cap in hand, and in spite of that indefinable "New China" look and manner of his that I didn't quite like, he was impeccable, and smart in his charcoal-gray uniform of thin, hot-weather silk, ribbed like whipcord, and with a high Chinese collar braided and frogged in black.

You wouldn't see a chauffeur as chic waiting outside

the Colony Club or Claridge's, or the Georges Cinq, or anywhere else. And he, too, was part of a stage setting, I thought, as I got in the car. But as the handsome, expensive Rolls purred toward the gate through the torchlit, fragrant garden, I admitted to myself that a stage setting as beautiful and deluxe as the one Cousin Elizabeth had earned for herself by all her years of hard work deserved, after all, nothing but appreciation.

I'd better enjoy it while I could. Another week, and I would be back at my job, thoroughly spoiled, and wishing more than anything I were still here. Another week, and I would be skimping on lunch money, and sighing for one of those trays by the pool that today I had scorned. Waffles, on a drugstore stool, would have lost their appeal.

Another week, and I would be riding on buses and cable cars, pushed around, and stepped on, with people's elbows and packages poking me in the eye. I would go back to a big, ugly old house empty of everything except silence and shadows. I would be eating in Ah Sam's kitchen, with no Ah Sam there. And I would be caring so little about anything anymore that I wouldn't even bother to spread a napkin, as a mat, under my plate on the oilcloth-covered table.

Hating the picture, I settled back in the car, newly grateful for all Cousin Elizabeth was doing for me, and humbly wishing I had been born with a quarter of her courage. Guts, a man would say. And that's what it took, guts, to rise above life as she had risen.

I stole a sideways glance at her classic, composed profile. Had she ever found the time to fall in love? Had there ever been a man in her life attractive enough, strong enough, to even momentarily make her ambition take second place? It made for interesting speculation.

Our Nuuanu drive was under heavy mountain clouds, and the car was pelted with rain, but as we approached town, the skies cleared. It was so warm I wasn't wearing a wrap, but again, there was that lovely, sweet-scented breeze I had first felt at the airport, swaying the palms that grew everywhere, and I could have heard their rustle had the noise of traffic been less, just as I could have heard green waves breaking.

Cousin Elizabeth gave an order to Sing. "We have time for a roundabout way to show you a little of the city," she explained, and from then on, instead of downtown Kalakaua, there were side streets lined with the pink and coral and scarlet of shower and flame trees, and the cool blue of the jacaranda, with leaves like ferns, and its dropped blossoms a thick cerulean drift on the sidewalks.

There were houses, large or small, set in gardens or yards crammed with jasmine and ginger and croton and *ti*, and a savage jungle of crimson and yellow hibiscus, the cerise and apricot of bougainvillea that made color as exciting as music.

At the edge of town Diamond Head—an extinct volcano, Cousin Elizabeth told me—rose in a high dark cone against the sky still streaked with sunset. Approaching it, we passed a large grassy, tree-shaded park, and a stretch of beach where swimmers still lingered and brown-skinned fishermen were surf-casting, with octopus and eel for bait. And Cousin Elizabeth told me that on dark, quiet evenings the night fishermen could be seen all along the coast, wading out with their gasoline torches strapped to their heads, and their hand spears.

So much to look at and exclaim over. I was almost sorry when we drove through handsome Italian iron gates into a garden of wide lawns. Then I was being introduced to my attractive host and hostess of the evening, and being taken around to meet twenty or more other guests, and being made a fuss over, hospitably and flatteringly, not only because Cousin Elizabeth was so well liked and important but because I was so much younger than anyone at the party, and because everyone had inquiries to make about friends in San Francisco known to me, even if not of my generation.

Had I been from Washington, D.C., or London, or anywhere else, there would have been inquiries. Immediately, one had the impression that here was a cosmopolitan world.

But Island tradition still predominated. My host and hostess wore leis, and they had one for me, of white gardenias, that Mr. Morrow put around my neck with an aloha kiss. The warmth of my welcome and the easiness and the gaiety of the evening were infectious. I began to enjoy myself, and I was all eyes, taking everything in.

Most of the women were in conventional spring dinner dresses, but a few wore *holokus,* long, fitted silk or brocade adaptations of the Hawaiian muumuu; a few wore gauzy sari-cloth dresses; others wore the slit-skirted Chinese *cheong-sams.* The men were in dinner jackets.

The house was charming, long and low, and from the wide lanai, wreathed in stephanotis and jasmine, you looked directly to the sea, and through an open door I caught glimpses of a drawing room where family portraits, local seascapes, what may have been a Renoir, and one or two modern art conversation pieces managed to look well together.

A long buffet table was set up at the far end of the lanai, and small tables for eight were scattered on the torch-lit lawns. After an extended cocktail hour, a nice, jolly older man steered me to a seat.

"I have orders to look after you, young lady; so wait here and I'll bring you some food." Before he left me, he introduced me to several women whose escorts were scouting at the buffet table, and while we chatted I looked around to see if Major Fenton was anywhere in sight. He was easy to find. He had not gone over to the buffet table but was standing by himself, leaning against a palm tree, and still drinking. He had been looking around for me with as much curiosity as I had been looking for him, evidently, because as soon as he saw me he raised his glass to me in an annoyingly intimate way, and strolled over.

"Surprised to see me, are you, Miss Allen? And tell me, are you enjoying yourself?"

"Very much." I made my answer brief and chilly, but there was nothing for it but to introduce him to the other women at the table. They eyed him with interest. He was more than presentable, with something of a manner, and, in a well-fitted, if worn at the cuffs and lapels, dinner jacket, and a maroon cummerbund, attractive in a raffish kind of way.

"May I sit down?"

There was plenty of room at the table and extra chairs that could be pulled up, but I glanced toward the lanai buffet with a pointed, "You haven't served yourself? You're not eating?"

"No. Drinking is keeping me occupied at the moment." Coolly, he sat down next to me.

"That happens to be someone else's seat."

"I shall be staying only long enough to ask you a question. Tell me, have you ever been in Hong Kong?"

"Why, yes, I was born there." The question could not have surprised me more with its unexpectedness.

"Then that's where I have seen you."

I laughed. "I doubt it! I left Hong Kong when I was a baby."

"Odd—I would have sworn . . ." The hard blue eyes scrutinized me as impersonally as they had scrutinized me at the beach. "I have seen you somewhere. I shall have to rack my memory."

"Perhaps I have a double." It was just one of those meaningless remarks people toss off when they haven't anything else to contribute to a conversation.

Major Fenton emptied his glass. "You haven't forgotten that my Pearl of Pearls will be dancing tonight?"

"If you mean Lani, Major Fenton, why don't you say so?" I snapped it indignantly, but it didn't bother him.

"Time for a sweetener," he remarked easily. "So until our next meeting, Miss Allen. Meanwhile I shall be trying my best to recall that double of yours." He excused himself to the other women at the table and strolled off, leaving them a little disappointed looking. He would be a success in Honolulu, with Cousin Elizabeth for a sponsor, I was thinking as the nice, jolly man, a Mr. Graham, came back to the table with a plate of food for me and one for himself. Lots of Japanese waiters appeared to fill wine glasses, and later to bring dessert, and then there was a faint sound of music off in the garden, somewhere, that gradually grew louder as Lani's brother and his friend, the Hanale and the Keoki she had spoken of, came in sight playing steel guitars, and Lani herself, strumming a ukulele.

Both boys were handsome in white duck trousers and white shirts, with red carnation leis around their shoulders. Lani wore a creamy plumeria lei, and plumeria flowers in her loose hanging hair. A narrow bandeau of glossy ti leaves bound her breasts, and more of them made her a scant skirt.

She was all smooth brown skin—her slim arms, her hands, her small, rounded hips, her thighs, her beautiful legs. She was smiling, and looked as component a part of the music she was making as of the blue water in which I had seen her sport. She put her ukulele down on the lawn. The tempo of the steel guitars changed, and the boys began to sing as well as play, and then Lani was dancing.

I sat entranced. The boys' voices, strangely pitched, soared with indescribable sweetness. As for Lani, her dancing made the so-called hula of the mainland nothing but an ugly, vulgar travesty.

As she swayed, her body was a palm tree in the wind. Her exquisite hands were birds, or waves, or flowers, or stars. They were a rainbow, arching. They were rain showers. They were the moon, and the sun.

And don't forget the background she danced against. The lush, fragrant garden, torch-lit, but flooded, too, with moonlight that cut a bright swathe across the lawns, and turned the sea, beyond, into cloth of silver.

Island magic. And what heaven it would be if Jim were sitting next to me instead of Mr. Graham, who could have been my father.

I was glad, glad, when the music and the dancing stopped. I couldn't have stood any more stirring up. I wished I could have turned off the moonlight.

Everyone was clapping for an encore. The boys broke into comic songs and Lani made a little monkey of herself, doing a dance and making gestures, not as proper as they might have been, that brought laughter from all the kamaainas at the table.

There was more clapping, and then the singing and dancing were over, but before the three of them left, Lani ran to the table where I was sitting and took off her lei and tossed it around my neck, and kissed my cheek.

"Aloha, Mees Allen! Aloha nui!"

Even the most newly arrived *haole* would have recognized it as the ultimate in an Island expression of friendship, and as all the other guests at the table applauded, and laughed at my overcome expression, Mr. Graham gave me an approving nod.

"You are in, Miss Allen! It isn't every visitor to the Island that gets that treatment. But what I want to know is, Where did you ever see that little girl before? She and the two boys aren't well known. I believe they are a new trio, just starting in, and this engagement tonight is the first big thing that's come their way."

I told him I had met Lani on Cousin Elizabeth's beach, without bringing Major Fenton into the picture. The party began to break up then, because, as Mr. Graham explained, just as Cousin Elizabeth had once remarked, "Islanders go to bed early because they get up early."

Cousin Elizabeth and I said our good-nights to the Morrows and walked across the lawn toward the long line of parked cars in the driveway. Just before we reached it, Major Fenton joined us.

"It was a worthwhile evening for me in several ways, Miss Beaton," he said to Cousin Elizabeth with a smile I did not at the time understand. An unpleasant smile. A little frightening, for some reason, I thought. Or was I imagining it, and imagining that in the moonlight his eyes were a harder blue than ever?

"My very warm thanks to you," he went on. "I not only made a useful contact—one of the powers-that-be wants to see my pictures, and has made an engagement for me to bring several into town—but even more important, my memory has been given a jog."

"Your memory?" Cousin Elizabeth asked it disinterestedly.

"The Hong Kong days are coming back to me. All those people we knew in common; I had forgotten a number of them, but for one reason or another, our evening here has begun to bring them to mind. And if I concentrate . . ."

We had reached the car, and when Sing opened the door Cousin Elizabeth got in, but Major Fenton was persistent.

"We must have a little chat about the old wartime days, Miss Beaton."

"I have put the war and the camp behind me, Major Fenton, and I advise you to do the same. It is not a pleasant subject. And revived memories can be dangerous."

"Painful, yes; but dangerous?"

"Yes, Major Fenton. Because they are apt to lead nowhere but to self-destruction."

It was dismissal in no uncertain terms. I got in beside Cousin Elizabeth, and Sing closed the door. I looked back as we drove off, and Major Fenton was looking anything but put in his place. His hands were thrust deep in his pockets. He was smiling.

"I dislike that man intensely." Cousin Elizabeth commented quietly.

"So do I."

We drove along in silence, and then Cousin Elizabeth brought up a subject I had been waiting to hear about.

"You and that beach girl. 'Aloha nui,' indeed! Really, Nan. Did you go to the beach again, today?"

"No."

"You stayed home as a sop to my straitlaced, old-fashioned ideas?"

I flushed at the gentle sarcasm, but I picked up my

courage enough to ask, "Would you mind awfully if I kept on going? Lani is like a child. I don't want to hurt her feelings by staying away. And I hate to miss the swimming. The water is so perfect, so divine. And my time here is dreadfully short. Only a week more, and I'll have to be leaving."

"Very well. Go to the beach, if you like. Let's say you have my permission, if not my approval. But after all, the damage is done. You have already met Major Fenton. And as long as you dislike him, I don't suppose there is any real danger of your succumbing to his doubtful charm. He used to think he had rather a way with young girls."

"You knew him in Hong Kong?"

"Only slightly. Even before camp days, he was doing a good deal of hard drinking. I don't know what happened to him afterward. But he was down and out when he turned up here and approached me for a loan of money. Instead, I gave him the beach place to look after."

She put a hand over mine.

"Do you see why I stressed sharks and coral and stingrays and currents?"

I laughed, and said Yes, but it did seem unnecessary for Cousin Elizabeth to have gone to that length. A little ridiculous, really. But I was glad I could go openly to the beach. Because I knew I would have gone back anyway, even if she had made an issue of it.

Hurt Lani? Throw away the friendship she had offered as simply and appealingly as her shells and her flowers were offered? Give up the blissfully languorous jade and lapis and turquoise water that on each visit lulled me, for a little while, and let me pretend my heart wasn't broken?

Not that a modern girl allows her heart to break. Or she ought not, because she knows better. A different story with an earlier generation . . .

I stole another glance at Cousin Elizabeth's calm profile. That subterfuge to keep me away from the beach . . . By any chance, by any, any remote chance, had there once been something between the Major and Cousin Elizabeth?

Chapter twelve

ANOTHER day at the beach and another. I was completely under its spell. "Pretty soon, you Island girl, same me," Lani predicted. She took pride in teaching me Hawaiian words. I learned *mahimahi* and *opakapaka* for the fish her father dropped in with now and again, as she explained, and that she stewed or curried, or served raw with ginger and soy sauce. I learned *kulolo* for the pudding she made from taro and brown sugar and coconut milk. I learned to say *all pau* when I refused second helpings at a meal, or when I had had enough swimming; finished, or done, is a loose translation. I learned, too, that I was both a *haole* and a *wahine*, a foreigner and a woman.

Her approach to that particular lesson was practical; you see *Wahine* on door, O.K., you go in. You see *Kane*, you keep out, that means men's door.

There was nothing I could do about Lani's speech in return. It couldn't imaginably have been less grammatical, and it was as spicy and salty with slang, and with

Hawaiian and Japanese and Chinese and Portuguese and Filipino words and expressions as her cooking. Plain English would have left her with no vocabulary at all.

I asked her once if she had ever been to school.

"School? Sure theeng I go school." She looked shocked. "All Island keeds go school."

"Did you like it?"

"Is O.K. Nice place. Nice teacher. But . . . I don' know. Da beach more betta."

I could see her point. And I could guess at the difficulties of a truant officer. If that indefinite "ten or eleven brothers and sisters" was an average family, keeping count and checking up wouldn't be exactly easy.

Two days after the Diamond Head party, Lani and I came out of the water in the middle of the afternoon to eat the guava ice cream that I had bought at the gasoline station and carried off in a dry-ice carton. It was Lani's favorite. She would sigh ecstatically over it, and devour it either on a stick, or in a saucer, to the last pink dribble.

When she finally put her spoon down, reluctantly, and I said I must hurry back to Cousin Elizabeth's, she announced she would walk to the car with me. She wanted to pick some plumeria blossoms, because Major Fenton would be back at sunset from a day spent painting and fishing; she didn't have to explain further. It was clear that a fresh lei and fresh flowers in her hair were her way of dressing for dinner and greeting a lover.

We would not have seen the other car—not mine—that was parked on the far side of Cousin Elizabeth's beach house if Lani had not happened to push aside a tangle of vines and reach through a thicket of hibiscus to reach for a branch of plumeria that was especially heavy with bloom.

I say "parked," but "hidden" occurred to me at the moment I saw the small, nondescript, any-make, beige-colored car. Someone had taken considerable trouble to find just that particular spot.

"Whose do you suppose it is?" I asked Lani, surprised and curious, and for some reason not liking all those concealing shrubs. "The house is shut up, isn't it?"

Lani nodded. "Sometime plumber come. Sometime roof man. No good, if old house stay empty. All time some-theeng break."

That was true enough. It was quite likely that Major Fenton had called in a plumber. The water pipes at the shack were corroded with rust and salt and gave only a slow trickle, and doubtless gave trouble, too, at Cousin Elizabeth's anything but new saltbox house.

But why did the car strike me as being deliberately hidden away? Perhaps the plumber brought a girl with him sometimes, and perhaps they now and again made themselves very much at home in the saltbox?

I was satisfied with that conclusion, and wouldn't for the world have intruded on them with an investigation. Lani and I said good-bye, and she closed the white gate after me, and we waved to each other as I drove off through the banana grove to the highway. I was thinking about the pink dribble of the guava ice cream and smiling to myself, and then raging at Major Fenton for taking advantage of Lani's enchanting childishness, when, half-way up the Pali grade, the small beige car passed me.

I almost swerved over the dividing line of my lane. It was a distinct shock to recognize Mr. Yin Wah sitting next to another Chinese who was driving the car that had been hidden in the beach house hibiscus thicket.

Or was it Mr. Yin Wah? Could I be sure, when the

small car had zoomed past so fast, and when almost all my attention had been given up to thoughts of Lani and the Major?

I was sure enough, in any case, to begin imagining things. Mr. Yin Wah following me to the beach house. Spying on me. And if he had spied today, had he spied every day since my arrival in Honolulu? Had those unpleasant eyes of his kept me under continual surveillance? Everywhere I had gone, had he gone, in that inconspicuous, one-of-a-thousand anonymous little car that had come to my attention only by the merest chance?

Mr. Yin Wah, following me. Tailing, it was called in detective stories. It meant that a person was being followed as closely as his own shadow. It meant the person was never alone. Not really alone. Always, there were eyes on him.

Just to think about it gave me the creeps. But what could I do? Face Mr. Yin Wah and ask him what he was up to? I don't have that kind of courage. And think how mistaken I could be about the whole thing. Think of all the Chinese who look alike. Think how many small, beige, nondescript cars there must be on the island.

It was after dinner on the lanai that evening that I tried not to mind making myself sound silly, by asking a question of Cousin Elizabeth.

There had been heavy showers earlier, and now, in the steaming, hot darkness, the smell of flowers was almost too heavy, and the dark, tall trees at the foot of the garden, without a breath of breeze to stir them, seemed to crowd in closer than ever.

"Is there any chance of Mr. Yin Wah's having been at the beach this afternoon, Cousin Elizabeth?"

It surprised her. She was lighting a cigarette and she

paused, with the flare of a match bringing her face out of
the darkness to give me a glimpse of her quiet eyes that at
the end of every day were underlined by the black circles
that always made me wish she wouldn't push herself so
hard.

"Mr. Yin Wah at the beach house? I can't imagine
anything less likely."

"I am almost positive I saw him." I told her about the
car hidden in the shrubs and the car that had passed me
on the grade. And then I came out with what was really
bothering me. "I wondered if he had been following me."

"My dear child! Come now. Aren't you going too far in
your dislike for Mr. Yin Wah? Poor man. He is ugly, and
he is crude, but he doesn't follow young women." Cousin
Elizabeth laughed, and blew a spiral of smoke. "He hasn't
time. We are much, much too busy these days for him to
indulge in extracurricular activities of that sort."

Another gray wraith of smoke gave off a heavy, sweet
breath, and then she was gently reproving. "For your own
sake, dear Nan, shouldn't you try to curb that imagination
of yours? You are too young for nerves. Too young, and
too healthy, and too normal a girl for that sort of thing."

What more could I say, after that? Nothing. So I just
sat there and drank my frappéed liqueur and hoped
Cousin Elizabeth wasn't too disgusted with me.

She was very much the Court Lady again that evening,
in dark, Peking-blue silk, banded in a wide gold-thread
embroidery of peonies at the high neck, and wide sleeves
and slit hem. She was wearing sea-green jade jewelry, the
best of jade, deep and pure in color. A necklace and a
bracelet on each arm were fastened with gold dragon
clasps. A ring was on one of her slim hands with its
lacquered, almond-shaped nails.

Just as you might have expected her to have the bound

"lily feet" of Old China, you would not have been surprised had she worn cloisonné and gold nail protectors on each of those fingers. And you could so easily imagine that instead of the cigarette in her hand she held a tiny bubbling water pipe, or that instead of tobacco smoke, you smelled the drowsy fumes of scarlet opium poppies.

For that matter, you could pretend you smelled sandalwood. How very much she had wanted to keep my fan!

I had not forgotten that curious little passage between us a few nights before, but because every day, every evening since had been so full, giving me so much to enjoy, so much to think about, it had faded into umimportance. But now that the fan had come to mind, I began to dwell on it.

If I had not rescued my fan, would Cousin Elizabeth have continued to crunch the delicate sticks, until, instead of only one being cracked, there would be nothing left of any of them, with the carved date, and the letters that spelled out "Edith," obliterated?

Though what her motive could be . . . Had she not liked Aunt Edith? Might that, just possibly, be the answer? I was remembering Cousin Elizabeth's difficult position in the Allen family, her childhood and girlhood as the "poor relation," and later her life as nothing more than a housekeeper-companion to Uncle John Allen's wife.

So much could go on in a family under a surface as deceptively smooth as silk. Might Cousin Elizabeth have been in love, once, with Uncle John? Perhaps, then, she had more than merely disliked Edith, his bride. Perhaps she had hated her, with the bitter taste of gall and wormwood in her mouth. And even though Edith was long dead, might the old bitterness have made Cousin Elizabeth's hands tighten on the fan?

It was all imagining, all a flight of fancy. I was really

letting myself go. But just possibly I might have hit on the truth, and on the chance of it my heart went out to Cousin Elizabeth. Love could be hellish.

When Cousin Elizabeth said her usual "Good-night, child," I put my arms around her impulsively. "You have been so good to me. I can't ever begin to thank you enough for letting me stay with you."

The large gray eyes looked not only tired but a little sad. "I have always wished you could stay an infant. I have always wished your growing up had not to be so inevitable."

"Why, Cousin Elizabeth?"

"One feels one can hold on to a baby. That one can possess it. Own it, wholly. And a baby is never a problem."

"I'm not a problem either, I certainly hope," I protested, laughing. "Not any longer. Not now, when I'm a working girl and finally standing on my own two feet."

"Of course you are not a problem—not an unsurmountable one. But I do a great deal of thinking about you. It was all so uncomplicated before you grew up. But now, with a grown woman to consider—and the future—and what's best to do, in terms of long-range planning. Oh, by all means, you should have stayed in your cradle!"

"Sorry I couldn't have obliged you, darling Cousin Elizabeth." I laughed again, and she smiled, ruefully.

"The time went so fast. Where did the years go?"

As I walked to my room, I was wondering why on earth Cousin Elizabeth should be giving me a thought, in conjunction with the future. Unless—and the wild thought struck me suddenly—unless she was going to make a will. Was she considering me as her heir? Or if nothing as fantastic as that, was she considering some kind of very generous settlement on me, now that we had met again?

Had she become truly fond of me? Did she respect me, now, for proving I didn't need the crutch of her money but could get along on my own? Had the difficult last few years she had imposed, the years when she had so abruptly pulled the rug out from under me, been a test?

But what if Mr. Yin Wah, her business partner, wasn't too keen about a new will? Just how strongly was he entrenched in Cousin Elizabeth's financial world?

As soon as I opened my bedroom door, my thoughts were jerked from Cousin Elizabeth and her money. The long, filmy curtains at the French windows were stirring. Stirring as though they had been brushed against an instant sooner. The French windows that led beyond the garden, across the lawn and past the tall dark trees to the driveway gate, and the road.

Had someone slipped away when they heard my heels clicking along the hall's bare polished floor? It had to be that. There was no wind, no slightest breeze on this hot, oppressive evening that could have stirred those filmy folds.

I ran to the window. It was ajar, and its outside screen was ajar. Whoever had slipped out had been too hurried to close it.

An intruder. No servant would have left the screen open so much as a crack. There were too many insects to swarm in from the hot, damp garden, too many huge, circling moths to flutter around the bedroom lamps. Cousin Elizabeth's servants were all too well trained for any such carelessness.

Quickly, I switched off the bedroom lights, stepped out onto the guest room's small, private lanai. Just as my eyes were able to pierce the darkness of the garden, a crouched-over, indistinct figure scuttled across the lawn to the cover of deep shrubbery. And then I heard a car start up, and the squeal of tires on a rain-wet turn.

Was I imagining things again? Uncertainly I went inside and closed the screen firmly, and hooked it, and drew the thin curtains that were hung full enough for privacy. It would have been too smotheringly hot had I closed the French windows.

I wouldn't rouse the house. I wouldn't go to Cousin Elizabeth with my tale, I decided. The crouching figure could have been a trick of shadow. The filmy curtains could have been stirred by my opening of the bedroom door or a draft down the hallway.

It was only when I undressed for bed that I knew, certainly, that someone had been in my room. Lui Lung, Cousin Elizabeth's maid, had left my nightgown and robe exquisitely folded at the foot of the bed, but as I went to the tall Chinese wardrobe that served as a closet to see if I had a fresh cotton dress for the morning, I saw that its doors, too, were slightly open. I threw them wide, with my first thought: Did they go through my suitcase?

The case was at the back of the wardrobe, on the wide, deep shelf. I flung the lid back. My return ticket. My traveler's checks. A hundred dollars in cash. A diamond wristwatch Cousin Elizabeth had sent me on my eighteenth birthday. A string of very nice cultured pearls with a diamond clasp she had sent for my debut. They were all there. But the suitcase had been rummaged through, and Ah Sam's fan was gone. Aunt Edith Allen's fan.

Who could possibly have stolen it? Only someone who knew that Cousin Elizabeth and I would linger on the lanai over our coffee and liqueurs. Only someone who knew the routine of our quiet, companionable evenings.

A servant? No. Cousin Elizabeth's staff had all day to

steal, if they so chose. Cousin Elizabeth was never home in the daytime, and I had been away for hours at a time ever since I discovered the beach.

There was no need for a servant to risk tonight's hurried rummaging. No need to leave telltale disorder behind. No need to rush away, escaping detection by seconds. No need to scuttle across the wet lawn into dripping shrubbery, and to speed headlong around the turns of a narrow, rain-slick road.

I was suddenly frightened, frightened beyond all reason. Was the car on the wet road outside Cousin Elizabeth's gate the same small beige car that had passed me on the Pali? If I let myself think it, even for an instant, where would further thoughts lead me? I mustn't think it. I mustn't.

My heart began a heavy thudding. Greed—you read in the papers constantly about greed, and what it does to people. What it puts into their heads. Quite often, it puts murder.

Common sense took over at that point, and helped me to almost, if not quite, laugh at myself.

Mr. Yin Wah might not be happy at the idea of his business partner's making a new will, or arranging some sort of trust for me, and Mr. Yin Wah might well be wishing I had never reappeared on the scene, but Mr. Yin Wah would not be rummaging in my suitcase for a sandalwood fan.

And as to who else would—it was beyond me. But I was remembering another night, a night in Cousin Elizabeth's San Francisco house when I had sensed an intruder, and my heart began to thud again. Had that been before or after Mr. Yin Wah had first come into my life? I wasn't quite sure. There had been so much happening at about that time, and only my evenings with Jim had seemed of calendar importance. But perhaps it would come to me.

Before I got into bed, I pulled the curtains wide and stood staring out into the dark, warm, heavily scented garden. The rain had begun again. I could hear it drum on the painted and gilded tiles of Cousin Elizabeth's pagoda-roofed house, hear it gurgle from the mouths of the dragonhead waterspouts.

The driver of that small beige car would have his windshield wipers on. Would it be pouring on the Pali, I wondered, and at the beach? The drumming would sound twice as loud on the tin roof of the shack. If Lani heard the drumming, and stirred, would she smile and murmur like a sleepy, dream-dazed child, and draw closer to Major Fenton?

Major Phillip Fenton, caretaker and artist. Major Phillip Fenton from Hong Kong.

Hong Kong. So far away, and yet, always, so close seeming. And if there once had been anything at all between him and Cousin Elizabeth, was he, too, somehow bound by that same scarlet cord of a sandalwood fan that somehow also bound together Ah Sam and Cousin Elizabeth and Mr. Yin Wah and me?

The skeins of that scarlet silk cord were too tangled for me to unravel, its knots too tightly tied for me to undo. I tried and tried. But it was like being all thumbs. The tangle only worsened.

Chapter thirteen

THE night was endless. People so often say, without half meaning it, "I didn't get a minute's sleep, I didn't close my eyes once." It was true in my case. And all the while I tossed between the rumpled, hot sheets and turned my pillow to the cool side, as I puzzled over the enigma of Edith Allen's stolen fan, my heart was racing. Because the vague and perhaps foolish apprehensions that had disturbed me since my first meeting with Mr. Yin Wah were now a concrete fear.

So understandably, he might want me out of the way, I saw now. So understandably, he had tried to keep me from a visit with Cousin Elizabeth. So understandably, he could have foreseen that his employer and I would become close to each other once we met again after all the years of our separation. And to an Oriental the fact that I was family would mean that Cousin Elizabeth would leave me her money.

Mr. Yin Wah quite possibly had made plans of his own

for all that wealth. He was younger than Cousin Elizabeth, judging by appearances, and by the law of averages would outlive her. And in Hong Kong he might well have a wife and children. A family of sons, and to Chinese thinking, even one son would be far worthier of the benefits of wealth than any female.

A new will could well come as the ultimate in disappointments to Mr. Yin Wah. Even a trust set up for me could be a blow. As the valued, indispensable partner of an enormously rich woman without family, wouldn't he have had every reasonable right to visualize himself as her heir?

My thinking was logical enough up to a point, but when it came to the disappearance of the fan everything was a muddle. It was much easier to imagine Mr. Yin Wah's wanting me out of the way than it was to imagine any possible interest he might take in a few carved sticks of sandalwood.

As I pictured the fan to myself through the hours of that fear-haunted, restless night, I kept seeing its carved date.

That year—1937. What had it meant to Edith Allen? What did it mean, now, to Mr. Yin Wah?

Take its importance to Edith Allen first. Begin there. And when you have found out, then go on to Mr. Yin Wah's interest. Yes, but who could tell me what that date meant?

A possibility suddenly occurred to me. Mr. Martin's office just might have a record of the date of Uncle John's and Aunt Edith's wedding. Marshall, Martin, and Hitchcock had been the Allen family's attorneys for years, in the old days. And if I telephoned Mr. Martin, it would be a starting point, at least, for my almost impossible attempt to link Mr. Yin Wah with the sandalwood fan.

It wasn't yet dawn; impatiently, I glanced at my little traveling clock ticking away on the bedside table, its illuminated hands refusing to move, it seemed to me. Even with the time difference between San Francisco and Honolulu, I had hours to wait before Mr. Martin would be in his office.

The same telephone number would give me Jim on the wire. "Mr. James Bradford, please. Miss Nan Allen calling."

But Jim wouldn't take the call, if I put it in. I was so sure of it I could hear the office secretary's cool, courteous dismissal of me: "I am sorry, Mr. Bradford is out of town." It was done all the time. I knew plenty about office calls.

Eventually the blackness outside the French windows paled, and slowly, with the rain over, the dripping garden began to glitter in sunlight, the myna birds were chattering on the lawn, and I could hear the morning trills of the bright-feathered birds in their cages on the front lanai. That meant Cousin Elizabeth, in a dressing gown, would be going out to share fruit from her breakfast tray with them, and that another day had begun.

Only a few more hours now to wait.

I put on one of my cool cotton shifts that Lui Lung kept washed and ironed and was at the front door when Cousin Elizabeth came out of her room, individual-looking and quietly smart, as always when she left for the office.

"Have a good day, child."

"You have a good day, too, Cousin Elizabeth."

I watched Sing Lee open the car door for her, and as she was driven away I was thinking how decent it was of her, how really gracious not to bring up the subject of the beach again, but to let me feel free to fill my day as I saw fit, without any feeling of awkwardness or of pressure being applied.

How fair she was. How tolerant, with her letting people do as they chose, even while she held fast to her own ideas. Jim would be bound to like her, bound to respect her. And if only he could meet her, could see us together, he would understand what I had sought, and what I had found on this visit.

Jim—always Jim. Forget him. You are being a fool. Yet I ate breakfast longing for him, aching for him. In this perfect spot, perfect if he were here . . .

My tray had been brought to me under the shade of what Fong told me was a hau tree. The wide spread of its drooping branches were supported on a trellis, and covering the uprights of the trellis, white orchids cascaded from pockets of moss and fern and shredded bark, dampened with the fine mist of a little fountain.

Jim and I, eating breakfast together.

It wasn't a spot conducive to the healing of heartache, and I wondered how I could swallow papaya and muffins and guava jelly, and drink coffee, without choking, or how I could read the paper Fong brought me. I wondered, too, if, always, for the rest of my life, I would get through the days as mechanically as I was eating breakfast.

I kept glancing at my wristwatch. Finally it was time to put in my San Francisco telephone call. I went back to the house, and in minutes Mr. Martin's secretary had put him on the line.

He seemed pleased I had called. "Glad you caught me. We're off to Europe tomorrow for a little vacation. . . ." Then he said Mrs. Martin was fine, and he hoped I was, and he wanted to know what kind of weather I was having, but as quickly as I could, I got to the point of my call. Did he know the date of Uncle John and Aunt Edith Allen's marriage?

It was a long minute, and I heard him tell the Long Distance operator to reverse the telephone charges to the office of Marshall, Martin and Hitchcock.

"Hello—still there? Yes, we've got the date in a letter from John. March six, nineteen hundred thirty-seven."

I knew he was ready to ask, "Why do you want to know?" and I quickly forestalled him. "I'm getting interested in family history," I tossed off as lightly as I could. It was all too complicated to go into with him. Too insubstantial.

"Why don't you ask Elizabeth? What's the matter, is her memory slipping?" It was all jocose nothings from then on with Mr. Martin. "You'd better get back in a hurry," he said. "Before you know it, a certain young man will start taking out a blonde." Then he was serious. "Think it over, Nan. Come back, like a sensible girl, and get things patched up. We'd have a lot happier vacation if we could leave knowing you were going to show a little common sense."

I could hear him so clearly, and he sounded so close, that I couldn't believe there were four thousand miles of ocean between us. All I could think was, Jim is just down the hall from him. Nothing would be easier for him or please him more than to put Jim on the line.

My pride was wavering. Quickly I said good-bye to Mr. Martin, with some inanity about debtor's prison because of his telephone bill if I didn't hang up, and when the receiver clicked at the other end of the line, San Francisco wasn't near at all, but seemingly in another world, not only an ocean, but planets away.

And what had I gained by my call? Nothing but stirred up longings and the verification of an unimportant date. So what, if 1937 was the year of John and Edith Allen's marriage? Just how did I expect to link Mr. Yin Wah with that date?

I thrust the question from me. Mr. Martin's fatherly, well-meant lecture and Jim's tantalizing, torturing proximity had undone me. I couldn't concentrate on the puzzling and improbable involvement of Mr. Yin Wah with Edith Allen, much less an interest in her fan. Nor could I make myself care whether or not Cousin Elizabeth was going to be financially generous to me. And, at the moment, I wasn't afraid any longer. Nothing mattered to me but my heartache. As far as anything else went, I was deep in an abyss of apathy.

I turned from the telephone too wretched, too restless to settle down to anything. Even Cousin Elizabeth's beach didn't appeal to me. I'd see Lani, and be jealous of her, jealous of a girl who had everything she wanted, while I had nothing.

By midmorning I was thoroughly ashamed of my self-pity and took myself in hand. Why not go into town and be a tourist until this black mood of mine passed? Anything would be better than sitting around, babyishly moping.

I put on my bathing suit and its matching cotton coat, stuffed my beachbag with a towel and sunburn cream and dark glasses and a comb and lipstick and my wallet, and drove off for the Royal. The water looked lovely, and I bought a seat on a catamaran, and along with a lot of other tourists had an hour's sail, out beyond the coral reef. As the water slapped at the bow of the catamaran and we heeled into strong breezes I pretended I was in San Francisco Bay with Jim, in the *Seabird*, which, of course, was the height of foolish, wounding self-delusion.

Jim at the tiller, Jim in navy-blue wool slacks and a

heavy turtleneck sweater. I in slacks and a borrowed pea jacket. The water gray, and running swiftly beyond the Gate. The wind that filled our sails icy, the spray that drenched us stinging with cold.

But this water was blue, blue. The offshore breeze was balmy, and smelled of flowers. The beach boys handling the catamaran were next to naked, their oiled brown skin glistening in hot sunlight, the tourists, in big lei-wreathed straw hats, screeching and carrying on every time the catamaran wallowed in a deep trough, or rode a mountainous swell.

Just Jim and I aboard the *Seabird*—Jim tying up at the pier when our sail was over, and I obeying the skipper's orders to "break out the stores, mate."

The spaghetti, the French bread and cheese, the red wine. The cry of gulls, the moan of a buoy, foghorns blowing. Gray fog enveloping us in a private world. And then the two of us driving back across the bridge, and Jim lighting a fire in the drawing room of the old Allen house. The two of us in each other's arms.

But the reality? Just me, alone, who had bought a ticket for nowhere, and who was entirely indifferent as to where the breeze blew her, and who would come ashore eventually to eat a solitary salad lunch in a big, impersonal hotel whose beauty and luxury couldn't begin to make up for my loneliness.

The loneliness was so awful when the ride was over and I climbed out of the catamaran that I went out of my way to throw a beach ball back to a little girl who had bounced it into the waves, beyond her reach. I would have been glad to play with her, but she couldn't be bothered with me. She had a pack of laughing, shouting children to play with.

I couldn't face the hotel's dining room or its luncheon terrace alone after all. Instead, I ordered a sandwich and ate it on the beach, under a bright umbrella. It wasn't a good idea. All around me, there were couples, people together.

My heartache only worsened, and with a final attempt to take my mind off myself, I walked through the hotel gardens to Kalakaua Avenue. And again among tourists, crowds of tourists, in gaudy muumuus and shirts, or bathing-suited like myself, I shopped for a present for Lani, and decided on a bottle of *pikake* perfume. The tiny white pikake blossoms, like carved ivory shells, were expensive to buy, the clerk told me, and rarer than most Island flowers. Lani would love the perfume, I knew, when I sniffed a sample.

The small gesture of a thought for someone else gave me a lift, and I began looking for a present for Cousin Elizabeth. It was difficult. She had already everything. But finally I settled on two small cloisonné enamel cigarette ash trays that would do as birdbaths for her bright, fluttering, little finches. A silly little present, but it was just something to show I had been thinking of her.

There was no use sending anything to the Martins, so soon to start on their holiday in Europe. But if only I could buy something for Jim. . . . A postcard stand offered much too much of a temptation. I simply couldn't pass it without stopping. And I ended up by buying a very large card picturing a girl in a gay-nineties bathing suit, with the inscription, *By the sea, by the sea, by the beautiful sea,* and I wrote on it, "You don't want this card, but I'm sending it anyway. Doubtless you have a waste-basket handy."

I signed it and bought an envelope and an airmail stamp for it and dropped it into a mailbox.

Would he bother to look up the next line of that gushingly sentimental old song that was back on the radio now? ". . . you and me, you and me, oh how happy we'd be . . . ?" Something like that.

If only I could make him laugh. If only I could make him take this Honolulu adventure of mine less seriously.

It was only when I had driven back to Cousin Elizabeth's house and had involuntarily paused to gaze across the lawn, toward the dark encircling trees, and the thick shrubbery, that the scarlet cord of Edith Allen's fan again presented its knots and its tangles, and that once more unreasoning fear touched me with a cold hand.

Whether or not the puzzle of whether Mr. Yin Wah had stolen the fan was completely beyond me to solve, my former baseless suppositions were convictions now. Mr. Yin Wah wanted me out of the way. I ought to run. I ought to hide. I ought to cry out for help.

But cry out to whom? Cousin Elizabeth would only laugh again, and make me feel a fool. And Jim was four thousand miles away, and couldn't care less.

Chapter fourteen

As I got out of my car, I saw Cousin Elizabeth on the blue-tiled entrance terrace. Standing among its lush ferns, its pots of gardenias, its wreathing jasmine, she looked as cool and as well groomed and smart in her linen suit as when she had left in the morning. "I am home a bit early, and I am feeding my birds before I go inside for my rest," she explained as I joined her.

The door of one of the pagoda cages was open, and of the four finches that usually were swinging on the gilt perches two had flown out to light on her shoulder and were snuggling close to her neck with affectionate twitterings.

She had been replenishing seed cups, and it seemed an appropriate moment for me to give her the cloisonné ashtray-bathtubs. They were tremendously successful. She exclaimed over them extravagantly and her thank-you was a light kiss.

"I adore presents. What a nice child you were to think

of me. And, do you know, I have been thinking all day how sad it is that you will be gone, so soon now. But there, I ought not to bring up such an unhappy subject."

When she had talked a while with the little birds with twitterings like their own, she put them back in the cage.

"Now for my rest and my bath. And then, oh how welcome our cocktails will be! You have no idea!"

"Was it another difficult day, Cousin Elizabeth?" I asked.

"More or less. Decisions, decisions . . . though it is the unresolved problems that are the most exhausting, actually, I find. Let's forget my day, though. It's over. And our long, lovely, peaceful evening ahead will help make up for it."

I couldn't, after that, bring myself to upset her by any mention of an intruder in my room, and certainly I couldn't tiresomely voice my fear of Mr. Yin Wah again. I simply couldn't. And so, as it turned out, it was not I, but Major Fenton who interrupted the quiet and the peacefulness, the congenial intimacy, of our evening.

We were having our cocktails on the lanai, Cousin Elizabeth in plum silk, I in a white piqué shift, and Cousin Elizabeth was outlining a quick, brief tour of Oahu and the other neighboring Islands that were a must before I went back to San Francisco. Pearl Harbor, the beautiful, moving mountainside cemetery for our Pacific War dead. Orchid nurseries. Volcano sites. Cattle ranches. Sugar and pineapple plantations. Fishing villages. Museums. Aquariums. Dolphin tanks. Art galleries.

"I'll have to make a dozen visits. I'll be like that bad penny that turns up so often." Just as I laughed, Fong, looking as upset as he had on the afternoon that I had arrived at Cousin Elizabeth's so unceremoniously, ushered Major Fenton onto the lanai.

"Did someone mention a bad penny? I'm afraid I am rather pushing myself in on you, Miss Beaton, but I've brought several of my pictures along, as I'm anxious for your advice. Which have the best chance of interesting that chap I met the other evening?"

It was as good an excuse as he could invent, I supposed, though why had he bothered with it? An easy insolence, a kind of boldness was written all over him, and I couldn't understand why Cousin Elizabeth didn't dismiss him with a freezing, "I'm sorry. I'm busy at the moment. I can't look at your pictures just now." It would have served him right. It was outrageous the way he was taking over, making himself entirely at home.

Without so much as a "May I?" he opened a large portfolio he was carrying, took out a number of canvases, and lined them against the house wall of the lanai. "Take your time looking at them," he said calmly. "I'm in no hurry to get back to the beach, and your property is in good hands, Miss Beaton. I have deputized my housekeeper as caretaker in my absence."

His housekeeper. It was inexcusable of him to speak of Lani that way.

"Bring Major Fenton a cocktail, Fong."

"Could it be a whiskey and soda instead, Miss Beaton?"

"Whatever you prefer. Will you sit down?"

I glanced at Cousin Elizabeth surprisedly. Why on earth . . . ?

Major Fenton chose a comfortable, high-backed peacock chair like ours, took his drink when Fong brought it, and nodded toward the pictures.

"Island birds, Miss Allen," he explained for my benefit. "Plover, pelican, frigates, cormorants."

The canvas I had seen in the shack was there. It could, fittingly, have been entitled "Survival," I thought. You knew the dark, strong, widespread wings of the bird would triumph over the storm. Battered and exhausted though it might be, the bird would find a rock or a cliff for refuge.

In a way, wasn't the man who had painted the bird rather like his subject? I wondered it in a curious and very brief instant of sympathy. Battered, and with the wind against him. But he was an impossible man, so why be sorry for him?

He was stretched out, lounging in the chair. When he had made the gesture of patting the pockets of his worn blazer for a cigarette, he reached into a box on the small table at his elbow and helped himself, and struck a match.

It was only because I had once thought Jim would like the picture, and was thinking it again, and wondering if I could afford to buy it, that I bothered to be civil to him. "How much do you ask for your pictures, Major Fenton?" I asked.

"As Miss Beaton can tell you, I believe in trying for top prices."

"Yes. Major Fenton has a distinctly businesslike approach to any transaction, even though he is an artist."

They were fencing. They were deliberately getting at each other. I didn't know how I knew, but I knew. There wasn't time to wonder what it was all about before the Major had turned to me.

"You and that elusive double of yours again. And not only the red hair and the eyes, but that white dress . . . Blast my sieve of a memory!"

"Why not be grateful to it? I should be in your place. As I said the other evening, looking back and dwelling on the past can be less than pleasant." Cousin Elizabeth's words, and the faintest edge to her voice distinctly suggested she wasn't interested in whatever reminiscences Major Fenton just might come up with. You could imagine him having had all sorts of adventures, the bawdy, sordid sort, or even out-and-out disreputable.

And though I knew how straitlaced she was, and knew I shouldn't encourage Major Fenton to go on, the thought of having a double was intriguing, and I wanted to hear more.

"There must be a great many redheaded, brown-eyed girls in the world who wear white dresses." I suggested it with just enough obvious interest to keep him on the subject.

"The odd thing is, the white dress, as a dress, isn't important. I don't see the whiteness that way. I'd say I see it more as a background, setting off your double's coloring."

He frowned reflectively, glass in hand. "You said you were born in Hong Kong, Miss Allen?"

"Yes."

"I knew a good many of the British and American set before the war. But times have changed. There's a new lot there now."

"I'd like to go back someday. When I was a child in San Francisco, my amah, who had come back with me, described it all so vividly I used to think I could remember it. The crowded streets climbing the hillsides, narrow as ladders. The masses of people. The noise. The smell. The junks in the harbor. Even the woven wire fencing around the camp."

"The camp?"

"I was born in the prison camp just before it was liberated." I threw a grateful glance at Cousin Elizabeth. "If it hadn't been for Miss Beaton, and for my amah, I wouldn't be alive now."

"Let me congratulate you. There were other infants less fortunate."

Fong passed a tray of hot hors d'oeuvres, and Major Fenton chose a large shrimp that had been fried in batter, but even while he was dipping it in soy sauce, I was aware of his eyes on me with an intensity that made me self-conscious.

He had nothing to say for a few minutes, and Cousin Elizabeth and I chatted inconsequentially, but when he had cooled his mouthful of hot shrimp with a long drink that emptied his glass, he stood up.

"Time I went along. But you haven't said what you think of my pictures, Miss Beaton."

"They all show a great deal of talent. I like them very much." It was said with sincerity, and I admired her for not letting her distaste for Major Fenton stand in the way of an honest appraisal.

"Thank you."

Major Fenton put the pictures into his portfolio, but before he went to the door Fong was holding open for him, he scrutinized me again. "Not a white dress. A white sheet? That's more like it. A rag of a sheet. Filthy . . . bloodied . . . and a smell of disinfectant. It's beginning to come to me. By Jove, if it isn't!"

"It's not the most attractive of backgrounds," I protested. "Can't you do anything better for my double?"

"It is Major Fenton, erstwhile surgeon, speaking. You must make allowances for his realism, my dear Nan."

Cousin Elizabeth was mocking him lightly, but then she gave a little shudder. "That dreadful camp. I still can't understand this fetish of yours for looking back, Major. Why not be satisfied with the here and now?"

He seemed not to have heard her. His probing gaze was on me again.

"Why not stop in tomorrow evening for dinner, and tell us what success you have had with your art critics?" Cousin Elizabeth went on. "We might even talk about a show. Possibly I could arrange one."

I was admiring her again, immensely, as he left. I couldn't have been half so decent to him, half so tolerant, and when we had heard his car start up, I put a frank question. "How could you possibly ask him back when you dislike him so much?"

"Why?" Cousin Elizabeth was turning the heavy jade ring she wore, and to admire it, she held a thin, almond-nailed hand up to the lantern light. "Because he interests me. Or should I say his future interests me? It interests me enormously."

Was she going to "take up" Major Fenton for the sake of his pictures? Were they that good? Well, he was a lucky man if Cousin Elizabeth's shrewdness told her to go ahead and back him.

Would he mention that double of mine again, tomorrow evening? Just so he didn't dwell on that gruesome bloodied sheet. It wasn't pleasant to think about. Still. It *was* intriguing to have a double, and only natural to hope Major Fenton's memory would get back in the groove so that my curiosity could be satisfied.

That curiosity of mine! It was endless. What else had I done all day but ask questions? I had been asking them since last evening when that filmy bedroom curtain had moved at the brushing past of an intruder.

I longed desperately to tell Cousin Elizabeth about my rummaged-through suitcase and to again confide my fear of Mr. Yin Wah. Both at the dinner table and on the lanai, later, I was on the verge of bursting out with it all, but each time I held back. Cousin Elizabeth looked too tired, and she was quiet, and not inclined to conversation. A little distrait, she seemed, and I was sorry that the evening hadn't been as peaceful and uninterrupted as she had anticipated.

The office back again, I supposed. And more of those decisions. Or, more exhausting, as she had said, some unresolved problem worrying her.

What a pity, what irony, that neither of us was enjoying to the full this house of hers, tonight, so crammed with beautiful things; this garden, this balmy, flower-scented garden; this paradise she had worked so hard to gain for herself. She in one chair, I in another, so close on the lanai, and yet so remote from each other, with our thoughts so afield, so unshared.

When I went to bed, my loneliness was far worse than my fear of Mr. Yin Wah. There were plenty of moments when I could say to myself, "You are imagining things, you are letting your imagination run away with you, as you have done so often before," but there was nothing I could tell myself that would alleviate my longing for Jim.

He could have been mine. He had been mine—for that little, little while. But he could have been mine always. And I his.

Oh, fool, fool, to have given him up for Cousin Elizabeth who didn't need me, who had a world of her own, and who was safe in that world. It was I who had no world. It was I whose safety was questionable. It was I who needed someone to look after me.

The last thing before I turned out my light, I took my

favorite, almost known-by-heart little book of Chinese poems from the bedside table. And painful though I knew a penchant for poetry can be, I searched out the lines I wanted, and through a blur of springing hot tears, read them.

> Who are the companions sitting alone at the bright
>   window?
> I and my shadow—the two of us.
> When the lamplight dies out and it is time to sleep,
> Everyone deserts and hides away from me.
> Alas! Alas!
> So sad and troubled am I.*

* From *The Penguin Book of Chinese Verse,* translated by Robert Kotewell and Norman L. Smith. Introduced and edited by A. R. Davis. Baltimore, Maryland, Penguin Books, Inc., 1962.

Chapter fifteen

I woke the next morning to what Islanders call liquid sunshine, a soft, warm mingling of rain and sun that means a rainbow arching wherever you look, against a sky that is blue, blue toward the ocean, and purply-gray toward the mountains—*makai way* and *mauka way*, directionwise, as Lani had taught me.

Just to think about her was a lift, and to escape from my loneliness for a little while, and to forget Mr. Yin Wah, I determined to spend the day at the beach, a day of swimming, and lying in the sun, and of shell gathering, and of listening to Lani's laughter.

I was on my way soon after breakfast. As I drove out of Cousin Elizabeth's gate, I watched carefully to see that no small beige car—or any car—might sneak from the thick concealment of roadside trees and shrubs to follow me. My eyes went again and again to the rear-view mirror, and I was gripping the wheel tensely, but all the way to the Pali I saw only tourists' buses and a highway patrol car and a mail van, and the side road leading to Cousin Elizabeth's beach was deserted, except for me.

Lani was picking plumeria blossoms from the trees at the saltbox house, and she rushed to greet me with an "Aloha, Mees Allen. Where you been, huh? Say, you know sometheeng? I unhoppy, when you don' come! All time I theenk, whassa matta, she mad, maybe?"

She was exactly like a little girl, delighted when a playmate appears to share her games and toys, and reproachful for an absence. And I was glad to see her. I felt better at once. My loneliness I could evade for a time, and fear took on a saner proportion.

It helped, too, when Lani told me Major Fenton had gone into Honolulu. He wouldn't be there to make me self-conscious under those scrutinizing eyes of an artist that seemed so strangely intent on filing away, for future reference, every detail of my coloring, of my features, of the shape and bone structure of my face.

That mysterious double of mine. I gave a little shiver at thought of her, as though someone had walked over my grave. In the absence of Major Fenton I wouldn't be giving undue thought to any of the undercurrents I was conscious of when he and Cousin Elizabeth were together. That fencing, that getting at each other, sometimes it was far more than a tone of voice.

When Lani and I went to the shack and I had changed into my bathing suit, I asked her if I might look at the canvases Major Fenton had stacked on the floor.

Fish and birds, with broad seascapes, or rocky pools, or quiet lagoons for a background; they were my kind of pictures, and they were Jim's kind, too. We had been to art galleries together, and I knew his likes and his dislikes.

The water Major Fenton painted was wet, and made

you think you could taste salt, whether it was lashed by storms or lying tranquil, at ebbtide, and where palms grew on a shoreline they swayed in a breeze you knew smelled of flowers and that made you think your hair was streaming, like Lani's when she ran along the beach.

Terrific! And I wished that I had plunged, and bought outright, the night before, the picture I thought of as "Survival." From now on Major Fenton's pictures would undoubtedly be priced altogether beyond me. I could well believe what he had said, that he would ask the top. Those hard blue eyes of his suggested a man who would know how to bargain, and see to it that he came out ahead.

I restacked the canvases, and Lani and I ran out on the beach and into the heavenly water. The sea was Lani's element. In its depths she ceased to be a laughing, playing girl and became a frolicking dolphin.

Later, when we walked along the shore looking for shells, I asked her several questions about the boy Keoki, her brother's friend who had played the guitar and sung at the Diamond Head party. Was he nice? Was his job a good one? Didn't she think him very handsome? The answer was Yes, to everything, and then I asked, "Do you like him?"

"Sure I like. But . . ."

"Does he like you, Lani? A lot, I mean? I wondered, the other evening, when you were dancing."

"Sure Keoki likes me! He's red-hot for me. All time wanna marry me."

"Then why don't you do it, Lani? I wish you would."

"Say, you crazy, Mees Allen? Me marry Keoki when I got my Doc?"

"Keoki is young. Major Fenton is old. You belong with

Keoki. You both like to make music, and your people are the same, and——'"

"You make talk all same my brudda. All time he give me what for 'cause I no want marry Keoki. 'Same kind peoples, you an' Keoki,' he all time tell me. 'More betta that way.' "

"Does he ever tell you Major Fenton might go away someday?" I hadn't the heart to say: might leave you. "But with Keoki you would have an Island boy husband, and maybe children. You'd be lucky. You'd have him for always, if he liked you as much as you say."

I put a hand on her arm. "Think about it, Lani . . ."

She pulled away. "All time I tell my brudda, 'Please shut beeg mouth.' An' you, Mees Allen, please, I no like you make crazy talk, same like Hanele."

She was only angry for a moment. Then she was laughing. Flinging back her long, wet hair, she began to run down the beach, skimming the sand like a shorebird.

"I race you to my Doc's house," she called back. "You hungry, Mees Allen? How you like kaukau, now?"

Well, I had said my say. If she wouldn't listen, she wouldn't. But just how long would the Major stay with her? I wondered as I ran after her. How long, if the signature "Phillip Fenton" began to mean something on a painting? That could make all the difference in the world. The right people after him. A studio in town, perhaps. Lani certain to be hurt, certain to come out on the short end of things.

I was all the more concerned for her when, back at the shack, she proudly opened the icebox to show me a special taro pudding she had made for the Major's supper. It was pathetic, when I knew so well he was dining with Cousin Elizabeth that evening. And it was pathetic to see her wash out his shorts and hang them on a line stretched between the hibiscus shrubs, and heat a flatiron to press a shirt, with the kitchen already almost unbearably hot.

Worst of all, though, was to see her string the plumeria blossoms into a fresh lei and put it, with flowers for her hair, into the icebox to wait until her "dressing for dinner" time arrived.

Why, why did girls have to fall in love? I wondered. The whole business of being a girl was wretched, unless you were the sensible sort. The sort who carefully avoided the risk of painful involvements.

I didn't tell her where the Major would be dining that evening. I had no wish to read the disappointment on a face so ingenuous that every thought, every emotion was mirrored.

Perhaps the Major would leave Cousin Elizabeth's early, and eat the pudding on his return. Perhaps the plumeria lei and the flowers in Lani's hair would not be unappreciated, and in spite of Major Fenton's dinner engagement would eventually be crushed against the pillows of the wide couch. At any rate it was not up to me to say more than I had already said. Why interfere? The crowded days were flying by. My stay in the Islands would be over much too soon, and it would be impossible to sway Lani in the short time left me. Besides, she obviously preferred to run her own life, just as I had preferred to run mine by refusing to listen to the Martins, refusing to listen to Jim.

Poor Lani. And poor me.

I was sorry and depressed about a lot of things as I drove back to Cousin Elizabeth's. And I was constantly glancing in the rear-view mirror, although puzzlement about Mr. Yin Wah's involvement in my life was even greater than my fear. If only I could think of any reason why my room and my suitcase should have been searched, and any reason at all why the fan should have been stolen. If only I had the faintest clue. But a clue simply didn't exist.

And no matter how dangerous a man Mr. Yin Wah might be, and how much he might want me out of Cousin Elizabeth's life, the question was, Why had he stolen my fan? It was beyond me. My thoughts were going in circles. I got nowhere. Over and over, driving the Pali highway, the question nagged me. Why steal a fan? Why? Why?

When I got back to Cousin Elizabeth's I garaged my car and went to my room and changed, and then joined Cousin Elizabeth on the lanai. I had been anything but anticipating Major Fenton's arrival, but it was a distinctly unpleasant shock when I found Mr. Yin Wah sitting in one of the peacock chairs talking with Cousin Elizabeth while Fong passed a tray of drinks.

He stood up with a brief nod of recognition and a curt greeting for me. How intensely I disliked those dark, goggling eyes! I had noticed his pudgy hands the afternoon of our meeting at the Fairmont, and thought them repulsive, but now I found them sinister.

They were huge hands, with splayed fingers, one clutching a glass, the other reaching into a bowl of salted macadamia nuts. I had to look away from them. Too clearly, I could see them closing around a throat instead of a highball glass, too clearly I could see him reaching out for some helpless victim instead of those nuts. Which of course was absurd, I tried to tell myself, and all Fong's fault.

Fong's fault? Yes, because each evening at Cousin Elizabeth's, if anything at all bothered me, with my thoughts carrying me away, too imaginatively or sentimentally, I was in the habit of blaming it on the icy rum drinks that Fong offered too temptingly, padding about with such quiet, zealous service. Immediately, he saw when a glass was empty. Immediately he was offering a full one.

This, then, this flight of fancy concerning Mr. Yin Wah's hands was just another rum-induced bit of idiocy. Of course it was. And it had not been Mr. Yin Wah scuttling into the shrubbery the night before last. It couldn't have been. Because Mr. Yin Wah was a trusted business associate of Cousin Elizabeth's, and no ogre, but simply a man who couldn't help his unfortunate physical appearance, and whose crudities were to be overlooked, considering his background.

"A sampan rat." He sat in his peacock chair, too big for it, and his large body seemed to bulge over the wicker sides, with nothing to say to either Cousin Elizabeth or me while he munched on the nuts and greedily ate everything Fong offered. In the way of food, that is. He refused a second drink, to my surprise, and let the ice melt in his first, and put it down on the small table by his elbow only three quarters finished.

I put my own glass down and shook my head firmly the next time Fong made his persuasive rounds. I was on guard against another drink. Already the warm, flower-scented night, and a moon, and millions of stars had stirred up an unwelcome heartache, and already my apprehensions, no matter how nebulous, how ungrounded, how foolish, were tightening their grip on me.

Unwillingly, my eyes had gone again to Mr. Yin Wah's huge, soft hands, and were fixed on the jade ring he wore, when Major Fenton was announced by Fong, and with an easy, assured greeting to Cousin Elizabeth, an overly elaborate bow to me, a nod to Mr. Yin Wah—whom he seemed to have met on some occasion or other at Cousin Elizabeth's office, he, too, sat down in one of the peacock chairs.

Those tall, beautiful chairs—I shall never want one. I shall never think of one without a sick shudder at the memories of Cousin Elizabeth's lanai that they will bring back for all the rest of my life.

At the time, I was wondering if a more unlikely group of people could possibly have been gathered together, and again and again I tried to understand Cousin Elizabeth's tolerance in putting up with either of the two men.

Major Fenton began to strike me as particularly obnoxious. At least Mr. Yin Wah could not be called a hard drinker. But the Major, on his arrival, was already flushed-looking, and his easy, presumptuous manner had a swagger to it and more than a suggestion of whiskey-fortified self-assurance.

His interview with the art critic had been a success, he wasted no time in telling Cousin Elizabeth, and when she congratulated him with a great deal of kindness that I could not have mustered, they talked pictures for awhile, with Mr. Yin Wah silent except for his noisy munching of everything Fong passed, and with me silent, too, thinking about Jim, and wondering if my postcard had arrived, and if it had cracked the ice, even the slightest bit.

My wishful thinking was broken in on by Mr. Yin Wah getting to his feet, and I supposed him to be taking leave of Cousin Elizabeth when he mumbled something or other; but instead of starting toward the garden path that led around the house to the driveway, and presumably to his car, he disappeared into the house.

Was he looking for the coat room and lavatory that opened off the hall, I wondered? Most likely—or, just possibly, had he another reason for going inside? A surreptitious reason? Whose room would he swiftly rummage through this time, while all the servants but Fong would be having their supper at the back of the house, and while Fong was padding only between the kitchen passageway and the lanai?

My curiosity was irresistible. I, too, stood up, murmuring something about needing a handkerchief, and whisked into the house. The guest coat room was at the far end of the hall, beyond the drawing room and the library, but Mr. Yin Wah had stopped in front of the lacquer cabinet where Cousin Elizabeth's curios were displayed, and he was opening its curved doors.

I darted behind the lacquer screen that shielded the drawing room from drafts, and through a fold watched and waited, holding my breath. What was he up to now?

I saw him take a small magnifying glass from a pocket of his linen jacket, and then he took a pink quartz figurine of a Buddha from a shelf and holding it up close to his thick-lensed spectacles, examined it minutely through the magnifying glass, running his fingers over it and turning it upside down. He put it back, then, and next picked up a carnelian snuff bottle and, removing its stopper, peered inside. An old, old, red cinnabar box came under his scrutiny next, and before he put it back on a shelf he tapped it as though to find out whether or not it had a hollowed-out false bottom.

He had just picked up a porcelain jar when a telephone bell shrilled somewhere, and on the chance, evidently, that one of the servants might appear with a message for Cousin Elizabeth, he closed the cabinet door, and in seconds was only a guest, pausing with casual interest to look at her curios before he shambled on to the coat room.

I waited until he came out, and then I slipped from behind the screen and, giving him a minute to get back to the lanai, followed after him. I was completely at a loss. If Mr. Yin Wah had intended to steal, he had had every chance. And if he had not intended to pocket any of those curios, why that hurried putting down of the jar, and his quick pose of a mildly interested guest?

Unmistakably, the contents of the cabinet were important to him; a magnifying glass is not a usual pocket accessory, and besides that, those pudgy, splayed fingers of his had examined each object with the same carefulness as his eyes.

By the time I got back to the lanai he was saying goodnight to Cousin Elizabeth, and then he shambled off down the garden path, those long ape arms swinging, his fleshy, soft hands dangling. Major Fenton was looking amused. "Not precisely Chesterfieldian."

"He reminds me of a great gorilla." My comment was emphatic. It was also the first remark I had made to the Major since his arrival, and he quirked an eyebrow.

"The redheaded *haole* heard from. Lani's little friend speaking up. Would you believe it, Miss Allen, I have been doing a good bit of thinking about you the past few days—and about those prison-camp days."

Cousin Elizabeth turned her large, quiet eyes on him. "Not the camp again, Major Fenton?"

He ignored the rebuke, and his hard blue gaze was on me again. "Extraordinary, one's memory. A chance jogging, and there's no end to the interesting bits that come to mind. And extraordinary the way those bits dovetail.

Which is to say I have finally pegged your double, Miss Allen. She was a young woman who died in that cesspool of a camp that Miss Beaton, here, would so much prefer not to discuss."

"Then why bring it up?" was on the tip of my tongue, but a curious excitement was suddenly possessing me. I leaned forward in my chair. Unconsciously, my hands gripped each other.

"You don't mean you knew . . . ?"

"I knew both Mrs. Richard Allen and Mrs. John Allen." Major Fenton tilted his empty glass and stared into it as though it mirrored the prison where I was born. "The young Allen wives—a pair of charming sisters-in-law. They were quite different in appearance. One was an ash blonde —am I remembering correctly, Miss Beaton? The other had hair the color of a sorrel mare's mane, or the coat of an Irish setter. Your hair has the same brightness, Miss Allen. And your eyes are the same. Brown, with gold flecks."

He broke off to reach for the full glass Fong offered, and to take a long swallow, and then I gasped, and stared at him, not believing my ears, when he asked Cousin Elizabeth, "Will it interest Miss Allen, do you suppose, to hear that I was the doctor who delivered her? Or perhaps you have already told her?"

Chapter sixteen

Might we go into that another time, Major Fenton?" Cousin Elizabeth's second rebuke was as coolly and unperturbedly spoken as her first, and for the moment it checked Major Fenton, and I was grateful beyond words for her quick sparing of me. I was staring at the Major aghast. I could see that bloodied, ragged, filthy camp sheet. I could see the girl who was my double, the girl who was my mother, dying. There was the smell of disinfectants, instead of Island flowers. My one thought was, "Don't let him tell me any more." I couldn't have stood hearing another word about my mother's terrible childbirth. Not then. Not while Major Fenton reeked of whiskey.

He sickened me.

Cousin Elizabeth reached out a ringed hand and at the touch of it on my arm I knew that she, too, was sickened, and I knew why she herself hadn't told me the part Major Fenton had played in my mother's death. With infinite understanding, with the most delicate perception, she had realized my inner cringing at thought of my mother in the hands of a dissolute, hard-drinking doctor who had lost the respect of everyone who knew him.

And yet—and yet—here was someone who had known my mother. An overpowering wish that I, too, might have known her made me lean forward again in my chair. "Am I really as much like her as you say, and as Miss Beaton has said?" There was longing in my voice, and it was not quite steady as I added, "I wish I had a picture of her. I wish I could see for myself."

"As a matter of fact, I was coming to that." Major Fenton took another long swallow. "A former colleague of mine and his wife were great friends of the Allens before the war. The three couples went about together a good deal in Hong Kong. My colleague's wife is dead, and he is living in a club, but there is just a chance he might have held on to a snapshot or two of those early days. He was a chap who was always taking pictures, a camera fiend, and——"

"Isn't it rather cruel of you to stir up false hopes, Major Fenton?" Cousin Elizabeth interrupted. "It seems a pity."

"Ah, but if a snapshot of Miss Allen's mother and aunt were to turn up, it would mean a great deal to her, would it not? And to you, too, Miss Beaton—come to think of it?"

He didn't give her a chance to answer, and to me, as he went on, his short laugh had a brutal disregard for anything Cousin Elizabeth might be feeling. "A souvenir of prewar days, let's say. But neither you nor I would need a memento of what followed, right? Not an hour of prison life could ever be forgotten. Not by me, certainly. That hellish camp. We could tell Miss Allen a thing or two about it, and what it did to people, if we chose. The lucky devils were the ones who died."

He was becoming maudlin with a third drink. There was no knowing what further ghastliness he would bring up, and I waited expecting the worst.

"Must you, Major Fenton?"

Cousin Elizabeth's question came coolly, evenly.

"Have it your way, Miss Beaton. Anything to please the ladies. Anything at all. That has always been my motto—need I remind you?

There was an insolence in his laugh this time that again gave me a curious awareness of undercurrents, of something between the two of them.

So many puzzles. As I was thinking it, he turned to me. "To go back to those snapshots. Shall I try to get hold of one for you, Miss Allen?"

"Oh, please, will you?" I almost begged it, much as I disliked the thought of accepting anything in the way of a favor from him. But a picture of my mother!

I had only a moment to hug to myself a sudden excitement, a quick joy. Fong, on a nod from Cousin Elizabeth, announced dinner. She hadn't wanted Major Fenton to have another drink, I realized, and she was reasoning that the sooner we sat down, the sooner he would be on his way.

How intensely she must be regretting the mistaken kindness of her invitation. And with what apprehension she must be realizing, too late, that dinner, and more to drink, could result in almost any unpleasantness.

The long polished table of dark teakwood, whose legs were carved dragons, was set with three wine glasses at each plate. There was sherry with the chilled soup. White wine with the curried chicken. French champagne as usual with the dessert, which, this evening, was a lemon sherbet snowed under by a drift of coconut flakes and resting on a nest of pale-green spun sugar, like the grass in Easter-egg baskets, with little meringue birds bordering it all.

Spun-sugar nests. I hadn't seen any since Ah Sam used to delight me with them. Meringue birds, with beaks of little bits of crystallized ginger and tiny chocolate eyes.

They took me back years. I was again the child Ah Sam had loved, and who had loved her in return. Ah Sam—my world. But now she was gone, and so was her fan, and I had nothing more tangible to remember her by than the sight of a spun-sugar nest, a meringue bird.

Back to the fan, again, back to Mr. Yin Wah. Back to puzzlement. But this was neither the time nor the place to attempt working out any sort of answer. Guiltily I realized I had been lost in my private thoughts, and was not helping Cousin Elizabeth to get through our difficult dinner. But I needn't have troubled to make amends with my hurriedly-tossed-in conversational nothings. Cousin Elizabeth, too, had been somewhere else in her thoughts, from the remote and pensive, and almost unhappy expression on her face that ordinarily reflected nothing but the serenity that comes with an inner calm and inner strength.

As for the Major, by then he was drunk, really drunk. That wasn't exaggerating his condition, which was unpleasantly apparent when he raised his champagne glass and, with the foaming wine spilling on Cousin Elizabeth's Chinese brocade table mats, stood up to propose a toast.

"To Miss Allen, the prison baby. And to the baby's beautiful mama, God rest her soul."

It was the end. The absolute end. Nothing, nothing would ever make me forgive him for bringing up, again, the horror that dreadful camp had been for my mother, the unforgettable nightmare of it for Cousin Elizabeth. I loathed his blue eyes, with their not-quite-focused glance at each of us in turn; I loathed his vacuous, foolish smile as he lifted the spilling glass to his lips and drank— alone—this inexcusable, insensitive toast.

Cousin Elizabeth was wonderful. Magnificent. She glanced at me, and an almost imperceptible shake of her head seemed to say, "Let it go. It's nothing. And I can manage him."

She got up and suggested quietly, "Shall we have coffee?" and led the way to the lanai, with the Major weaving a little in his walk, and sitting down abruptly in the first peacock chair he saw.

When Fong came with the coffee tray, Cousin Elizabeth had him put it on a table, and when she dismissed him, asked me to pass Major Fenton a cup after she had filled it, and then passed me a cup, herself. I admired her for sending Fong away. She was saving face for Major Fenton before he could make any worse spectacle of himself.

"Will you get my checkbook and pen, please, child?" she asked me, then, as she lighted a cigarette, very much the Manchu Court Lady, all dignity and poise in her high-backed chair, and with her brocade and her jade and the ivory cigarette holder that should have been a little opium pipe. "They are on my dressing table. I want to be Major Fenton's first patron."

She turned to him. "May I have the picture of the cormorant fishing? And you must tell me what price you are asking."

She was handling him marvelously. She even had one of her gentle smiles for him then. ". . . and if I told you I am very tired, Major Fenton, would you forgive me for suggesting that you go home after our little transaction?"

Major Fenton was attempting to pull himself together, and he stood up when I left to get the checkbook, although he had to steady himself with a hand on his chair back; but when I had returned, and while Cousin Elizabeth was writing a check, the coffee cup in his hand crashed to the floor of the lanai. It was empty, so there was no splatter, but fragments of porcelain were everywhere.

"Sorry—frightfully sorry," with little coherence and less balance he apologized, and stooped to pick up the pieces. I seized the chance to whisper in an urgent aside to Cousin Elizabeth, "Send him home this minute. Get rid of him. You've been much too decent."

"I shall have to send him with Sing. It would be criminal to let him drive himself."

Major Fenton was back in his chair, a few pieces of the shattered cup in his hand. He was looking at them stupidly. He didn't know what they were, I thought disgustedly, and he didn't know where he was. In another moment, slumped in his chair, he would be asleep. Noisily asleep. Already his breathing was heavy.

"Don't be too hard on him, Nan." It was as though Cousin Elizabeth had read my thoughts, and her quiet admonition spoke of a compassion I couldn't share, and with which I was impatient; but nevertheless it shamed me a little.

"I am not excusing him, but none of us are perfect. And is there anything more pitiful than a man who has thrown his whole life away because of drinking too much?"

"What started him off tonight, do you suppose?" I asked.

"The success of his pictures, I imagine. It wouldn't surprise me to hear he had been stood several rounds of drinks before he got here. And unless he gets hold of himself, there goes his work, and his chance for a fresh start."

Cousin Elizabeth pulled the silk bell cord that dangled from the wall by her chair, and at the two sharp tugs both Fong and Wing hurried onto the lanai. It was too late, now, to attempt any further face saving, and Cousin Elizabeth gave a quiet order to her houseboys.

With their yellow faces expressionless, they padded to either side of Major Fenton's chair. He refused to let them touch him, and got to his feet unaided, and stood swaying, and smiling his foolish, drunken smile.

"Running me out, are you?" he asked Cousin Elizabeth.

"I told you I am very tired, Major Fenton."

His glance turned to me. "The red-haired haole . . . nice girl . . . nice to Lani . . ." He lurched and would have fallen if the two Chinese had not grasped his arms and steadied him. This time he did not resist them. He was still looking at me. "You, and a sorrel mare, and that girl in camp." The words came out thick and slurred on his tongue. His face was suffused, the bold, hard blue eyes were glassy. Again he lurched. Again Fong and Wing steadied him. Now he seemed to be trying to remember something, with his gaze on me again. "The camera chap —must write him. Worthwhile, jolly worthwhile—Ian . . . Ian Grant. Old colleague . . ."

We watched him stumble away with Fong and Wing holding him up, and we could hear his garrulous, meaningless talk until the garden path curved toward the front terrace.

I was sorry for him, I realized. Terribly sorry.

We heard Cousin Elizabeth's car come around from the garage and then, in a moment, there was a swish of gravel on the driveway and the receding throb of an engine on the road leading to the Pali.

As though she had contained herself only waiting for those sounds, Cousin Elizabeth gave a long sigh, and for the first time that evening I saw she had reached the limit of her forbearance. It made her seem more human and more on my own level. She had been a saint.

"Enough is enough." She lighted another cigarette and inhaled deeply. "I couldn't have stood another word about the camp—and you might think that after all these years, when it's all water under a bridge . . ." She inhaled again with a long, dragging pull at her cigarette. She looked done in and old, in spite of the soft and usually flattering glow of the lanai lanterns. "Sometimes I could almost agree with Major Fenton that the ones who died were the lucky ones."

I looked away from her and made a pretense of picking up more shattered bits of the Major's coffee cup. Her face was revealing too much, and I was remembering all that Ah Sam had told me—when I was old enough for its horrors—about the prison camp.

The semistarvation. The numbing cold of winters. The sweltering heat of summers. The rats. The stench. The fevers. The dysentery. The beatings. And more—the rapes.

Had the ultimate in humiliation and hideousness been Cousin Elizabeth's lot? It had happened to dozens of other women in that camp. And the very dignity and tranquillity that lent her a distinction all her own might well have been an incentive to her captors to bring her low.

Was that the fundamental reason why any discussion of

camp days was unbearable to her? Was that why she had never discussed my mother with me, or Aunt Edith, at any length? Did she think her own experiences in prison even less enviable than theirs?

If only I knew how to let her know my inexpressible regret for it all. There was nothing I could say, but Fong, with understanding and practicality, brought us a fresh pot of hot coffee, and in a few minutes Cousin Elizabeth looked better, as though she had been able to relegate Major Fenton to nothing more than a drunken dinner guest, and so forget him.

I was glad for her as I sipped the frappéed crème de menthe Fong brought us every evening, and only wished that I, too, could do some forgetting.

There was a full moon, and under it the garden was silvery, and without shadows. No one could creep along the shrubbery tonight unobserved, and no one would be foolish enough to try, I was thinking; and then, with the scent of jasmine and gardenia a sweet, cruel stab, Jim was in my thoughts. Reflection along that line hurt too much, and it was a relief when the garden's perfume brought Lani's plumeria lei and the flowers for her hair to mind.

They would wilt, unnoticed. Major Fenton would return to Lani sodden and stupid, and barely able to stand. Would she give up the wide couch to him while he slept off his drunkenness, and she herself sleep on the matting floor? Probably.

I could imagine the moonlight shining into the beach shack. I could imagine an inert figure stretched out on the *hikea*. I could imagine Lani curled on the mat of woven leaves—the child Lani, who gave away love so lavishly and easily and with so much laughter.

When Cousin Elizabeth and I finally said good-night

and went to our rooms, I was still thinking about Mr. Yin Wah, and Jim, and Lani; they, and the moonlight flooding through the French door into the garden kept me tossing for a long time, and I was just dozing off when the telephone extension on my bedside table began to ring and ring. Sleepily startled, I reached for the receiver.

"Yes? Hello? Hello . . . ?"

Cousin Elizabeth, in her bedroom, had answered, too. And we both heard what a highway patrol officer was saying.

Poor Lani. Oh, poor Lani. Cousin Elizabeth's car had crashed. Sing had escaped, but Major Fenton was dead.

Chapter seventeen

TEN minutes after the telephone call, Cousin
Elizabeth came to my room in a silk dressing gown and
embroidered Chinese slippers, to tell me further details
of the accident. She had twisted her long, thick plait of
hair into a hurried but neat coil, removed whatever night
creams she used on her face, and touched her mouth with
lipstick, and though obviously shocked and upset, as
would anyone be, to hear of a fatal accident, she was
honest, and made no hypocritical show of undue regret.

"I don't consider him a great loss. I am only sorry for
my share of the responsibility. It wouldn't have happened
except for the wine at dinner. I shouldn't have allowed
Fong to serve it. Though how I could have foreseen . . ."

Major Fenton, in the back seat of the car, had roused
from a stupor to insist, on an unreasonable, absurd whim,
that Sing drive back to the beach by way of the old Pali
detour so he could see the view by moonlight. To humor
him, Sing agreed. Next, the Major was demanding bel-

ligerently that Sing stop the car so he himself could drive, and they had just approached the Lookout, with Sing trying to placate him, when he had reached over the front seat and seized the wheel.

Sing, doing the only thing possible, slammed on the brake; but the heavy car skidded, and knowing a crash was coming he had jumped, seconds before the car slammed into the Lookout parapet.

There was nothing to be done for Major Fenton, and Sing had rushed to the new road and flagged down a passing car. The highway patrol had taken charge, then, and the Major's body had been removed to a mortuary in town.

"Does Lani know?" I asked, heartsick for her.

"Lani?"

"The girl who . . . the girl at the beach."

"The girl who has been living with Major Fenton?"

It was a direct, factual way of putting it that distressed me.

"She was very fond of him, and if you knew her, you'd understand; she doesn't just . . . well, just sleep around with everyone. And she is like a child," I hurried to justify Lani.

"A child? Nonsense. She is quite old enough to know better. In my opinion, at any rate. But to answer your question, the police notified her and her family. One of the ambulance crew is a Hawaiian boy who knows them, and knows the situation."

"Where is she? At the beach, or has she gone back to her family?"

"I don't know. Why do you ask?"

"I want to see her. I'll go first thing in the morning."

"It would be very kind of you, but is it necessary to involve yourself, considering who and what she is?"

"I'll never forget her calling me 'Mees Allen, my friend.' And if that's the way she thinks of me . . ."

"You might tell her for me that I shall be glad to pay the Major's funeral expenses. I don't suppose he had a penny put away. And as I said, I am sorry about my responsibility for it all."

"It was just one of those things, Cousin Elizabeth. You weren't to blame." I offered what comfort I could, but Cousin Elizabeth wasn't willing to take the easy way out.

"He would be alive if he hadn't stayed for dinner. But what is done, is done. And as far as the girl is concerned, she will have to leave the beach. And at once, if she has not already gone. It is all very well to make excuses for her, my dear Nan, but after all, she is trespassing, and she *is* a little tramp."

If that was Cousin Elizabeth's viewpoint, what was the use of arguing? None at all. So I made no attempt to defend Lani further, but when Cousin Elizabeth went back to her room, and I waited for morning to come, I could think of nothing else but the laughing child who no longer would have a reason to wreathe flowers, or to pin them in her hair.

When the sun came up, I was staring into the garden, which was soaked, and steaming with a sequence of mountain showers that came and went, and that had caused a rainbow to arc against the pink-flushed sky; but I wasn't seeing the garden. I was seeing the beach, and the sea, and the quiet, small waves of the early-morning low tide, and the Major's canoe, high on the sand, a derelict, now.

When at last it was time to get up, I found I was dawdling over dressing, dawdling over breakfast, with a dread of what lay ahead. What could I say to Lani? What words could I find? But as soon as Cousin Elizabeth had gone off as usual to the office, driven by one of the yard boys, instead of the shaken Sing, in the station wagon the staff used for marketing, I drove my own car out of the garage and took the road that led to the beach.

As I drove along, I was sickened by thought of Sing and Major Fenton on the narrow, rain-slick detour to the old Pali Lookout. It was all too easy to picture broken glass and crumpled metal, too easy to picture that windswept gap, that terrible drop—down . . . down . . . and a hurtling body.

It was a relief to leave the Pali behind, even with its new wide, gentle, safe grading, and reach the shore road, with Cousin Elizabeth's property ahead—though what to say to Lani? I still didn't know.

As I parked under the plumeria trees, I saw that someone else had come to see Lani; a sports car painted in orange-and-white zebra stripes and with a very large exhaust pipe, and a cut-down look to it, was parked in the shade, too.

I walked to the shack and knocked, and then went in through the open door. Lani's brother Hanale and his friend Keoki were sitting on the wide couch. Both had their black hair slicked back, with the ridges made with wet combs still showing. Both wore the very clean shirts and white duck trousers and immaculate white buck shoes they had worn at the Diamond Head party. Hanale was fingering mournful chords on his guitar and singing softly to himself. Keoki was leaning back, halfheartedly swishing a fly swatter, and with a faraway look on his face, keeping time with the tap of one foot to Hanale's strumming. Open beer cans were on the floor beside them, conveniently in reach.

"Is Lani here?" I asked.

Both nodded, wordless, toward the kitchen, and then I saw Lani. She was wearing a muumuu. It was the first time I had seen her in anything but a sarong or a hula skirt, and, like the boys, she had a dressed-up, special-occasion look about her. A heartbreaking look.

She was at the ironing board, pressing a man's white shirt. And I knew whose it was, and who would wear it, without being told.

"I'm so sorry, Lani. . . ."

She looked up from her ironing, briefly. "Sure . . . sure." It was all she said. She went on with her ironing, pressing one cuff and then the other. Then she put the iron back on the stove, and waited, and when it sizzled at the touch of a finger she had wet, she took it up again to press the collar of the shirt.

All the while there was the sound of that melancholy strumming, that soft singing, and the slap of the fly swatter, the tap of a shoe. Nothing else. I just stood there. At least she knows I came, I kept telling myself.

When at last the shirt was finished, Lani reached behind the curtain that served as a closet and took from a wire hanger a pair of gray flannel slacks and a striped regimental tie, and from a hook on the wall the navy-blue blazer with the brass buttons. She put them over her arm, with the carefully folded shirt, and went to the icebox and brought out the plumeria lei of the day before, in a cellophane bag. Only then did she turn to me. "So long, Mees Allen."

Her eyes had no tears. Her face was blank.

"Lani . . . Lani dear . . ."

"More betta we make talk bimeby, Mees Allen. Too much *pilikia*—beeg trouble—here now. An' the Major, he need his clothes. Come on, Hanale. Come on Keoki. We gotta move now, you keeds."

Before she went out the door, she took a long look around her at the wide couch and the table, still set for two, and last night's supper, and at the stack of canvases. Then, without a backward glance, she walked to the zebra-striped car. She would never set foot in the house again, not ever, I knew. Cousin Elizabeth wouldn't have to order her out.

When they drove away, she was wedged in the middle, with Hanale at the wheel and Keoki and the guitar on the other side, and I watched them go, wondering, What next for Lani, when the Major had been buried in his clean white shirt?

Would she take Hanale's advice? Would she listen to Keoki? Give in to him? It was anyone's guess. But she would have to have a man in her life, some man—that I knew, because she was Lani, half a loving child, overflowing with affection, half a woman, amorous and amoral.

Before I drove away, I took what I thought, then, would be my last glimpse of Cousin Elizabeth's beach. No more than Lani would I want ever to return.

The Major's canoe was pulled high on the sand, just as I pictured it to myself, under the shade of the gently swaying coconut palms, where wet shells glistened and crabs scuttled. Everything was the same as I had seen it on a week of other mornings, yet everything was different now. And as I walked to my car, I knew I would never forget the *ssh, ssh* of the quiet water, and the rustle of palms, and the fragrance of yellow plumeria blossoms, and I was wondering, wondering why Lani's sea gods had so cruelly snatched away her happiness.

I was hoping, too, that for Lani there would not be too many sailor and soldier pick-up dates on Kalakaua Avenue. Not that for her future. Not that, no matter what else it held.

When I got back to Cousin Elizabeth's, a late lunch was brought out to me at the swimming pool, and served under the big blue umbrella, but I couldn't eat. I was still in the shack kitchen where Lani had tested her flatiron with a wet finger.

"*Pilikia,*" she had said. Big trouble.

I kept wondering what she would do, where she would go, after she had been to the mortuary. I hoped Hanale and Keoki would take her to a drive-in. I hoped they would buy her fried shrimp, and her fill of the pink ice cream she loved. I wanted, with all my heart, to see her as Lani the child, being comforted as a child is comforted. I wanted, with all my heart, to picture her dancing again. But all I could see was that sizzling iron, that white shirt. I was haunted all day.

I was more than tired of my own company by the time Cousin Elizabeth came back from the office, and hugely grateful that she, as well as I, had no wish to bring up any mention of the accident either at cocktail time or dinner, nor afterward on the lanai, and our only mention of Major Fenton was when I asked her, "Had you ever heard of the Captain Ian Grant he spoke of, 'the camera fiend'?"

"Everyone knew everyone else in Hong Kong, in the old days."

"I wonder where a letter would reach him?"

"A letter?" Cousin Elizabeth sounded mildly surprised.

"I want to write him, on the chance of his having those snapshots Major Fenton spoke of."

"The chances of finding him are one in a thousand, I should think. He could so easily have died in the war, or, for all one knows, be living in Rio, or Capetown or London—anywhere at all in the world."

"True, but——"

"But you are determined to find him?"

"If I can. First, I'll write to the Governor of Hong Kong——"

"But Hong Kong is enormous! And people have been coming and going constantly, ever since the war. Thousands of them must have been lost track of, in the shuffle. Even military personnel."

"If the Governor's office can't find him, I'll write to London, or wherever the British Army Headquarters are."

"There must be dozens of Ian Grants. It's not at all an uncommon name."

"I'll keep on writing until I have sifted out the one I want."

"You will be spending a fortune on stamps, I'm afraid." Cousin Elizabeth was gently ridiculing me. "Besides which, my dear child, you'll have writer's cramp. And even if you do find him, and even if after all these years he still has a picture of your mother, how could you possibly tell what she looked like from a faded, yellowed snapshot?"

"If he ever were a real camera fiend, he would have taken care of his pictures, presumably, and, anyway, snapshots, no matter how old, can be wonderfully restored."

"My stubborn Nan! Well, have it your own way—just so the stamps are yours, and not mine." Cousin Elizabeth's voice was amused. "And tell me, is this to be an immediate project?" She was concerned, then. "I don't want to see you disappointed. And you are bound to be, you know."

"I'll write that first letter tonight, before I go to bed. I'm longing to get it out of my system. And if, in the end, I get nowhere, it would have been worth the try."

"Now really, Nan! Not tonight. Go to bed and get a good sleep. Last evening was—shall I say, exhausting?"

I put down my liqueur glass and stood up. "Writing the letter will help me forget last night. And I can't wait to get in touch with that man. If he still exists."

"A very small needle in a very large haystack, my dear."

"But just think, if I'm lucky . . . And if Major Fenton has helped me find that snapshot, I'll forget all the things I didn't like about him. I could forgive him anything, I think, poor man."

"Poor you, in my opinion, Nan."

"Why poor me?"

"Because of your insatiable weakness for involvements —and because of the unnecessary complications you make for yourself."

"Such as my mixing up in your life, Cousin Elizabeth?" Now it was my turn for a little affectionate ridicule. "Such as hunting you up, after all these years?" I gave her a quick kiss. "That, for my involvement with you! It turned out pretty well, I'd say. I'd risk it over again, anytime."

"Speaking of involvements . . ." Cousin Elizabeth was lighting a cigarette as she spoke. "I asked you once before if there was a man in your life. Anyone in particular, that is. Did you answer me quite truthfully?"

"No . . ." I confessed it reluctantly.

"Where is he, in San Francisco?"

"Yes."

"Do you hear from him?"

"No."

"I have wondered about you. Somehow, you give the impression of being a rather detached girl."

"Detached is the word. I'm the cat who walks alone— not from choice, I might add." It had a bitter ring to it, and because she was sorry for me, or so I supposed, Cousin Elizabeth was quick to ask if the Martins kept an eye on me and saw that I met people, and didn't become a hermit. "They will be glad to see you back, I expect; they are counting the days, I don't doubt."

"They are in Europe."

"Oh? But surely you must have other friends who will be glad to see you?"

"I could stay on here, in Honolulu, or anywhere else, forever, without a single soul knowing or caring if I ever came back to San Francisco." My answer was a burst of self-pity, and then I had the grace to laugh at myself. "It's not that bad. I'll be ready to pick up the pieces when I go back, and there are plenty of people who will see I start having fun again. You needn't worry a bit about me, Cousin Elizabeth. Nobody dies of a broken heart these days."

"You are quite certain this man in your life wouldn't come looking for you if you stayed on here indefinitely?"

"Quite certain." The bitterness was there, again. I was ashamed to have let anyone else in on my hurt, and I said good-night hurriedly to Cousin Elizabeth.

The trouble with life in Honolulu was, I decided as I went to my room, that the warm, starry nights, the scent of flowers, the rustle of palm fronds, the sound of the surf, all hurt too much. They kept your loneliness an open wound. And they made your going to bed at night, your getting up in the morning completely automatic and useless procedures.

I might as well be dead. . . .

Poor Lani. Poor Major Fenton. Yes. But Cousin Elizabeth was right. Poor me, as well.

Chapter eighteen

THE next day was Saturday, and Cousin Elizabeth did not go to her office. She had a late breakfast in her bedroom, and I wandered around the garden at loose ends, missing Lani, missing the beach, and most of all, missing Jim. Then, in the middle of the morning, Fong came back from the mailbox at the gate with a large envelope for me postmarked San Francisco and with the return address of Jim's office. I tore it open in a rush and took out the most absurd, the most zany of cards. There was a drawing of a little forlorn-looking man with a sad, turned-down mouth and outstretched arms, a Charlie Chaplin sort of little man, and the verse under him read,

> Like a waffle needs syrup,
> Like a hot dog needs mustard,
> Like strawberries need cream,
> Like a bird needs a nest,
> I need you.

And in a corner Jim had written, "Trying to stay mad, but no luck, and the effort is killing me. What are the chances for kissing and making up? I love you."

My crazy, divine Jim! I wanted to laugh, and I wanted to cry as I rushed into the house to my bedroom and a telephone. I could hardly dial correctly, in my joyous flurry, but at last I got an operator and sent off a radiogram, brief but to the point.

IN ANSWER TO INQUIRY CHANCES EXCELLENT. ALL MY LOVE

When I remembered it was Saturday and Jim might not be at his office, I sent a duplicate to his club. After that, I rushed down the hall to Cousin Elizabeth's bedroom; I simply had to share my wild happiness with someone. I couldn't possibly keep it to myself.

Jim. Jim. Oh, Jim! I hardly took time to knock at Cousin Elizabeth's door, and I didn't wait for a "Come in," before I grasped the knob and burst in on her.

She was standing with her back to me by her dressing-table, but I saw, in the mirror, before she quickly whirled around, what she held in her hand, and I saw the expression on her face.

She was clutching my sandalwood fan, and the bitter-ess, the torment, that ravaged her face had turned her into a stranger.

"My fan . . . !" I exclaimed it bewilderedly. "Where did you find it? Who took it out of my suitcase? And oh—it's broken!"

That a single delicate ivory stick should have been cracked a few evenings ago had distressed me enough; this was worse, an actual pang, to see that two other sticks had snapped.

Before she answered me, her face had already gone smooth and calm, and was the face of Cousin Elizabeth again. I had imagined that other face of a stranger. I must have imagined it. And her lifted eyebrows, gently implying the reproof I deserved, were making me realize how thoughtlessly and rudely I had burst in on her privacy, uninvited and unannounced.

"Where did I find your fan? Lui Lung brought it to me only a moment ago, with a confession. She took it from your suitcase several days ago, merely to admire it, when she was looking to see if by chance you had another linen dress on hand. I asked her to look; I thought you might be running short, and I was going to surprise you with one or two new ones, for a little present. One needs so many changes in this climate. Unfortunately, she dropped the fan, and when she saw the broken sticks, she was too frightened to tell you, and without stopping to think how silly she was being, she ran out of your room with it, and kept it until this morning, when her conscience got too much for her. Needless to say I gave her the sternest of lectures. She's groveling, and she will be coming to you with the most abject apologies."

"It doesn't matter. I hope you weren't too hard on her."

Somehow, I managed to get it out even though a spate of far-out, wildly improbable conjectures were flooding over me.

Was it possible that Cousin Elizabeth herself, and not Lui Lung, had taken the fan? To have dropped the fan was not apt to break the sticks, but a hard crunch—that was something else again. The kind of hard crunch by long, slender fingers, heavy with a weight of jade and pearl and carnelian, such as I had mentally visualized the night I took the fan out onto the lanai.

Had the sight of the fan, that evening, rekindled in Cousin Elizabeth an old passion? Had its faint, lingering breath of the Orient stirred old fires that long ago ought to have been cold ash? Was she still eating her heart out for John Allen? Still hating Aunt Edith Allen? Was jealousy still consuming her, even at this late date? And had some form of exquisitely cruel self-torture driven her to hunt out the fan so that she might gaze, again, on its carved wedding date, its five inlaid letters that spelled out "Edith"?

But what was I thinking of! It couldn't have been Cousin Elizabeth who had rummaged in my suitcase. Fastidious Cousin Elizabeth, demeaning herself to that extent? No. Never. I must be out of my mind. Nor could it have been anything but a contortion of the dressing-table mirror, some curious effect of light and shade that had masked Cousin Elizabeth's face with the face of that stranger.

When she put the fan in my hand, she was looking at me questioningly, as though she sensed more to the situation than I had told her, and I stumbled through the briefest of explanations; I would have felt idiotic to drag Mr. Yin Wah into the picture. No one enjoys being scoffed at, no matter how gently the scoffing is done.

"The fan means a great deal to me. I was upset when I missed it. But I didn't want to say anything. I didn't want to bother you."

"Nonsense, my dear. You should have told me at once. I could have immediately gotten the truth from Lui Lung and saved you days of concern. You foolish child. What did you think had happened to your fan? Wherever did you think it had gone?"

This was my chance to tell her about Mr. Yin Wah and

unburden my definite fear of him, and the temptation was great, in spite of not wanting to be laughed at. But before I blurted out about those gauzy curtains stirring at the French door and about a large, thickset figure scuttling into the concealment of shrubbery, the sound of a car driving away in a hurry, and my ransacked bedroom, I caught it all back. There was too much I suddenly wanted to think through and puzzle out for myself. Someone *had* been in my room. It would only be frustrating to listen to Cousin Elizabeth's well-meant, reasonable efforts to convince me I had imagined it all.

It was an awkward spot to be in, but while I was trying to think up some sort of hurried answer to her question, Cousin Elizabeth smiled, a little sadly. "A fan that you cling to, and the hope of a snapshot—if only you knew how much I wish you needn't be hurt by all this preoccupation with the past. I haven't thought of anything else since last evening but your stubbornness about that letter. Did you write it in spite of all my persuasions otherwise?"

I was vastly relieved at the change of subject. I had had enough of the fan for the moment. My astonishment at seeing it in Cousin Elizabeth's hand and my startled glimpse of what the mirror had done to her face were not what I cared to think about at the moment.

"I am going into town this morning for the first of those airmail stamps you spoke of," I answered her, with an attempt at a light touch. "Let's hope the postage rates don't go any higher. If finding Captain Grant is going to be as difficult as you predict, I shall have to take out a bank loan."

"You won't reconsider? Why not tear up the letter? Consider it something you've gotten out of your system, by writing it—and forget the whole thing. Even if you get in touch with Captain Grant, and even if, by a miracle, he still has a snapshot, do you think for a moment that a twenty-five-year-old, or older, picture will bring your mother any closer to you? How could it? Snapshots are not always flattering, and at best what would you have but a girl looking ludicrous in outmoded clothes, and with an outmoded hairdo? And to an idealist like you, need I say more? Don't you see for yourself that you are only asking for disappointment and a hurting letdown?"

She was right, and for an instant I wavered. But only for an instant. And it was the fan, safely mine again, that strengthened my determination. It, too, had come into my possession by the most devious and unlikely way, so why shouldn't a snapshot turn up, just as unexpectedly? And it wouldn't matter what the girl in the picture looked like. She would be my mother. She would have taken form and substance. She would be an actuality.

"I know it's foolish of me, Cousin Elizabeth, but the snapshot is a thing with me, now, and I won't be satisfied until my letter has gone down the slot in a mailbox."

"Then I shan't keep after you about it anymore, my dear." Cousin Elizabeth pulled one of the tasseled bell-cords that were everywhere in the house. "Would you like your car brought around? No need for you to walk to the garage; it's very warm. And as long as you insist on going into town, I advise you to start before the heat gets any worse."

"I'll go right now."

"Do. And if you are back in time, we shall have a lovely cool lunch by the pool."

I left her to go to my bedroom for the straw bag that matched my casual sandals and that held my purse and wallet, and for the letter to Captain Grant, and it was only then that I realized I had not mentioned Jim's card to Cousin Elizabeth. The tormented face I had seen in the mirror, and the fan, clutched so tightly in Cousin Elizabeth's hand, had made me forget the reason for my ecstatic rushing into her room.

Those crunched, snapped ivory sticks; had they, in fact, revealed a raw hurt of Cousin Elizabeth's that still bled, or had I allowed the flight of my always hard-to-control imagination to soar higher than any kite, this time?

There was one way to find out the truth—in part, at least—and on my way to the front of the house I detoured to the servants' wing, where I found Lui Lung sitting placidly mending an embroidered pillow slip on the lanai off the servants' dining room, while Gee, the cook, who was her husband, and Fong and Wing sat at a table drinking bowls of midmorning tea—their coffee break, and sampling egg rolls and pork tidbits.

I got nowhere, questioning Lui Lung. She chose not to understand a word of English. The others were of no help when I attempted to use them as interpreters. As the Chinese do, they were backing each other up. If Lui Lung had broken the fan, and chose not to admit it to me, they would never give it away. Not one of them would have told on her.

I was furious with them, with their imperturbability, their pidgin English, purposely a little less intelligible than usual, their expressionless, unreadable faces, glistening with sweat while they emptied their steaming tea bowls, forked up the pork with their chopsticks.

Lui Lung, Mr. Yin Wah, Cousin Elizabeth? I would have to decide for myself which of those three it had been. If only I could eliminate Cousin Elizabeth from that trio. If only I hadn't burst in on her, caught her, so cruelly, off guard.

That tormented face. No use to pretend to myself it had been a distortion of the mirror. No use, either, to pretend I had only imagined the crunching grip of ringed fingers on the fragile, brittle sticks of my poor, precious fan.

My full admittance of what I had seen, and all its implications made me sorrier for her than I could ever express, and in thought I was back again in Cousin Elizabeth's San Francisco house and remembering how somber I had always found it, how joyless and depressing. Was it Cousin Elizabeth's childhood resentments, her girlhood jealousies, and the beginning of adult bitterness and heartache that had permeated the house like a miasma? And when I brought Aunt Edith's fan into the house, had it wafted a hint of Cousin Elizabeth's unhappiness to further chill those empty rooms?

I shivered, as I had shivered once before, almost seeing unhappy Cousin Elizabeth, her hand on the banister of the hall stairway, and seeming to feel that chill, that depression again. And with a surge of gratitude, I gave thanks for Jim. Jim, who was mine again.

To be in love, rapturously in love, is, I suppose, to be almost wholly selfish and completely self-centered. I found it comparatively easy to dismiss Cousin Elizabeth from my mind—other people's unhappiness didn't concern me, now that my own was over, and I could even forget Mr. Yin Wah and aggravating Lui Lung as I went to the front door to wait for my car to be brought around.

Yes—and I could almost forget Lani—almost, but not quite.

As I crossed the front terrace, where the little birds were hopping and chattering in their cages, I saw that the car had already been brought around and parked for me in the shade of the thick, high shrubbery that blocked sight of the driveway from the rest of the garden. And I remember opening the door of the driver's seat and starting to slide under the wheel. But that was the last I was to remember with any coherence, for hours and hours.

Someone's hands were closing on my throat. Someone's thumbs pressed hard. I felt myself sinking, down, down, into agonizing blackness, and heard a horrible, choking gurgle.

When I regained consciousness, I was not in a car. I was in a strange room somewhere, gagged, and with my hands and feet bound.

Chapter nineteen

I was not yet engulfed in total pain—that was to come later—but my head ached with a steady pound, pound, and the thin plastic cord that was knotted around my wrists and ankles cut into flesh. My mouth was dry and stretched, my tongue thick, from the wad of cloth that gagged me and was knotted behind my head.

I was lying on a four-poster bed in semidarkness. Wooden shutters were closed at the room's two windows, and the dimness gave no indication of what time it was, or any clue to how long I had been lying there.

Eleven o'clock, perhaps a few minutes after, when I had opened the car door—hours ago, had it been, or only long, unending minutes? Not to know either that, nor anything else about what had happened—the why, the who—compounded my awareness of being utterly helpless.

If it was only minutes, I would not yet have been missed at Cousin Elizabeth's. "If you get back in time, we shall have lunch by the pool." That meant I could be lying here, wherever I was, for hours on hours before Cousin Elizabeth became anxious about me. I had stayed in town to shop or sight-see, she would think, when lunchtime came and went without me.

At first, there was only heavy silence in the room, the silence that permeates and becomes part of any room that has been unoccupied and closed for more than a few days. Then, only vaguely recognizable, there was a faint, rhythmic sound that could have been tidewater lapping somewhere. Next, and all at once, there was the loud race of my heart as realization of my situation struck, and the vacuum of unconsciousness filled with a terror that was absolute.

Why? Why? And who? To think, or, rather, to try to think, was so great an effort that I began to wonder if I had been drugged, and if that could explain the room's faint, hospitalish smell of chloroform or ether.

Oh, God—dear God, where was I? And who had done this to me? And why? Dully, unanswerable. I asked and reasked those questions, and a monstrous, anonymous Someone began to loom as frighteningly as though he were in the room.

What would finally happen to me? The same thing that had happened to those other girls, in newspaper stories? Decent girls. Quiet girls. Respectable girls.

Or had I been kidnapped, and was I being held for ransom, because I was a cousin of the rich Miss Elizabeth Beaton? In my abject terror I looked about me, as though, in that dim, shut room, I could somehow find an answer to my agonized questions.

The bed under me was spread with a patchwork quilt. A maplewood chest of drawers, an old one, stood against one wall. On it was an oil lamp and what looked like a big, old-fashioned family Bible. There was a straight-backed chair in a corner. A small, round, maple-framed mirror hung over the chest, and on the wall opposite the bed there was a steel engraving of a haloed Shepherd and a flock of sheep.

Straw matting covered the floor. Of two doors, one was closed, the other was ajar, held open by an iron doorstop in the shape of a rooster, and gave me a glimpse of a white-painted bathroom.

None of it had an answer to offer, nor a hint of an answer, but now I wasn't caring; with my return to full consciousness, pain was mounting intolerably in my arms and legs, which had been cold and numb and dead-feeling until now.

I knew I was moaning, though the only sounds that came through the gag were guttural, and barely audible. My tongue, thick and enormous-feeling, seemed to fill my dry mouth, and to swallow was agony.

Dragging, terrible hours passed. I began to count from one to sixty. If I could get through another minute, and then another. Several times, I must have fainted, or perhaps succumbed to a lingering effect of whatever drug my kidnapper had used. But whenever I was conscious, my eye went, alternately, to the closed door, and to the half-opened door. Through either of them the Someone who had done this to me might at any instant appear. And eventually, my slowed, groping search for an answer told me who the Someone would be.

Mr. Yin Wah, who, I had sensed from my first meeting with him, would be a danger to me. Mr. Yin Wah, who had followed me over the Pali. Mr. Yin Wah, who had ransacked my bedroom.

Through one of those doors his shambling, gross body,

his big, heavy-featured face with its coarse, thick lips and its pockmarks would come nearer, nearer, as I lay bound. The dark eyes that were sharks, swimming behind those heavy-lensed glasses, would fasten on me. The soft, fat, manicured hands wearing the two jade bands would reach out.

In my terror I was babbling, inwardly, to Ah Sam for help, and to Jim.

Jim . . . Jim . . .

After that, sight of the Shepherd in the steel engraving started me saying the Twenty-third Psalm, and then I was crying out to Jim again, as the patchwork quilt I was lying on reminded me of two lines from my little bedside book of read and reread poems.

> Night after night I ever keep for him the half of
>   my quilt,
> In expectation of his spirit coming back to me in
>   dreams.*

For weeks, ever since our rift, I had been keeping the half of my quilt. Night after night I had longed for him. Jim . . .

> Like strawberries need cream,
> Like a bird needs a nest . . .

Off and on the horrible blackness took over, but always when I came to, my eyes sought, in turn, the two doors. Slowly, something about the iron-rooster doorstop began

* From *The Penguin Book of Chinese Verse*, translated by Robert Kotewell and Norman L. Smith. Introduced and edited by A. R. Davis. Baltimore, Maryland, Penguin Books, Inc., 1962.

to seem important to me, vitally important—if only I could concentrate.

Think. Think hard. Pull yourself together. Try . . .

An iron cockerel with spurred legs, and with tail feathers and a comb. But what had that to do with me, and the agony of my cramped legs and arms, the chafing of my bound wrists and ankles, or with the thirst of my dry, gag-stretched mouth?

An iron rooster with an erect, serrated comb . . .

If I could get to it, if I could throw myself off the bed to the floor, and crawl to that cockerel, I could use the comb as a knife to cut the cord around my wrists.

The attempt would inflict still more pain on myself, and how could I bear more? But could I bear with any less agony the ghastliness of lying, inert and helpless, while I waited for that Someone, who would be Mr. Yin Wah, to appear?

I doubt if I was in a state to think through what I was attempting when I rolled over to the side of the bed and, with a desperate hunching of my shoulders and a wrenching twist of my hips, let myself drop to the floor.

I remember hearing the thud of my deadweight body. I remember my awful fear that the Someone would have heard it, too. And I shall never forget the minutes of waiting until I dared make another move and, inch by torturing inch, began to drag and hump and roll myself across the matting toward the bathroom door.

I used my shoulders and my knees, even my chin, for propulsion. My chin, scraped raw on the matting, began to bleed. Twice I sank into blankness again, and came back to find the floor had become a hill I was trying to climb. A high, high hill. And for each upward gain, there was a slipping back.

When, at last, I reached the half-open door, I collapsed —spent, and longing to give up. The tantalizing nearness of the cockerel wouldn't let me. I rested until it was physically possible for me to move again, and then, shoving with my forehead against the door so that it would swing back, and the doorstop would stand free, I rolled over on my left side, the side nearest the cock, and raised my wrists until the cord that bound them grazed the heavily cast, deeply cut comb.

Then I began to saw my wrists back and forth, back and forth. Continuously, I warned myself, "Don't saw too hard; don't risk toppling the rooster."

Miraculously, it stood steady on its base.

Forward, backward. Forward, backward. I don't want to think about the ache of my arms and shoulders. When the cord finally parted, I collapsed again, but the will to free myself was stronger than my exhausted longing for a merciful return to unconsciousness, and I made myself sit up and rub my wrists and arms and flex my fingers until their circulation painfully returned. My wrists were as bloody as my chin; now and again the sawing had cut into flesh instead of cord.

As soon as I could move my hands, I pulled out the gag in my mouth, a man's wadded white handkerchief, and then I tore at the knotted cord around my ankles. The knots had been carelessly tied; obviously the Someone had assumed there was no possibility of me freeing my hands to get at them.

For a few minutes after the cord dropped away, I couldn't stand up. My legs were all pins and needles, with the return of circulation as excruciating as it had been in my arms. When I finally got to my feet, I clutched hold of the knob of the bathroom door to keep upright, and after a moment I staggered to the other, closed door, and found it, as I knew I would find it, locked.

I was now certain I was alone in the house. I had made a good deal of noise throwing myself over the side of the bed and inching across the room. The Someone would have heard, by now. Unless he had merely been entertained by my painful struggles, unless he was waiting, and laughing, and taking his own time.

I began to pound crazily on the door, and to sobbingly demand that it be opened, until a last vestige of common sense told me I was only adding to the Someone's amusement, if he were listening, and, if he weren't, I was exhausting my last strength for nothing, with the two windows of the room still to be examined for any possibility of escape.

When I had made my still unsteady way across the room, I jerked up the matting blind of one of the windows and unlocked the lower sash. Pushing it up, I unhooked its mesh screen. Next there were latched, white-painted outside shutters to open. And then I was staring out, dumbfounded.

Through clumps of yellow plumeria trees I could see a low stone wall and quiet, shallow water with the glint of late-afternoon sun on it. Where the wall ended, there would be a little sandy curve of beach, though I couldn't see it because of the sea shrubs that blocked my view, and there would be a canoe pulled high on the sand, under softly rustling coconut palms, and a tin-roofed shack with hibiscus crowding the door.

Chapter twenty

I was in Cousin Elizabeth's saltbox. That much I knew. But who had brought me here? Who had locked me in this bedroom that spoke of New England missionaries with its plain, sparse furnishings? The questions Who? and Why? that I had been asking myself over and over were persistently clamoring for an answer, but I had no time now to give to further conjecture or guess. The Someone would come back. Surely he would come—unless he intended to abandon me to starvation in this solitary, closed house, from whose deserted beach the caretaker had gone, and Lani too. Was it then, and then only that the Someone would return, to dig a hole or throw what was left of me into the sea?

Or had he other plans? Plans that depended upon his keeping me alive—until such time as he was finished with me?

Oh, God! In terror unimaginable, and with every newspaper horror headline I had ever read again rushing to mind, I scrambled painfully to the sill of the window and dropped to the lawn of thick matted grass that circled the house. I came down on it hard, and at the drop that was fresh agony to my ankles and legs, and that sickeningly jarred my splitting head, I began to cry again. Then I was running, stumbling blindly, toward the shack. My one idea was to get as far away as I could from the house, and to avoid the white gate and the banana-grove lane that led to the highway, where, for all I knew, the Someone might be turning in.

I had no plan, no realistic plan thought out. I was too overwrought for thinking, too muddled, and all of me hurt too much. But a primitive instinct to hide possessed me, and I was remembering the front door of the shack, always swinging and slamming in the smallest breeze, and never closing properly because the Major hadn't bothered to repair its hinges or its latch, and I was remembering, too, the wide couch with the tapa-cloth covering that fell to the floor. I would cower under the sofa until dark, and then—if the Someone had not come seeking, and found me, I'd slip out and run down the beach. Beyond the cove, and the limits of Cousin Elizabeth's private property, there would be a fisherman's hut, or a town dweller's weekend house. And this was Saturday; there would be people to take me in, and get me to a telephone. I'd be safe and Cousin Elizabeth would come.

When I had rounded a corner of the shack, my legs were sagging under me and I sank on the threshold of the front door, which was swinging on its rusted-out hinges, and knew I hadn't the strength to drag myself to the couch.

"Hey! Wassa matta, lady?"

Keoki, in a flower-patterned loincloth, his hair sleek

from a swim, had put down the guitar he was restringing, and jumped from the *hikea* to rush to me.

"Hey! Wassa matta, you, huh? You gonna pass out?"

"I can't walk—everything hurts . . . I can't get up. . . ." I gasped it incoherently, and without waiting to hear more, Keoki lifted me in his arms and carried me inside the shack to the couch. Then he stood staring at me, his eyes lively with curiosity.

"Saay . . . ! Wha' kinda fight you been in, keed? Some fella, he beat you up? Jeez . . . ! You don' look so good."

"Help me, Keoki—help me—don't let anyone come . . . !" I clung to him frantically as I told my story. And when I finished, I was sobbing. I fell apart rather badly. Perhaps because, to add to everything else, I had not eaten since breakfast—that had been only coffee and a slice of papaya —and now, as I could see by the crimson and gilt of the sunset sky, and by the outgoing tide of the quiet ocean, it was almost evening.

More than food, though, I longed for a drink of water. I begged Keoki for it, and when he filled a jelly glass from the top of the sink, I took great gulps. After that he rushed to bring me a banana and a big bowl of super-market poi, out of a can. The poi was glutinous, and faintly sour-tasting in my haole opinion, and would need getting used to, but I devoured it gratefully and raven-ously. While I ate, Keoki opened a can of beer for himself, and briefly explained why he was at the shack. He had driven over from the Ahkina house a short hour ago. Lani had asked him to empty the food out of the icebox and bring back her things: her sarongs, her ukulele, her shell collection, which he would find in a coffee can on the kitchen shelf.

Those shells. Like the plumeria lei and the taro pudding, they broke my heart for Lani. Those shells that she had gathered from the beach to offer up to "dem, out there." How cruelly her gods had let her down. . . .

I was thinking it as Keoki broke off his explanations, put down his half-empty beer can, and jumped to his feet to announce, decisively: "We gonna beat it, keed, and fast! We gonna make tracks before maybe dat no-good fella, dat sonna beetch, come back after you. How I know if maybe he try to pull rough stuff, huh? How I know if maybe he got a gun?"

"No . . . please, no! I'm afraid to go back to the highway. We might meet him along the road coming in. It's too narrow to turn—he could block your car. . . ."

I was in a panic.

"I ain't no dumb guy, keed." Keoki looked disgusted with me. "Who says we take my car? I a got betta idea. We take the Major's canoe, and paddle down shore to Lani's mudda's and fadda's house; then Hanele, he drive you home. And some big surprise not to find yuh, huh, if that joker comes back?"

"Oh, Keoki, a terrific plan—but let's hurry!" I staggered up from the couch. I was wild to leave. That sweet word, "home"—I could have hugged Keoki for using it. "Home," that meant Cousin Elizabeth looking after me, and safety.

"Let's hurry!" I urged it again as I steadied myself, wincing at each difficult step, but Keoki was giving orders. I was to stay in the shack, out of sight until he had pushed the canoe into the water. ". . . but when I holla, you travel, keed—fast."

He sauntered with careful casualness out of the shack, pausing outside the doorway to pick a red hibiscus flower, and putting it behind his ear as he glanced toward the saltbox house. Then, with the same elaborate casualness, he sauntered to the canoe, pulled high on the sand, under the palm trees. And dragging it to directly in front of the shack, he launched it into the shallow water of the outgoing tide.

"Get moving, keed!"

At his shout I kicked off my straw sandals and on wobbling legs I tottered outside and waded into knee-deep water. Then, with Keoki steadying the canoe, I half crawled, half fell into it.

The sting of salt in my cuts and abrasions was like a whip of flame. As I huddled in agony, Keoki swung over the side. The canoe tipped—perilously, to my thinking—then righted itself as Keoki began to paddle. Out beyond us were jagged reefs and white-crested water, and in my ignorance of what course Keoki would take, I shut my eyes tightly and began to tremble again. Then I heard Keoki laugh. "You got the shakes, keed? Take a look. How you like this trip? A bathtub ride, huh?"

My eyes flew open. We were paralleling the shore in water as quiet and safe as the water I had swum in so often with Lani. I laughed, too, hysterically, and from reaction tears started to come again, but after a few minutes I got hold of myself.

I needn't be afraid. I needn't be afraid of anything, ever again. Oh, thank you, thank you, God. And as the prow of the canoe cut smoothly, silently, through the placid water, a delicious lethargy, a delicious calm, crept over me—the aftermath of taut nerves and strained body—and I could almost forget the burning smart of saltwater, my pounding headache, the hurting of my throat when I swallowed. They didn't matter.

Tomorrow there would be the police, interviewing me, I knew, and newspaper reporters. But when that was over,

I would take the first plane back to Jim, who had said, "I love you."

Twilights are short in the Islands, and as I gave myself up to blissful thoughts of a reunion with Jim, and to a rapturous sense of peace and security, the sky paled from its sunset flaming and became the gray of moonstones.

Keoki began to sing as he paddled. Standing naked except for his malot, his strong, hard-muscled body shadowed by dusk, he was an Island boy out of some book of Polynesian legend.

Keoki, warrior and maker of music, and navigator. An Island boy, one with his world. When the sea spoke, or the trade winds, they spoke in a language he understood. When a wave broke, or a palm frond rustled, he heard songs only he, and his own kind, could hear.

And like Lani, he had his Island gods—the words he was singing in his strange, haunting Hawaiian falsetto were like the words of a chant. If he was petitioning his gods, I hoped they would listen. I hoped they would give Lani to him.

Perhaps they had taken the Major from her only because they held something better in store for her. I wanted to think so. I longed for her "big pilikia" to go away, and for her to learn to be happy again.

The moonstone sky was black now. Stars, stars, stars, were tossed—gold confetti. A moon silvered the wake of the canoe. The scales of a leaping fish shimmered. A porpoise fin was a dark glint, surfacing from darker water.

Keoki had paddled perhaps five miles when he paddled still closer in to shore toward a tiny cluster of lights.

"Lani's house," he announced. "That make you feel good, keed?"

I assured him, fervently, that it made me feel very good

indeed, but a qualm or two began to bother me. My arrival would be awkward; how could I be anything but an unwelcome intruder? This was the night before the Major's funeral, and Lani wouldn't want to see me, nor would her family appreciate having a complete stranger walk in on them, I would be just that to them, a haole stranger. An outsider. A mainland tourist, patronizingly curious about Islanders and their personal lives. Critical, and almost certain to be rigidly and intolerantly disapproving of Lani's relationship with the Major—a relationship they had not merely quiescently permitted, but which they had, in fact, arranged.

There would be nothing for it but to be as tactful as possible and to leave the instant one of them would drive me to a telephone. Or to be less of a nuisance, perhaps I could borrow a car? No. I'd be afraid to drive alone in the darkness . . . afraid . . . afraid. I would be seeing the Someone lurking behind every bush or rock along the road, lying in wait for me beyond every lonely curve.

The awful terror that had possessed me in the saltbox house gripped me again, and I was imagining all the horrors of assault as the canoe rode the swell of a wave and, with Keoki paddling hard, shot toward the shore on a rush of white foam. Just before it grated on sand, Keoki sprang out into the water to beach it.

"Hi, Hanale!" He shouted it toward the lights. "Is me, Keoki . . ."

"Hi!" There was an answering shout. "Wass on your mind, beeg boy? Where'd you get canoe? Who yuh rob, Kanaka?"

Through the blackness I could see the outline of a little house and several indistinct figures running toward us, and it was the one in the lead who was holloing the joking questions.

I was intent on trying to get out of the canoe without tipping it, and had steeled myself for another wade through saltwater and its burning smart against my ankles and scraped knees when an arm reached out of the blackness to steady me. And just at that moment a flashlight was focused.

"No—oh, no!" The scream caught in my throat and came out a terrified whimper as I shrank away from the grasp of a heavy, thick hand. The flashlight had shown me a wide jade band on yellow-skinned, fat, manicured finger, and had glinted on thick-lensed glasses. And the dark eyes behind the glasses were like slowly swimming sharks. Sharks with no need to hurry, which could afford to take their time.

Chapter twenty=one

"Why you bawlin', keed? Why you scare? Nobody gonna get you. Dey no come. Not when we here. Dey don' dare."

I heard Keoki from a long way off. And I heard Mr. Yin Wah reiterating, "It's all right, Miss Allen, it's all right."

When the horrible sinking sensation of my brief faint passed and I opened my eyes, Keoki was carrying me, limp in his arms, up the rickety steps of a little tin-roofed house that was set high on stilts to keep it above the swirl of seawater when the tide came in. In the light of an oil lamp its unpainted board sidings, bleached by salt air, were the gray of driftwood.

A huge woman, a mountain of a Hawaiian woman, barefoot, and in a bright printed muumuu, her coils of strong, iron-gray hair thrust through with clusters of the little purple vanda orchids that crowd like weeds in every simple Island yard, filled the doorway.

"Hi, Mrs. Ahkina."

"Hi, Keoki. You got Lani's friend there?"

"Sure thing, I got her."

"Mees Allen . . . !" Lani pushed past her mother.

Big-eyed, brown-faced children of all ages swarmed onto the little porch to stare at me, and then, as Lani's mother lifted me from Keoki's arms as though I were a baby and carried me inside to a couch that, like the couch at the shack, was covered with tapa cloth, Keoki began holding forth, dramatically, to a huge-shouldered, stocky man in a palm-leaf-patterned shirt, ragged shorts, and barefeet, whom I later found out to be Lani's father.

Hanale was there, too, as interested audience, but Mr. Yin Wah had stayed out on the tiny porch. I could see him. He had lighted a cigarette, and was gazing out to sea.

Why had he come here? How had he known he would find me? What sort of lies would he tell the Ahkinas? And if he offered to drive me back to Cousin Elizabeth's, they'd let me go with him. They would believe the lies. Believe him, before they believed me.

The shaking I couldn't control seized me again, and Mrs. Ahkina, taking control, ordered everyone out of the room but Lani. Her big, beautiful, motherly eyes were full of questions, and so were Lani's eyes, but they asked none of them as they got me out of my water-soaked dress. They sponged me with warm water from a kitchen pot they brought in from somewhere, and washed the blood from my cuts and scrapes. All the while, Mrs. Ahkina was soothing me, crooning over me in a sweet, rich voice that seemed to come from the very depths of her huge body.

And I had worried as to my welcome!

When Mrs. Ahkina had smoothed my hair back from my face with a comb from her own thick coils, she slipped what evidently was one of her own muumuus over my head. It was at hand, folded over the back of a chair, and it smelled nice, of soap and sun, as though it had just come off a clothesline. The yards and yards of it swallowed me up, and when I smiled, weakly, at the ludicrous fit, her brown, good face lighted up, and the mounds of flesh that were her breasts and upper arms and stomach quaked as she laughed, pleased that Lani's friend, the haole, was showing signs of feeling better.

She propped me up on the couch with a huge, wadded armful of clean washing that had the same smell as the muumuu I wore—shorts and shirts and little gay cotton dresses and underpants, and sheets and towels, and Lani took the cap off a bottle of Coke for me, and fed me slices of dripping-ripe pineapple.

I was wiping juice from my mouth with a dampened towel when there was a knock at the door. Mrs. Ahkina opened it and Mr. Yin Wah came into the room.

"I must speak to you, Miss Allen. It won't wait. . . ." With a brusque nod, he let Lani and her mother know he wanted to be alone with me, and before I could protest, they were gone. I tried not to cringe away from him, but I couldn't help it, as he drew up a kitchen chair and sat down, all too close to the couch for my liking.

"I am a Special Services Agent, Miss Allen," he said, abruptly. "I have shown my credentials to the Ahkinas and to the young man who brought you here, and I shall be glad to show them to you, if you wish."

"A Special Services Agent?" I repeated it blankly, and then, in a rush, my fear of him crystallized. "Keoki or Hanale will drive me back to Cousin Elizabeth's. I won't go with you. . . ." A torrent of wild accusations burst from me. "You searched my room, you followed me, you kidnapped me. . . ."

I was close to hysteria as I shrank away from him. In another instant I would cry out to the Ahkinas and Keoki. "Why . . . why? That's all I want to know, why? Tell me—you've got to tell me—and when Miss Beaton hears . . ."

"I searched your room and I followed you, but it wasn't I who kidnapped you. If my deductions are correct, it was Miss Beaton's driver, Sing, though as yet I do not know his reasons, nor who put him up to it. But I do know of what your cousin is guilty, Miss Allen, and it is for this that I am here to tell you."

"Guilty?" I parroted it.

"An explanation that will not be pleasant for you." Mr. Yin Wah lighted another cigarette as he stated it stolidly.

My heart, which earlier that long, ghastly day had pounded so hard with terror, lurched and turned over. None of the hideous truth had yet been revealed either by words, or by the closed, expressionless moonface of the uncouth man opposite me, but a sickening premonition seized me. Fear for myself was as nothing, now. Something worse was coming—something unspeakably terrible. The palms of my hands were suddenly sweating, and yet I was cold, cold, although the room was stifling with the lingering heat of the Island sun, beating unshaded on the tin roof all day.

"What do you mean?" My voice shook, and was barely audible.

Mr. Yin Wah's answer was neither softened nor evasive.

"Miss Beaton is the head of a large Chinese dope syndicate. She has been operating out of Hong Kong for the past few years, and selling to an international market. I work with the Narcotics Bureau of the United States and with the British Crown Colony officials in Hong Kong. My office has suspected her for some time. We now have sufficient evidence, and tomorrow a warrant will be issued for her arrest."

"I don't believe you! You don't know what you're saying. Miss Beaton runs a dope syndicate? It's not true. It couldn't be true. I won't listen. Oh, wait till I tell her!"

I was off the sofa, and in that swathing, tripping-up muumuu, I started for the door.

"Wait, Miss Allen. Sit down."

I obeyed, without his putting a hand on me; the dark eyes behind the thick glasses held me, hypnotized.

"Facts are facts. You will have to accept them."

"There's some mistake—some terrible mistake."

"There is no mistake."

"But dope!" My lips could hardly frame the word. "Not dope."

"To traffic in narcotics was a logical next step for Miss Beaton."

"A next step?" I was parroting again.

"She has been suspected of dealing in forged passports and visas, and of smuggling refugees from Red China into Hong Kong. She has also been suspected of operating a concern that smuggles oil and gasoline from Hong Kong to neutral Macao, for purposes of resale to Red China. Another group in which she is financially interested brings in gold bars from Siam, with the same outlet."

"None of that makes her a dope seller. I still don't believe you."

"Let me say again, that facts are facts."

I turned to stone, I could neither move to leave the room, nor could I get out words, as Mr. Yin Wah's guttural voice with its British intonation went on and on.

"The smuggling and the forgeries failed to satisfy her

abnormal craving for power. She has never been satisfied with money only; she has made a fortune out of her legitimate export business, but power is what she is after. Power and more power. The ultimate in power."

I couldn't drag my eyes from his eyes. They held me, and mercilessly refused to let me go. Brutally, they compelled me to stay, that none of the horror should be spared me.

"Her ambitions are limitless—and mad. She knows that the bribery and corruption of officials has played an ugly part, before this, in my country's history, and she knows that by playing her cards correctly she can control an enormous amount of money circulating from the illegal sale of opium and morphine and heroin. Money that can take her to the top. The top her self-delusion believes in, and craves. Because she sees herself as a second Tzu Hsi . . . And may I remind you, Miss Allen, that Tzu Hsi—a woman of equally boundless ambition—was that Dowager Empress of Boxer Rebellion days who chose to entitle herself Heaven-born and of Divine Authority, the Vice-Regent of Heaven upon Earth."

To my spellbound eyes Mr. Yin Wah was all at once metamorphosed as he spoke of the Dowager Empress. He became one of those character dolls in the window of a Chinatown bazaar; a teacher doll in sober black silk, a black silk cap on his head, topped with a coral button, a braided queue down his back, a tuft of beard sparsely sprouting, his arms folded as he expounded.

". . . a Heaven-born, ruling with absolutism. A Heaven-born who, having made gracious descent from the celestial world, dwells among his subjects, smiling upon them as the sun chooses to shine in the Season of Peach blossoms, but, at will, sometimes frowning upon them, and causing them to wither away, as the frost withers the leaves in the Season of Bare Branches."

And then, after that, he was once more Mr. Yin Wah, a Special Services' Agent in a well-pressed, expensive, tropical-weight silk suit. He added, "Enough opium, enough heroin and morphine peddled, and you can buy all the power in the world, Miss Allen."

It was like a long-playing record—on, and on, and on.

"When she first became a suspect, my office sent me to her with a false lead on a shipment of heroin available for bringing into outer Red China from Burma and Thailand, to be sold in Hong Kong for re-export to the United States and Brazil and Europe. You may or may not know, Miss Allen, that to Red China, foreign-exchange money is a lifeline, and in return for my information the bargain was that Miss Beaton would take me into partnership. She would supply the funds for further shipments, I would contact the various sources and arrange the ultimate sales. She was too clever to trust me at first with any concrete facts of her involvement with narcotics. I had to move slowly. But in the end I had a conclusive case against her."

"A spy—an informer . . ." An uglier word burst from me. "A—a stool pigeon! There's nothing lower." It was only a token sop to the loyalty that slowly, painfully was draining from me.

"I disagree. A purveyor of narcotics is the most despicable of all in any rating, Miss Allen."

The last word was his. Cousin Elizabeth was indefensible, and I knew it, just as I knew I had been listening to the truth. I might loathe him. But he had told me the sickening truth.

"I am going to her now, to inform her she will be

officially under arrest in the morning, and that her house is now surrounded by my men to prevent any attempt at escape. But after I have talked with her, she may see you alone, if she wishes to, and she may see her attorney. Would you care to come with me, Miss Allen? You would prefer it, I presume, to a meeting in the police court, tomorrow, when she is arraigned?"

"Yes. I'll dress, if you will wait."

He got up, and before he left the room, I asked, "Do the Ahkinas know? Does everyone know?"

"You are the only one who knows except my men. The Ahkinas know only that I came here to ask if your friend, their daughter, knew where I could find you. I have been looking for you all day, Miss Allen. But I shall go into that later."

When he had left the room, I put on my crumpled, stained, still-wet linen dress. I had no shoes. In a daze, in a state of shock, I was trying to tell myself that when I saw Cousin Elizabeth I would wake, and the nightmarish accusations would be nothing but untruth piled upon untruth. There would be lantern light on the lanai. The garden torches would flare, golden in the soft trade wind. The scent of jasmine and ginger and gardenia would be everywhere. The bright myna birds would be chattering in their gilded pagoda cages. Fong would bring coffee in the Crown Derby cups, and frappéed crème de menthe. And Cousin Elizabeth, with her quiet, grave eyes, the gentle smile I could remember from childhood days, would be waiting for me. Cousin Elizabeth, to whom I had become "Nan, dear."

I was trying, trying, with all my heart. It didn't work. Deep down I knew I was going to have to accept and live with reality.

I tried to say some sort of reasonably coherent good-bye to the Ahkimas and Keoki, and thanked them, somehow, before I walked with Mr. Yin Wah to his car. Lani and Keoki came with me. The visibly impressed Keoki ran ahead to open the car door with a flourish, and I could guess what he was thinking. "Brudda—! Dat haole keed gettin' to ride wid a boss fella from da Secret Service!"

Lani said nothing. She had been subdued and silent all evening. Her tomorrow morning would be cruelly hard, too, as well as mine, I remembered. I reached for her hand, and she squeezed mine in return. Then Mr. Yin Wah started the car, and he and I were on our way to Cousin Elizabeth's house, with the Pali ahead of us. We drove in silence until we came to the turnoff that would lead to the saltbox house, when I asked, dully, "Why do you think it was Sing who kidnapped me?"

"He may have counted on wringing ransom money out of Miss Beaton. Double-crossing and blackmail could be the root of it. I can only guess. It would not surprise me to find that he is one of Miss Beaton's underlings in the narcotics racket. Regrettably, he is out of our reach for the moment, but we shall soon catch up with him."

Sing from New China. Only a boy. But already corrupted. Corrupted by Cousin Elizabeth.

"Where is he?"

"I put my men on to him before I went to look for you. They found your car at the International Airport. He may have left the Island by any one of a dozen flights. With a ticket bought under an assumed name and a falsely made-out passport—they can be had—he could be on his way to any place in the world. However, it won't be difficult to pick him up."

"Why were your men looking for him?"

"It goes back to my search for you. He was last seen driving your car when it should have been you driving it."

"But how did you know I should have been driving? I don't understand. I don't understand anything." It was all a hideous muddle, none of it, not a word, was comprehensible.

"We have had you under surveillance for months, in San Francisco, Miss Allen. We fully expected Miss Beaton to use you as a plant. What could be more convenient for a Hong Kong drug merchant than a young niece in a port like San Francisco with a Chinese servant who could serve as a go-between?"

"Not Ah Sam, too!" This hurt beyond bearing. This made it all a hundred times worse. As I cried out my anguished question, I clutched beseechingly at Mr. Yin Wah's arm, and the car swerved dangerously.

"Don't do that again, Miss Allen. And you needn't worry. Your servant was entirely cleared in our books. But when she died, we took an even greater interest in you. You would have provided, innocently or not, an ideal outlet for drugs if Miss Beaton had chosen to use you."

"How? How, possibly?" I couldn't take any of it in.

"Gift packages could have been sent you. A fortune in heroin, alone, could have been stuffed in the hollow stems of those plastic flowers Miss Beaton's factories turn out. Heroin in the seams and hems of the beaded, sequined dresses she contracts for. Heroin in the paper wrappings of a roll of silk. In a New Year's box of lichee nuts or sugared ginger. The possibilities are endless. And it would have been a simple matter for her contacts in San Francisco to get into that big house of hers that was empty all day, and remove the drugs, with you none the wiser."

"You mean, while I was at my job they could have come?"

"Exactly. We had our own operators in the house half a dozen times, checking up. And not only in the daytime."

The old Allen house—my grandfather's house. There, while I slept, strangers had prowled and searched. Oh, horrible . . . horrible.

"When I tell you that we are currently looking for seven hundred and fifty thousand dollars' worth of heroin due to have arrived a week ago in Honolulu, and as we are convinced it is somewhere in Miss Beaton's house, you can perhaps now understand why your bedroom was searched? You could still have been a plant."

"But if you are her partner, if she trusts you?"

"Because of greed she has reached a point where she no longer wishes to divide her profits. This is a strictly private deal of her own. I have every reason to believe that very soon, now, she would have dissolved our partnership. With finality. Her henchmen would attend to me."

"Don't . . ."

"She is what she is, Miss Allen. But to go back to Sing and your car, and my search for you this afternoon. I had watched your cousin's house all morning from behind the trees at the gate, on the chance she would go out and I could get into the house again for further searching. I saw Sing bring your car around from the garage, and I saw you come out of the house and walk toward it. But when Sing drove it through the gate a few minutes later, alone in it, or so it seemed, it struck me as odd. It bothered me. I went to the house and inquired for you from Fong, who told me you had left to take your car into town. I alerted my men by radio to look for your car. When they reported they had found it at the airport, without Sing, and also reported a smell of chloroform on the floor of the back seat, I very much wanted to locate you. I immediately thought of the beach house. I knew it was empty. I had followed you there a number of times when you visited the Ahkina girl; Miss Beaton could have concealed the heroin in your car, and it gave me an opportunity for a thorough search. Given time, car upholstery can be opened and the inner tubes of spare tires examined, and the chassis gone over. I also knew, of course, that the beach property had been without a caretaker since Major Fenton's death. Which meant, I took for granted, that the shack would be unoccupied. There was also the factor of distance and timing; Sing could have taken you to the shack and still have reached the airport before my men picked up the car.

"And another factor, Miss Allen—the isolation of the beach house. Whatever Sing's intentions toward you, he would know the value of that. I couldn't puzzle out his game, but I was convinced you were being used as a pawn. I forced my way into the house and into the bedroom where you had been locked. Beside a smell of chloroform on the bedquilt, there was a faint smell of perfume—of the perfume you use, Miss Allen. A very fresh, light scent, with an oil-of-lemon or verbena base. We are taught about perfumes in my work, and I recognized it from my search of your bedroom at Miss Beaton's.

"I then found the gag and the sawed-through cords in the bathroom. And let me congratulate you on your ingenuity. It was the iron cockerel, was it not?"

"Yes."

"Extremely clever of you. I then went to the shack. No one was there, but I found a pair of sandals with a San

Francisco shop label in them, and there was a freshly peeled banana skin and a recently opened poi carton in the sink. And outside there were the marks of a canoe having been dragged to the front door of the shack, from farther up the beach. It all added up to a hope that Miss Ahkina or her brother, whom I had seen at the shack when I followed you a day ago, might have helped you escape. I found out where they lived from the service station on the highway, and went to their house. When they told me about that young man, Keoki, having been at the shack, I was reasonably certain you would turn up with him, more especially, as I presumed you would want to get in touch with your cousin as quickly as possible, and the Ahkinas were the nearest people who could get you to a telephone."

This, too, had gone on and on. His deductions meant nothing to me; we were on the Nuuanu side of the Pali by now, and as we neared the road that would wind to Cousin Elizabeth's house through the forest of *koa* and ironwood trees, I was again trembling violently. I felt sick. I wondered if I would be sick in the car.

Mr. Yin Wah drove through Cousin Elizabeth's gate and parked at the front entrance.

"There is no need to go in, Miss Allen, if you find it too difficult. Will you be able to go through with it?"

I nodded, mutely, fighting nausea. I would have to see her; if she attempted to defend herself, I, in decent loyalty, was obligated to listen. She was Cousin Elizabeth. I owed her my life—she had saved me from death in the prison camp. I owed her Ah Sam. I owed her all the happiness, all the security of my childhood, my girlhood.

She was Cousin Elizabeth, who was my family.

Chapter twenty=two

I watched Mr. Yin Wah go toward the terrace. In the light of its pierced-ironwork wall sconces, the gilt and the lacquer of the eaves, the glazed ceramic dragons, the blue and green tiles, the temple gong that Mr. Yin Wah was striking were, as they had been from the first, details of an illustration. "The Entrance Way to the Inner Courtyard of a Chinese Lady." When I turned the next page, there would be the Lady herself.

God . . . God. How could I face her? What was there to say?

There was no breeze stirring. The air was hot and muggy. The stars that earlier had been so bright and close were blotted out now by mountaintop clouds, heavy with rain to come.

The night was so still I could hear the little birds stir in their cages, covered now with squares of persimmon brocade weighted at each corner with amber beads and gold silk tassels. I could hear a drowsy chirp or two. The driving in of the car had wakened them. But soon their heads would be under their wings again, and they would sleep until morning. But who, in all the terrible mornings to come, would take those tasseled covers off their cages? Who would open the door of those gilded pagodas with bathwater in the bowls I had bought for Cousin Elizabeth? Who would watch them preen their bright feathers? Onto whose shoulder would they flutter? From whose hand would they peck, and scatter seed?

The ghastly wait dragged by, I don't know how, until Mr. Yin Wah came back to the car.

"She wants to see you."

I made myself follow him to the lanai. It was all as I had pictured. For a moment, the ugliness, the sordid, evil truth was only a nightmare. I would waken from it. But the moment was short. Cruelly short.

Wearing one of her elegant, beautiful Chinese dresses, she was leaning back in her peacock chair, a cigarette in her long, ringed fingers, her large, grave eyes reflective as she watched a thin gray, heavily scented spiral of smoke dissolve.

"Well, child . . ."

My feet were bare. My dress bedraggled. My ankles and knees and elbows and chin scraped and bruised. Her eyes swept me up and down. Her brows lifted.

"You haven't taken time to change?" Then she smiled at me with the calm, sweet smile I knew so well. "You will get over this, my dear. Just remember that, for me, it has all been very exciting, very rewarding. And I have always known it could end this way—always been prepared."

I had been turned to stone, driving with Mr. Yin Wah. I was still stone. I couldn't move. I couldn't speak.

Her eyes were on my cuts and bruises again.

"Sing was a novice with chloroform, and you were very clever about cutting cords, Mr. Yin Wah tells me."

I found my voice. "Why did Sing kidnap me?" I had to know. I had to know. I clenched my hands and waited. Horrible, oh, horrible to learn the truth from those gently curving lips.

"What a tiresome girl you are, Nan, with your propensity for asking questions and your determination to get to the bottom of things." She laughed lightly. "You insist upon an answer? Very well. After all, why shouldn't I tell you? It won't change things—at this point. And 'in for a penny, in for a pound . . .' But do sit down, child; you look exhausted."

She tugged at the bellpull and Fong pattered out onto the lanai. "A frappé for Miss Allen and for me. And will yours be a Scotch and soda, Mr. Yin Wah?"

"Thank you, yes."

Her gentle smile was for Mr. Yin Wah, then. "I imagine you, too, will find this quite entertaining. Hong Kong comes into it. The old war days."

Her eyes followed the spirals of smoke again. "It all began a long time ago, my dear Nan, in the Allen house in San Francisco. I loathed having to accept the Allen charity. I burned with jealousy of the Allen money, the Allen position. . . ."

With her first quiet, even-voiced sentence, a reel of film began to be projected; scene after scene flashed before my eyes. San Francisco was the background first, with an inwardly resentful, unhappy child growing up in the old Allen house with the two Allen brothers, and even then knowing how to dissemble, and smile, and ingratiate herself.

I saw Cousin Elizabeth, a young woman now, breaking

her heart over John Allen, and masking her consuming passion for him.

Richard Allen's quarrel with his father, and his departure for Hong Kong. His father, angry and hurt, announcing to John and Cousin Elizabeth the terms of a newly drawn will. The bulk of his large fortune to John, and to John's children, if he married, with a lifetime allowance left to Cousin Elizabeth, but if John died without issue, the Allen money would go to Cousin Elizabeth.

John's departure, then, for Hong Kong, too, on Allen and Company's business. Both he and Richard marrying English girls. And on his father's death, John Allen sending for Cousin Elizabeth as companion-housekeeper to his young, delicate wife, Edith. Cousin Elizabeth living with them, her love for John Allen turned to a corroding bitterness, her jealousy of Edith Allen a secret, gnawing torment.

Richard Allen marrying another English girl, Anne. Then the war. John and Richard killed by sniper bullets. Both of the Allen wives, Edith and Anne, together with Edith Allen's old Chinese amah, and Cousin Elizabeth, in a prison camp.

The film unreeling, unreeling . . .

I saw Richard Allen's wife, Anne, die of malnutrition and malaria. I saw Edith, John's wife, die in childbirth the same day. And I saw the British Army surgeon who delivered Edith sign a false birth certificate. It declared Edith and John Allen's child to be the daughter of Anne and Richard Allen. And I saw Cousin Elizabeth pay the surgeon for his falsifying with American gold dollars.

Clever Cousin Elizabeth, so quick to see and to snatch at the once-in-a-lifetime opportunity that had come her way! Her turn, now, at the Allen money, against all odds, and her turn at last to even old scores. With John Allen dying, supposedly, without children, Cousin Elizabeth became Grandfather Allen's sole heir.

And Edith . . . Who was Edith but a dead woman? Where was her charm, her prettiness? Consigned to a grave. And what and where was John? Dead. And not even in a grave. Rotting on a jungle road, somewhere between Hong Kong and his tea plantation.

And she was alive—alive, and rich!

I saw her warn the old amah who wailed by the dead Edith's cot as she hugged a newborn baby in her arms. "Remember, Ah Sam: one word, and I shall turn you over to the prison guards. I shall tell them you have stolen food from the commissary. They will kick you, and beat you until there is no skin left on your back."

After that, with the war over, back to San Francisco again, and a second warning to Ah Sam.

"No talking, ever, or I will have you sent back to China, and you will never see your Missee Edith's child again."

Still the film unreeled.

Miss Elizabeth Beaton establishing an image of herself in San Francisco as the kind, devoted, and wonderfully generous guardian of the Richard Allens' orphaned daughter. The child who was no blood relation of Miss Beaton's, and "cousin" only by way of the most distant family connection. The child to whom Miss Beaton affectionately referred to as "my little Nan," but who had been baptized Anne, after her "mother," with a christening in the cathedral, and an intimate little reception afterward in the Allen house, given by Miss Beaton for close, old friends of the Allen family.

Then Miss Beaton sailing for Hong Kong again, to rebuild the firm of Allen and Company.

It took little more than five minutes for the film to unreel; as I listened to Cousin Elizabeth, so calm, so detached a narrator, I shrank in my chair, sick, and crushed. My mother . . . Ah Sam, ignorant, submissive, worshiping Ah Sam . . .

"Shall I go on, child?"

"Yes . . ." I could just barely get it out.

Cousin Elizabeth sipped her crème de menthe, then lighted another cigarette.

"Poor, sensitive Nan. I am afraid this is all too much for you—but if you insist. . . ." She smoked meditatively for a moment. "Perhaps, if it had not been for your fan . . ."

"It was you who took it?"

"Of course. It was most awkward to have it turn up on your arrival. I knew Ah Sam had treasured the few possessions Edith Allen brought to camp, but I thought she had eventually sold them all for food. And the moment you showed me the fan, I realized I must begin to make plans; I was sorry, in a way—you seemed a nice child— but one must be practical. To be entirely fair, could you really have expected me to sit by, and allow your insatiable curiosity, your unending questions to endanger all that I had so carefully built up over the years? The fan could no longer be allowed to whet that truly monstrous curiosity of yours. It must be destroyed."

She picked up her glass again and held it to the glow of the paper lanterns, seeming to enjoy the greenness that was like wet emeralds, before she went on.

"But may I confess to a weakness? Though I more than once started to crush the fan, I invariably stopped just before it was too late. I had discovered that by allowing the fan to exist, I was in possession of a most gratifying reminder of who had come out ahead, in the end—John and Edith Allen, or I. You do see how much this could mean to me?"

I had no answer.

"You can see, too, surely, that your persistent questions, and your insistence on delving into this and that, were making you something of a problem to me? Yes. And quite as irritating a one as Major Fenton was becoming."

"Major Fenton?" I forced out the question.

"He had been blackmailing me ever since his arrival from Hong Kong two months ago. Not with outright demands for money, but with constant hints that when he was ready, he would bring up the prison-camp incident. To placate him, I took him on as caretaker for the beach house, knowing a place to live by the sea was vital to him for his paintings. It seemed to satisfy him, until he unluckily saw you, and his interest—and his memory—stirred. It *was* naughty of you, Nan, to go there against all my warnings. The whole thing, really, could be called your fault."

I let her say it; I didn't try to contradict her. Cold and sick and stunned, I waited to hear what would come next. With awful prescience, I almost knew.

"His interest was so aroused that he forced me to have you invited to the Diamond Head party. It was from then on that he began to put two and two together. And he realized that his mention of that snapshot would make me more than willing to pay him whatever he asked if he saw to it that it never reached you. One glance at Edith Allen's picture, and you would have known whose child you are. The 'Anne' fiction would never have held up."

She sipped from her delicately stemmed, frosted crystal glass again, and her gentle smile was regretful. "Such a very great pity you ever flew out here, Nan dear, to complicate things so unfortunately. You must admit I tried my best, for years, to keep you at a wise distance? But you would come; you would have your way. It was unfortunate, too, that Major Fenton, in his drunken sentimental appreciation of your friendship with his little beach girl, gave away Captain Grant's name. Immediately, I realized to the full how much else he could give away. He simply had to have a car crash—you do see that, don't you?"

"You planned it?" I was staring at her as though she were a venomous snake I had come on.

"Sing's greatest asset was his willingness to carry out orders, my dear. When it came to your case, though, he disappointed me. I had never for a moment expected he would back down. And I am truly sorry about your cuts and bruises, and the whole frightening experience Mr. Yin Wah tells me you have been through. Sing was to have drugged you—painlessly and fatally—and left you in the beach house until I was entirely certain the Ahkina girl had vacated the caretaker's shack for good, and then he was to have gone back and buried you. The Island grasses and shrubs grow quickly, you know—a grave would have been hidden in no time. However, Sing seems not to have been up to it, quite. He is young, of course—and hasn't had his hand in long. . . ."

Had she gone mad? Or was it I who had lost my sanity? I didn't know. I didn't know. . . . Here we were on the lanai where, in the soft yellow light of the paper lanterns, Cousin Elizabeth and I had talked, evening after evening, and grown close. And this was Cousin Elizabeth now, in the peacock chair.

Which one of us? Oh, which one?

". . . so there you have it," the gentle voice was continuing. "A rather long story. I hope it hasn't bored you, my dear. I hardly think so. And just one thing more. Are you perhaps wondering why I have told it to you?"

She waited until my wordless nod satisfied her.

"You couldn't guess? It hasn't occurred to you that, in the end, I have been given a last chance to score even more magnificently than I ever dreamed, against Edith Allen? This hasn't been a comfortable session for you. I have hurt you rather badly, and the hurt will be lasting. It will leave a scar. But after all these years, someone besides myself deserves a painful time of it. So why not make Edith Allen's child suffer? Edith wouldn't like that. She was a soft, tenderhearted little thing."

She put her empty glass on the table beside her chair and stood up. "You will excuse me, child? My affairs need winding up, and I haven't a great deal of time left."

She put a hand lightly on my shoulder as she passed me. I drew away from her. And my shrinking pleased her, because it was Edith Allen's child whom she had been empowered to hurt, and whom she had caused to draw in her breath with a gasp of repulsion, a shiver of sick horror.

She stopped in the doorway. "Will you and Mr. Yin Wah come to my room in, shall we say, ten minutes? I won't keep you, but there is one last bit that will round out what I have told you."

With a cigarette in her hand, a smile that was a little amused curving her lips, she went into the house through the door that led to her suite. Mr. Yin Wah was there, then, from the hall.

"You heard?" I asked.

"Yes." With this curt answer he sat down in one of those high-backed, woven wicker peacock chairs, imported from Hong Kong, that I never want to see again. It creaked under the weight of his heavy body, but that was the only sound on the lanai. Neither of us spoke until Mr. Yin Wah looked at the watch on his wrist.

"She asked for ten minutes. We have given her fifteen." He heaved himself out of the chair, and I got up, apprehensive of the further revelation she had in store for me. And yet I knew I had to hear, had to. . . . The compulsive curiosity that gripped me, and dragged me to her door was beyond my controlling.

I knocked, and when there was no answer, I knocked again. Still no answer. Mr. Yin Wah pushed me aside and opened the door.

She was lying on the dragon-embroidered, Imperial-yellow satin coverlet of her enormous carved bed, that was mounted on a sort of dais. She had put on a long, high-collared, wide-sleeved, Imperial-yellow satin robe over her Chinese dress. Her arms were crossed on her breast, her hands thrust deep in chrysanthemum-embroidered, cuffed sleeves. Her pearls and jades and carnelians were around her neck and wrists and in her earlobes, and were thrust through a heavy, meshed black silk snood that netted her chignon.

From a freshly lighted cigarette that burned in a jade ash tray on the nightstand, the spirals of gray smoke rose like incense.

Her large, staring open eyes were blank, but her mouth still wore a smile. A smile of triumph.

She, a Heaven-born, with a divine right to power, had commanded Death, the Black Tiger, into her presence, and her command had been obeyed.

Chapter twenty=three

My knees buckled. I was clinging to the edge of a heavy teakwood table for support. This ghastly, hideous day—this unending day. Would it never be over, even though it was dark, and by clock time, it was late at night?

Mr. Yin Wah stooped to pick up a small, carved snuff bottle and its fallen-out stopper that had dropped to the floor from a tapering-fingered hand that hung over the edge of the bed.

"Poison?" I breathed.

"It looks like it." He put the snuff bottle in his pocket, reached for the telephone on the nightstand, and began dialing.

I can't remember with any clearness what happened immediately after that. There were the headlights of cars turning into the driveway, and of an ambulance, and I saw the servants gathering in the hall, and I heard the thin, high wail of Lui Lung as she crouched at the foot of the Empress bed. Then Mr. Yin Wah was telling me to pack a bag, and dazedly, I put on a fresh linen dress, and shoes, and made up my mouth with bright lipstick, and patted face powder over my scraped, bruised chin. It was all mechanical. All because people in the real world, a world I didn't belong to anymore, would be looking at me.

My hand was shaking, and I didn't know who it was, facing me in the dressing-table mirror. It couldn't be Nan Allen; none of it, none of it could have happened to Nan Allen, who was the cousin of Miss Elizabeth Beaton.

I walked out of the house with the chirp and trilling of the finches in their cages unbearable, and the heavy, sweet smell of the garden noxious to me—a permeation of all things evil, all things twisted and perverted, all things decayed and rotted.

Mr. Yin Wah put me in his car and drove me to Waikiki, and the Royal, and by some miracle of influence, managed to engage a room for me. Surprisingly, he was being kind.

"I shall have sandwiches sent up to you, Miss Allen. Then try to get some sleep. I shall want to see you first thing in the morning."

Sleep? Mr. Yin Wah was suggesting the impossible, I thought as I undressed. Would I ever sleep again, with the shock and horror of the past few hours always in my mind, and never to be forgotten? But when the sandwiches came, and a glass of sherry, I ate and drank, and crept into bed, and in my exhaustion, knew nothing until morning, early morning, when the telephone by my bed shrilled.

"Yes?"

It was Jim. When he had gotten my wire, he had taken a late night flight. He had called Cousin Elizabeth's house as early as he dared and had been told of Cousin Elizabeth's death by Fong, and told where I was; he was downstairs, now.

"May I come up?"

"Oh, Jim . . . Jim. Yes!"

I sobbed it into the telephone and then I threw on a kimono and was at the door to let him in, and to cling to him as his arms went around me.

Everything happened in a rush, after that. When Jim heard what I had to tell him, he telephoned his office and arranged to stay on through the week that followed, with its inquest, and private burial, and lawyers' sessions.

Due to the express wish of the Special Services Agency, and the cooperation of the coroner's office, the cause of Cousin Elizabeth's death was released to the press as being due to an accidental overdose of a heart stimulant. It would be easier, that way, to trap any confederates she may have had, unknown to Mr. Yin Wah and his men, if they made an attempt to get their hands on the $750,000 worth of heroin still concealed in her house. And Mr. Yin Wah had gone to the Ahkina family and asked them not to discuss with any outsiders my experience at the beach house.

Cousin Elizabeth's will left bequests to all her servants sufficiently large to give them each a small income for life. She left the San Francisco house to "her cousin, Nan Allen," and money enough to be called a fortune. The remainder of her enormous fortune and all her beautiful possessions were to be divided between various hospitals and museums in Hong Kong and Honolulu and San Francisco. And how plain to see that even though she had lived aware of risk, and prepared for the day of downfall, she had gambled on the odds of never being found out, and chosen to believe that even after death the image of a generous, civic-minded and family-conscious Miss Elizabeth Beaton would serve as a lasting cover-up.

Nothing could make me touch a penny of her money— money that had come from the sale of drugs—nor her jewels or household furnishings. But I kept the funds made by Allen and Company, which were rightly mine as the daughter of John Allen, not of the disinherited Richard Allen, and I kept the old Allen house that my grandfather had built with the untainted, honorably earned money of the original Allen and Company.

Jim saw it that way, too; we are both traditionalists, and we both were brought up in old houses. Neither of us think we would feel at home in any other kind. So we are going to live in the Allen house and make it a happy, shadowless place again. We can do it. We know we can. And with Grandfather Allen's money I shall build and endow a hospital-home for the old people of Chinatown, and a plaque over the door will read, "In loving memory of Ah Sam from her foster daughter."

But that is getting ahead of myself.

Jim and I were married in Honolulu's St. Andrew's Cathedral a few hours before we flew back to San Francisco. There was no reason to wait, as long as the Martins were still away, and it was fun sending them a cable, and imagining their delight and excitement.

I wore a new white shantung dress, bought in about five minutes—I didn't want to wear anything I had worn at Cousin Elizabeth's—and a sort of bow-with-a-veil thing on my head, which wasn't exactly my type, but it was bridelike, and Jim seemed to think it was becoming. But he says he likes me best in the black sleeveless wool dress and jacket I wore to the Moon Gate on the first night he ever took a redheaded girl to dinner.

Lani and Keoki came to see us off. In spite of all the strain of the past week and its crowded hours, Jim and I had driven out to say good-bye to the Ahkinas and Keoki —who seemed to be their more or less permanent house guest—in my rented car. Mr. Yin Wah had arranged to have it brought to the hotel, and had also sent me my suitcase, as nothing could induce me to set foot in Cousin Elizabeth's house again.

I could never, with any honesty, say I have acquired a liking for Mr. Yin Wah, but neither will I ever cease being grateful to him for those last private minutes he granted Cousin Elizabeth, knowing her as he did, and guessing what she would do.

He didn't do it for Cousin Elizabeth, Jim says; he did it for my sake.

In return, I was able to do something for him. I was lying awake in the hotel bedroom, being sorry for Fong and Wing and Cousin Elizabeth's cook, and the little Lui Lung, who had all worshiped their mistress and given her years of service, and being sorry for the finches, and wondering who would take care of them. I was remembering their pagoda cages and the blue-porcelain bath bowls, when in a sudden, illuminating flash, I knew I could tell Mr. Yin Wah where to look for the hidden heroin. And when I telephoned him—late at night as it was—his men, who were on duty at Cousin Elizabeth's house, found it at once under one of the cages' lift-out gravel pans.

To go back to the airport, though.

Lani had been so pitifully subdued, so unsmiling, at home, that I hadn't dreamed she would make the effort to come to the airport. But there she was, barefooted, in one of her sarongs, and there was Keoki, barefooted too, his teeth very white when he grinned at us, and all the strong, brown, near-nakedness of him rather terrific in his G-string malot.

Both he and Lani had an armful of leis to put around our necks with ceremonial aloha kisses for me, on my cheek.

When Keoki informed us he was leaving for Kona that afternoon, on his new job, Jim told him that we would be in Kona, too, one of these days, and would hire a tuna boat from his boss, if Keoki promised to go along and show us how to pull in the big ones.

"Will you meet us there, Lani?" I asked her in a little whisper while the men talked fishing. " Say you will, dear Lani. Please . . . ?"

Slowly she nodded. "I theenk maybe yes," and I was glad for her that the next time we met she would again have a flower in her hair.

When we had boarded the plane, we stood on the landing steps, waving and waving until they were moved away and the cabin door was closed.

"Keoki will come in handy to teach our children to swim," Jim said as we settled in our seats and fastened our safety belts. "And if we have a daughter, Lani can teach her to dance and to sing the Island songs."

"What about her moral influence on those stuffy Boston Bradfords?"

"We shall just have to risk it."

We were both laughing when the plane took off. It swung over the ocean, and before we gained altitude I could again see the water that was lapis and jade and turquoise, and the toppling crest of waves rushing shoreward in white foam to Waikiki Beach, where tall palm trees swayed in a soft, fragrant trade wind. And behind, I could see the dark, forested, rainswept mountain slopes of the Nuuanu Pali.

I wouldn't be afraid to come back to the Islands, I knew in a quick surge of confidence. Cousin Elizabeth had hurt me for always, but I could seal off the hurt by letting myself remember only one thing about her: a truth she had given me to cherish—the truth about a name—my mother's name: *Edith*.

I leaned forward, my heart full, for a last glimpse—for now—of Honolulu. A double rainbow was arching in the moist blueness of a sky where, always, a golden sun and silver showers were rivals.

"Aloha, Hawaii!" I whispered. "Aloha—aloha nui!"